The Hidden Mountain

PETER PINKHAM

MFDC PRESS

All rights reserved.
Copyright 1998 by Peter Pinkham.
Cover by Glen Group.
Library of Congress Catalogue Card Number 98-065272

ISBN: 0-9662661-0-2

Printed by Thomson-Shore, Inc.

For Linda, who is neither yet both

No one had more influence on this story than my favorite Abenaki Indian, Stephen Laurent and his late wife, Margaret, who provided vital inspiration and immeasurable help. My deepest gratitude; without them there would have been no book.

My heartfelt thanks to those who read the novel as it developed and let me know when and where I'd gone off track — which was more often than I had hoped. When it gave them enjoyment, I felt it tenfold.

*Happiness springs from the climb,
not the view from the peak*

Prologue

THE MAN ENTERED the pine-paneled room and crossed to the window. A weak sun had fire enough for warmth. He pulled a chair into the shaft of afternoon light and moved the telephone to a table beside it. In a few minutes he unbuttoned his cardigan. Waiting. After a while the ring came.

"Yes?"

"It's now officially an accident."

"No comment about skid marks, or the lack of them?"

"It's being put down to an unfortunate mixup at the traffic light."

"Hmmm..." It was no mixup of course, but part of a well thought out sequence of events, of which this was just a part. He'd gone over the crashing of the cars and what had happened since many times in his mind and knew he was picturing the scene as clearly as one who'd been there. The darkened streets, slightly glistening from an earlier rain, the sudden rush of the big Chrysler from a side street, its headlights flicking on just before impact. Was there any flaw in his plan? He shook his head; ridiculous thought. There are always flaws.

"Tell me about the Carver funeral."

"It took place yesterday. I attended of course. Wallace Carver was better known than I thought; the church was overflowing. Are you sure we haven't made a mistake?"

"Don't go soft on me now. Were there any suspicions?"

"None."

"Hudson Rogers?"

"Still in Salem Hospital. He'll be there another day or two."

"Does *he* have suspicions?"

"No. Too overwhelmed with grief for awareness of anything else."

"The details we discussed?"

"Are being taken care of."

"Good."

He replaced the phone and sat back in the chair, reviewing the conversation that had just ended. 'Don't go soft on me,' he'd told the other. He knew he was considered an emotionless stick, but it was life that had toughened him; he hadn't come into the world that way. One who knew him as well as he permitted anyone to had written he was "like a hardwood tree, tough outside and just as tough in," with any warmth of human spirit — if indeed it existed — being sunk in his roots. Not so. Right now it was all he could do to keep going, with the loss he'd suffered. For the briefest of moments he allowed himself to dwell on it. Then he cursed his self pity. Weakness wouldn't get him through this. Keep your mind on what you must do, he told himself. His scheme was born of desperation, which made him uneasy, and it was based on his reading of the character of one man — a man by the name of Hudson Rogers. And that made him uncomfortable.

Though he'd done so all his life, he now hated the necessity of working through others. Was it a mistake? No, damn it, he'd been left no alternative! It was destroy or be destroyed. So far, his gamble had paid off.

Now came the part he most disliked. Yet experience had taught him early that sometimes the very best thing one could do was wait, and he'd become good at it. He'd have to be content with that.

He went out, closing the door behind him.

It was Monday, May 5.

Chapter 1

IT WASN'T THAT the house was a mess; it just wasn't the way Wally would have left it. The unevenness of the books on the shelves would have offended Wally's sense of order. In his North Shore home each book came to the front edge of the shelf no matter what its depth. Here, a drawer in the big mahogany desk was part open as was the door to a kitchen cabinet. Not Wally.

Someone had been here since. Hudson dropped his bags in what was obviously the master bedroom and went out on the little deck. Beneath him the ground dropped away sharply, disappearing behind some lacy hemlocks. The air was cool and pine-scented, and, though it must be several miles to the mountains across the valley, he could see no other signs of habitation. Fine. He felt no need for people. A youthful Catholic belief in a saintly heaven had undergone substantial revision as he visualized it populated by humans he had encountered over his forty-one years. If *their* souls were going to be saved, the hereafter was apt to be played out on a bingo card. Like life.

His thoughts were punctuated by several loud caws. Quoth the raven nevermore: *Voren karknul niekagda* — the Russian translation gave Poe's poem a fullness of body that English could not. But the crow had it right. Nevermore was when he would hear Sylvia's bittersweet greeting, "we're home!" to friendly but empty houses. They'd wanted children. Now it was just as well.

"I'm sorry, Mr. Rogers. Your wife took the full impact of the crash." Words of finality spoken by an unknown doctor that brought a pain far deeper than the physical wounds he'd suffered himself, and reduced his world to ashes. Was there something he could have done? He shook his head savagely. He'd been over it so many times. They were returning from Wally's 75th, Sylvia beside him, the birthday boy in back. Her father had been in rare form. All but retired, some new project had taken a decade off his step and lifted his voice out of the dry self-assurance lawyers affect.

Sylvia was delighted. Since her mother died, Wally had retreated to his "forest" — a genealogical library of local family trees, traced back, Sylvia said, nearly to Adam.

Suddenly headlights from a side street. An impact that seemed to stretch his body beyond limits. Then nothing. They'd told him Wally had also died instantly. Hudson's little Toyota had been hit square on the passenger side and bent into a V from the force of the blow. The other driver had escaped with minor cuts and bruises. No liquor involved; apparently confusion at the traffic signal.

There had been no warning, Hudson reminded himself. Had it to happen again, he still could not have braked in time. A late afternoon breeze set an empty birdfeeder swinging. He'd put birdseed on his grocery list. He went back inside, glancing at his image in the full-length bedroom mirror. Hudson's light brown hair as yet showed no signs of graying, but dispirited brown eyes and a slightly pudgy face over slumping shoulders gave his well-padded six-foot-two body the look of a melting store dummy. He tried to straighten his back and a jolt of pain ran from still-tender ribs where they had been battered against the car door. He had never really been injured before, at least not enough to be hospitalized. Though not a physically active person, he'd never felt like an invalid.

Wally's desk looked as though it had been ready for judgement day long before its owner: paper clips in their compartment, pencils freshly sharpened and file folders neatly labeled in alphabetical order ... but only if "W" led off. Though all the rest seemed in order, the folder in front was identified as "White Mountain National Forest," coming just before "Academies" and Accountant." It was empty. Wally seemed to have kept his genealogy material in Massachusetts. This was all personal stuff.

Hudson stared at the pile of envelopes he'd found in the mailbox. Who was to open them if he didn't? Wally had no longer an interest in affairs of this world. The house was now Hudson's responsibility as was Wally's substantial investment portfolio — all of which he would have traded for sackcloth and ashes to revoke that fateful first day of May. A seat belt was pitiful protection against a crushing blow to the side. Cars were supposed to be hit head on, where air bags provided defense. But Sylvia ... Hudson caught himself up. He couldn't remember ever sighing before and now he sounded like advanced emphysema.

Most of it was junk mail and discarded. He opened an envelope from the Town of Bartlett. Tax bill marked paid. He studied the receipt. Wally's land was listed at 12 acres. This seemed a lot to Hudson, who was brought up on streets where anything over an acre was an estate. He tried to picture where the acreage was in relation to the house. Driving in, the nearest neighbor was in no danger from thrown stones. Wally's house would be classified as contemporary — that loose category of all houses built since WW II that had any individuality. It sat well back from the gravel road and at its end. Beyond, it petered out to rutted woods road. The house itself was almost completely hidden by leafy beeches and stout evergreens that could not have seen a woodsman's ax this century. Nearly flat in front, the land fell off just beyond — opening up views of New Hampshire's rolling hills and craggy peaks, even to the rooms in the finished basement.

The knock on the front door pulled him up from his rather pleasant immersion in a feeling of isolated loneliness. At first he decided not to answer it. He knew no one north of the Massachusetts border 100 miles away, and that distance seemed about right. No one had any business with him or, for that matter, knew he was here. Ridiculous, his car was right outside. Another emphysema breath and he got up to open the door.

"Yes?" His greeting was as discouraging as he could make it without actually slamming the door in his visitor's face.

"Saw you drive up. You're not Wally's kid." Short, seventyish, ruddy faced and not at all put off by Hudson's manner.

"Very observant. Since Wally had just one child and she's ... not here."

"Son-in-law. Thought you'd be younger. Wally said his daughter'd made a good choice."

"So good he let her get killed."

"Not your fault from what I read. Just came by to tell you the geese you might see around ain't wild in case you're a hunter. I raise 'em and sometimes they wander."

Hudson felt a stirring of interest. "You're the next door neighbor."

"The only neighbor on this road. Wally and I are the two houses. We both of us got enough of people in Massachusetts — him in Marblehead, me on the Cape."

"I was just looking at the tax bill which says Wally has 12 acres and wondering where they are."

"I'll show you the line between us. Can't tell you how yours lays out — it *is* yours now isn't it?" Hudson shrugged and gave a slight nod.

The corner proved to be an iron stake buried under leaves and pine needles. "Surveyor name of Wheaton did my place when I added a few acres last year. Maybe he's got something on yours. You must have a deed."

"I left all that stuff with the executor. He just gave me the key and directions."

"Well, you could also get a general idea from the tax map at Town Hall."

"Thanks. Oh, by the way, you haven't seen anybody at the house recently, have you?"

"Why? Any problem?"

"I don't think so. It just looks like someone's been there. Since Wally."

"Just the gas company. About a month ago. Should have left a bill on your door knob like they do mine."

When Hudson returned to the house he checked both basement and kitchen. The stove was electric and the house had an oil furnace. Nowhere in the house was there a use for gas.

Chapter 2

THE PATH FIT his mood. A barren landscape darkened by a high thick bower of pine branches that quickly snuffed out any green plant with the temerity to put down a root. Dry rotting pine needles underfoot, scattered broken branches like the picked-over bones of a prehistoric monster. He adjusted his pack, feeling a sharp complaint from his ribs, and set off. Soon the day brightened as he began to climb through hardwood, and later the trees fell away completely as he neared the summit. It wasn't much of a climb as hiking trails go, but Hudson found himself feigning intense interest in an ordinary fissure in the ledge so a young amazon scampering past up the Black Cap trail wouldn't notice his apparent need for more air than city lungs could accommodate. Obviously a budding athlete. Racing through life, she'd never appreciate the pleasure of just sitting as he now did. A mosquito whined a landing approach. He slapped at it.

Was it just the few days in a hospital bed? Maybe everybody starts to deteriorate after forty. He would not have said his life was sedentary, but he'd never felt the urge to experiment with machines that enabled one to ski for hours in the winter wonderland of one's own living room. He and Sylvia were quite content to curl up with books of an evening, not feeling any the worse for not having soaked a set of warm-ups. Sylvia ...

He rummaged through his knapsack and pulled out the obligatory orange. He never ate oranges. He'd watched healthy hikers neatly peel them on television, but his hands were sticky from juice by the time he got the first wedge in his mouth. The valley below ran north and south. Across it was the mountain range called by the single name, Moat. To his right were the Presidentials with the white cap of Washington presiding. Somewhere between was Wally's vacation home.

The gas company knew nothing about a delivery. As a matter of fact, the truck that normally serviced that area had been in the shop for most of May. Was he considering a change to gas?

The amazon's parents — didn't warrior women leap into the world fully grown, or was that Minerva — had finally caught up with their energetic offspring and were spreading out a blanket for lunch. Hudson leaned back on the rock and turned his face to the sun. At least he could look healthy when ... When what? He'd tried returning to work. He couldn't. That phase of his life was over. He'd left house, business and neighborhoods of memories with scarcely a thought, throwing a week's supply of clothes in bags that had accompanied Sylvia and himself down the Danube, up the walls of Dubrovnic and into Portuguese Algarvian villas, and headed North. Wally had often talked about the White Mountains and his "cabin," and since it was now his...Was there anyone to admire a new tan? Was there in fact a single face he wanted to see again? Both his parents were gone. The advantage of having a first child late in life when one could afford it, had been balanced by the reality that they wouldn't be around to get to know it very long. They'd loved Sylvia...He stood up quickly to shake off his thoughts and immediately regretted it as his legs started to cramp. He hobbled from one foot to the other to the amusement of wondergirl and her attendants. The thought of doing a hike every day was now a lot less appealing than when it had been suggested by his partner on whom he'd dumped his share of their little business. Somehow the visions of back to nature never included the inhaled bugs, sweaty wrinkled socks in unfamiliar sneakers and quivering muscles that turned walk to a totter.

But it *was* beautiful. From the forests below came the rattating of a woodpecker. A flash of blue was perhaps a jay; the village of North Conway hardly noticeable in the sweep of the Valley of the Saco River. From here the scene was not much different from what early explorers would have viewed. Did they find anyone when they arrived?

He'd brought a newspaper to read, but the financial pages seemed so out of place in this setting that he put it aside. Across the valley were several cliffs over 100 feet high that might have been created by a giant ax. There was actually a back road to the top of one which he had driven up the day before. Standing atop the steep drop, the urge to do a swan dive into oblivion was almost irresistible. Curiously, when another sightseer commented that hang gliders used to launch from the cliff, his old fear of heights reasserted itself, and he backed away from the edge. Who was he to deny a heaven to others when he himself was only prepared to die if he didn't get hurt in the process.

A few drops of rain ended his reverie, and he began the trek back to his car, noting with pleasure that his long stride kept him well ahead of a middle-aged couple and their eight year old daughter.

* * *

Wally's attorney had asked for an inventory of Wally's Bartlett house, so that evening it began. Dinner had been eaten before the fieldstone fireplace, where a cozy fire took an unseasonable chill off the June night. Wally's library illuminated a new face of the man. Where his Massachusetts home contained mostly the dry tomes of genealogical research, here were glimpses of another soul; history books of course, but also the *Bhagavad Gita, I Ching, Candida* and the *Rubaiyat*, and old stories of mystery and adventure, *The Last Of The Mohicans, Murders In The Rue Morgue,* and several Nero Wolfe novels. A side to the old boy he'd never realized. He picked up a book of John Cheever's stories from a side table; perhaps it would do for bedtime reading. As he opened it a bookmark fell to the floor. On closer inspection it was just a piece of paper presumably used to mark Wally's place in the book. Hudson turned it over. It had one word printed on it in block letters:

STOP

At the top was a rip and a hole as if hung from a nail and torn off. Stop what? The paper was crinkled as though it had been out in the weather. With a frown, Hudson opened the front door. In the center at eye level was a single nail. He closed the door. Perhaps it was a note left for the postman, indicating mail to be picked up. He flipped through the other books on the shelf. No "bookmarks." He remembered the book next to Wally's bed and mounted the stairs. As he picked it up he saw right away there was another paper marker. This one had the same hole and tear and read:

STOP
OR
ELSE

There could be several unknowable reasons for the notes, but one thing seemed certain. Someone was warning Wally not to continue with something, and Wally was so impressed with the threats that he used them for bookmarks. Well, whatever it had been was no longer important. E. Wallace Carver, attorney and philosopher, had indeed come to a dead stop.

Chapter 3

WHEATON SURVEYS WAS on Bear Notch Road, just a few blocks from the center of Bartlett village. At the blinking light was a foundation where the Bartlett Hotel used to be before it burned. Wheaton's door casing had a hole where presumably the bell used to be. A knock brought no response as did a second. Though surrounded by well-kept New England houses, the Wheaton residence seemed to be held together only by its ancient coat of paint. A gravel path led to its rear, and Hudson decided that was sufficient invitation. In back was a sturdy barn, reflecting the philosophy that if you take care of your animals they will take care of you. The animals had gotten much the better of the bargain. A striped kitten ambled out of a bush.

Between barn and house stretched a clothesline to which a woman was attaching blankets.

"Excuse me," Hudson began and promptly stopped as the woman gave a startled "yip." Grey eyes with black hair tightly pulled to an enormous bun.

"I'm sorry. There wasn't any answer at the door. I'm looking for Surveyor Ben Wheaton."

"He's not here."

"I only wanted some information.. Are you Mrs. Wheaton."

"No."

"Ah ... can you tell me where I can find him?"

"I'm his daughter. What do you want?"

"I was hoping Mr. Wheaton could give me some information about a property I've just ...acquired." Was that really a clothespin that held her bun together?

"Name?"

"Well, my name wouldn't mean anything to him. The property was owned by Wallace Carver. I don't know if Mr. Wheaton ever did a survey of the Carver land, but he did for the next door neighbor and I thought ..."

"Name?"

Good God, what an idiot. He had no idea what name his crusty neighbor went by.

"We're on Swallow Hill Road," he replied weakly. "I think we're the only two properties on it."

She stared at him. There was a feeling of disquiet about her. "I'll look." She picked up the clothes basket and went in the back door. This did not sound like an invitation to follow. He sauntered toward the barn. Several stalls underneath, a hayloft above and a big open space where presumably the hay wagon or tractor would be kept. Though sturdily constructed, the barn leaked daylight through the sideboards. Must be a bit chilly when the January winds blow. Come to think of it, he'd never seen a barn with insulation. Was a pig's skin that warm? A horse's?

"Mooney." He jumped. She had several maps in her hand. "Your next door neighbor whose name you don't know." She read, "Augustus R. Mooney, parcel in Bartlett, New Hampshire." She looked up studying him. "Carver abuts to the south. There is nothing in the files for that." She offered the plan.

The boundary between Mooney and Carver was clear enough, but there was no indication of the size or shape of the latter parcel. He handed it back.

"This is how Carver looks on the town tax map." She unrolled a large paper and indicated a parcel.

"What's this," he asked about lines that formed one boundary.

"The Saco. Carver seems to have," she studied it, "four hundred and sixty feet frontage on the river."

"The Saco. That's pretty exciting. Is it swimmable?"

She sighed. "There are places. Do you want a photocopy of this or not?"

"Yes, please," he said. Unbalanced. That was the word that came to mind. Her head with the giant bun was perched on a long, thin neck, seeming ready to topple the girl over if she shook her head.

It occurred to him half way home that he had again failed to get a name. The last was probably still Wheaton, unless she had been a lot friendlier at some time in her life. Though he couldn't shed his own feeling that he himself had acted as much an ass as he considered most other people to be.

Lawrence M. Cook. Good work. Get the name right at the start. Though offhand he couldn't think of a reason why he cared what the manager's name of the First Conway Bank was. Well-built for his sixty some years, Cook was round-faced and small-eared, the latter nearly covered with bushy white hair.

"There you go. Pleasure to have your account."

"It won't be a big one. Just for bill paying."

"New in town?"

"Yes."

"So am I, and it's my fourteenth year."

"Father have to be born here to be a native?"

"Grandfather. What do you do?"

"Good question. Right now I'm recuperating from an accident. And years of laziness."

"Know what you mean. Come work out at the club. Nautilus. Took it up a few years ago and the bod's never felt better. Chess for the mind. You play?"

"Yes. Like to sometime."

"Here's my card. Call me."

Back in Wally's living room — it would be a long time before he could think of it as his — he studied a well-worn hiking map for trails. Easy trails. On the far side of the Moat range was a lower peak; one which the Appalachian Mountain Club book said was accessed by a seldom used trail. At its summit someone had drawn a circle with a cross in the middle in pen and ink. Owls Cliff. Good. A decision was made for him for the morning.

Owls Cliff was the name on the map, but it might have been the John Hancock elevator shaft by the time he was through. Brunel Trail began gently enough, through deep woods and along several Forest Service roads — or was it the same road winding around? Then a somewhat steeper ascent that brought him to an open field. A forest fire? Clear cutting? Whatever, there was a view of the valley below, and the trail seemed to level off, wandering through a scraggle of bushes.

With what was surely the cliff passing to his right? No way. He shook his head and reversed direction. Back in the woods he soon picked up the yellow trail markings again — heading almost straight up. He sighed and started to climb. An hour later, covered with perspiration, on his hands and knees scaling a wooded Matterhorn, his breath in short gasps, his heart nearly leaping from his chest in an effort to keep up, he thought, Good God, no wonder this miserable goat track isn't popular. He'd scratch instructions for the next climber what to do with his bones.

At last he came across a path to his left that opened suddenly on a downhill slope to an awesome view of a huge valley nearly surrounded by rounded mountains and jagged cliffs. He sank down gratefully in the shade of a scrawny maple, unscrewing the top to his container of water.

As a little life returned, he explored his conquest. No visible circle with an X in the center. Perhaps this was a favorite spot of Wally's. The cliff was but a small point of land, and he soon noticed he was not alone. Though the back was unfamiliar, the clothespin bun on the hiker seated on the edge could belong to no one but the girl who was probably a Wheaton. Had he been seen? He doubted it. With her back to him she seemed absorbed in her own thoughts, knees drawn up to her chest. He turned as silently as he could to exit.

"You sounded like a steam engine coming up. I heard you all the way from the main trail."

"I didn't know anyone was up here."

She turned her head. "So it's Mr. Mooney's curious neighbor." She turned back.

"I'm surprised to find anyone else here. I somehow didn't think this would be a popular climb with hikers."

"It isn't. I came for other reasons." Not an encouragement. He turned to leave. "My father died here."

"Oh." He leaned on a tree. "Recently?"

"This spring. His body was found at the foot of this cliff." She turned her head. "Come over here." He approached cautiously. "Come on. It's not dangerous. Stand right there."

For a fleeting moment he wondered if she was going to try to land another body in the same spot. Measuring wind drifts or something. "Yes. I can see quite well from here. What am I supposed to be looking at?"

She pointed. "This is solid ledge; a good firm lip to stand on. Even a safety net of saplings below. Would you accidently fall from there? Not even would. *Could* you?"

"Did your father?"

"A fine woodsman, good climber. Spent most of his life outdoors. Ended it falling off an ordinary cliff."

"Maybe he had an attack. Did he have heart trouble?"

She sighed. "The only trouble with his heart was it didn't have room for...others."

"Was anyone with him when he...had his accident?" Her head gave a small negative shake. "Don't surveyors usually have someone with them on jobs?"

"Here?" Her voice was pure scorn. "This is government land." She swept an arm. "As far as you can see in any direction, it's all White Mountain National Forest. He wouldn't be out here on business."

Hudson was unwilling to give ground. "He might have been working for the government."

"Occasionally the National Forest adds some land around its edges," she explained patiently as to a child. "Sometimes they even swap land, giving up an unimportant piece for a more strategic one. But we're in the middle here. No surveyors required. Understood?"

"So he jumped." It was cruel, but he'd had enough condescension, and it was time he went on the offensive.

Her eyes opened wide, but he saw not anger, but sorrow and perhaps doubt. Her shoulders slumped. "Maybe he did, I don't know. I'd...we'd kind of lost touch."

Contrite, "I didn't really mean that. If he wanted to end things, why come way out here? Was this a special spot?"

"No," she hesitated. Then with more assurance. "No, I'm sure not. We were pretty close when I was young. We often went hiking, and I used to help him with his surveying. I know his favorite places."

"Are you a surveyor?" Hudson felt a change of subject was in order.

"My role was carrying the theodolite. I developed muscles, but not much knowledge."

"I'm having a little trouble finding the boundaries of Wally Carver's land. Perhaps you would be willing to help me find them."

"I don't think so," she rose. "And I'd better start back." She picked up her knapsack and walked a few steps. Then turned. "Why are you so interested in Mr. Carver's land?"

"I guess it's mine now. He was my father-in-law. There was an automobile accident last month. He was killed...My wife died in the same crash. So that left me."

"I'm sorry." Her eyes were opaque. "I'm not very...When would you like to walk that land?"

"Tomorrow, if you're free. I mean if you have the time. I'll be glad to pay for any help."

"I'm not a surveyor. I won't do it for money. I'll be at... your house at five A.M.."

"Fine. Is the sun up that early?"

"Tomorrow is the longest day of the year. And there are thunderstorms forecast for the afternoon."

Seeing no reason to linger on the mountain top, he followed her back toward the trail. Weird kid. She couldn't be more than twenty-five, if that, he guessed. And yet she seemed to have absorbed all the world's bitterness. He took a look back at the view he was leaving, tripped and fell on his face with a loud, "Hunnff!"

"Are you all right?" she called.

"I think so." He sat up carefully.

"Not much used to being out with Mother Nature, are we?"

He rubbed his leg. "We tripped over this stick here." She came back to look. "And that doesn't look like Mother Nature's."

A square piece of wood protruded two feet above the ground and was buried deep enough so that Hudson's weight hadn't dislodged it. She knelt and studied it. There were figures and some writing on one side. She looked up. "I don't believe this." She looked again at the stake. Almost to herself, "How could it be." Then with conviction, "That stake was placed there by my father.'"

"It looks like a surveyor's stake. But you said..."

"I know what I said. We're in the middle of the White Mountain National Forest. There's no private land for miles. Everything around belongs to the government. What was he doing here surveying?"

There was no answer but the wind whispering to the trees.

"Come in. I've just put on coffee."

Longest day or not, the sun was not yet visible. She looked bright and alert as if she'd been up for hours.

"None for me. I've had tea." She looked around the living room. "You go ahead. I'll look through the bookcases."

When he returned from the kitchen, cup in hand, she had a book in her hand and was smiling over what she was reading.

"I think that's the first time I've seen you smile."

With his words it promptly disappeared. "Your father-in-law had excellent taste in his reading. This is an old favorite of mine." She held it up so he could see the words *Bhagavad Gita*.

"You're a philosopher?"

"A seeker."

"What are you seeking?"

"Peace. An answer. What we're all looking for. Or do you already have all the answers." More than a hint of sarcasm.

"I guess I'm not even sure what the questions are. Even then I don't always ask them. For example, I've never even asked your name."

"I have several. Cilla will do."

"Several? You've been married?"

"Several first names. My last name is the same as my father's. Wheaton."

"I'm Hudson Rogers." He stuck out his hand.

She replaced the book on the shelf. "Are you ready to start?"

He withdrew his unshaken hand. "Right. I'll just get rid of this cup." Christ. These New Hampshirites were as friendly as the granite they lived in. Maybe it's insulting in local custom to offer the right hand. Like an Arab his left. Well, that's what he wanted. Distance from people. And he'd have little difficulty retaining that status with Cilla the Bun.

He rinsed the cup and left it in the sink. She was studying a piece of paper when he returned.

"I stopped by Town Office yesterday for a copy of the deed. I've drawn it out. We'll start at Mooney's southeast corner."

The iron pipe was the only reference point he did know and led the way there. He noted Cilla had a compass, and she set out at a confident pace.

"A lot of ledge here," she commented after they reached the area where the land arose again.

"How can you tell?"

"Look at the trees. They can't put down enough root to fully develop." And indeed they seemed stunted and bent rather than straight and tall.

"Is that bad?"

"If you want to put in a septic system it is."

Hudson, who, if he had thought about it, would have felt municipal sewers were an indigenous part of the landscape that greeted the pilgrims at Plymouth, considered that there might be more to building in the country than framing in a house. "Pretty expensive then to dig a well, huh?"

"Actually not." Why had he been certain that no matter what view he expressed she would take the opposite. "Going through ledge you save on casing. Provided there's water here at all."

And a little further on, he did hear water, catching glimpses through the trees of what was surely the Saco. There was something mesmerizing about a brook flowing through woods. Here it was more a river — over thirty feet wide — with a small abandoned cabin on the far side the only sign in either direction that the spot had ever been visited by humans. A shack really, with a crumpled red and white curtain at the one grimy window...he stopped, rubbed perspiration from an eye and looked again. No. Blurred vision had made it appear the curtain had moved.

Large slabs of rock invited one to sit, but Cilla was off downstream. Where the undergrowth was heavy she used the river, jumping from rock to rock like a mountain goat, with her bun like a black horn. He followed, though more a lumbering bear. Hudson's quickness on his feet had been a major edge on his college wrestling team. That and powerful shoulders had won him several titles in the 190 pound weight class. The shoulders were still strong, though with a little more padding — if thirty pounds was a little. But there was no longer the spring in his step, he acknowledged. And the rocks seemed more slippery than they looked. He paused, studying a particularly lengthy leap that Cilla had taken with little difficulty. Male ego, normally well submerged in Hudson, was being raked close to the surface by the surveyor's daughter.

He didn't miss by much. Great, he thought as he sat in knee-deep water. No points for close.

"Are you all right?" He could see his middle years stretching into old as increasing numbers of people asked if his deteriorating body would be able to keep up one more time. "I think so." He clambered to dry land. Twinges from his ribs and his left ankle told him his pride wasn't all that had suffered. He removed the sneaker and massaged his foot.

"Where on earth did you get those things?" Cilla's tone was not sympathetic.

"If you're referring to the sneakers, I found them in a closet. What's wrong with them?"

"Probably nothing if you're out for a yuppie run. In the woods you need something with more protection — that won't turn on you. Can you walk?"

"Of course." He started to get up.

"First put your tennis shoe back on and lace it up as tight as you can." She found a substantial stick while he was — once again — following orders.

"I think we'd better go directly to the house and put some ice on that."

He decided resistance was futile. This woman was as bossy as Ethel, a nurse his parents had hired for him when he was eight. The diagnosis had been rheumatic fever, and the cure was a sentence to endless weeks in bed with the Witch of the East as jailer. His heart — the organ most at risk with this ailment — was undamaged, but he still shuddered at the sound of her name.

The journey back was less painful than humiliating, gimping along behind, but it felt better than he'd admit to sink into a leather chair as Cilla put together an ice pack. Comfort. At least he'd have that in his declining years. He sighed. Three months ago he was a healthy, contented suburbanite in the prime of life. Happily married — a state which had come as a surprise to him. At 28 he'd felt maybe he'd never find that mythical love that seemed to settle so easily on others. A bachelor life was not unappealing. He had always been his own best friend. Then came Sylvia. Probably not much younger than the woman of multi first names now in the kitchen. What a difference in his life, now and then. He had come to count on Sylvia's presence, a warm glow that illuminated his life, for an all-too-short twelve years.

"You'll probably have to find someone to push your wheelchair." She presented him with a towel wrapped around crushed ice.

He sat up straighter. "What do you mean?"

"Well, you're getting along in years now and obviously becoming accident prone."

"I'm forty-one. That may seem old to you, but it's barely half as long as I expect to live."

"Which makes you middle-aged." Had there been a hint of amusement as she turned to the bookcase? "May I borrow this book? My copy is in New York." She held up the *Bhagavad Gita* .

"Do you have a place in the city?"

"New York State. Near Syracuse. I live on an enormous estate. Seven hundred acres and a main building with fifty-six rooms." A far away look crept into her eyes.

He sat back. "It belongs to you?"

"It belongs to God."

"A convent?"

"An ashram." She noticed his look. "Where I live of my own free will."

"What does one do there besides...ah, worship?" He couldn't keep the condescension from his voice.

"Well, of course there's the lamb sacrifice each full moon, but mostly we just copy things on papyrus in our candlelit cells."

"Sure. But why would ...someone want to stay in a place like that?"

"To work on one's karma. It's a peaceful life."

"Karma. Then you believe in reincarnation. That what you do in this life affects who you are in the next."

"Or what."

He caught her look. "And you're thinking I'm in tough shape for my next."

She moved away. "I don't know you." Clearly implied but unsaid was that she also had no desire to.

He tested his ankle. "I don't think I've done much damage. Can you recommend some easy hikes for someone just starting?"

"Where's your map?" All business.

He produced Wally's tattered one. "I don't know if this is out of date."

"The mountains haven't moved." She opened the map and traced her finger down it. "There's a short climb near where...oh!...Did you make this cross where my father...on Owls Cliff?"

He shook his head. "Somebody else did. It was the reason I decided to go there."

She held the map to the light. "There's something written next to it."

He hobbled over. "You're right. It was so faint I hadn't noticed it. Seems to be just letters and numbers." He took the map from her, paper and pencil from the desk and copied the writing..

She took the paper. It read:

K8EKK8AKKEK

"The 'K's could be kilometers," she said. "And 'E's east. But what would the 'A' be," she puzzled.

"Looks like an old Red Sox scorecard when Clemens was pitching." She gave him a look. "Not a serious comment," he added quickly. They were after all discussing the place her father had died. "Is it important?"

"I don't know," she replied, mostly to herself. "There's something familiar about it...Why should there be a mark on that particular hill. It's not on a standard trail. In fact, it's quite out of the way...And these letters and numbers seem to refer to it." Exasperated, "Oh I'm just seeing ghosts!" Then, as though arriving at a decision, "When they told me about my father's accident I came here intending to spend only enough time to settle...whatever needed settling. But when I arrived everything was all wrong."

Hudson stifled an urge to interrupt. For Cilla Wheaton, this was practically an oration.

"Though he'd retired three years ago, Dad was in good condition. He'd always been active. There was absolutely no reason for him to fall from that ledge." She stopped. Then slowly, "There's something else. Dad wasn't the neatest person, but his files were always meticulous. He used a number system with a separate index on five by eight cards. The files were all out of order, as though someone had gone through them and put them back without reference to the system. When I checked them against the index I found one file was missing."

She paused for so long that Hudson prompted, "So, if you had the index you must know what file was taken."

She studied him, debating. "It meant nothing to me at the time. But when you came to the house I began to wonder. And now...The name on the missing file was E. Wallace Carver."

* * *

Chapter 4

THE OFFICES OF John Fanstock Realty were in the center of North Conway, on a side street across from Schouler Park and its historic railroad station. He crossed the street to it with only a slight limp. After Cilla's startling announcement of a connection between Wheaton and Carver, the subject of Hudson's conditioning program had been forgotten. They'd gone through Wally's files to see if he had stored any information on Wheaton. There was nothing.

Hudson told her his feeling that someone had also searched the Carver house, though there was no way of telling if anything had been taken. Cilla said the name Carver had been unfamiliar to her. But then she'd been away for nearly ten years. Any number of customers could have come and gone during that time.

"Have you been in the ashram for the whole ten years?" he had asked, trying to picture himself locked up for an entire decade.

"Oh no," she'd replied. "I was at school in the Berkshires for three years, then at Bennington. The ashram has been my home for just over two years."

"What do you really do there? I mean isn't it kind of...just the same routine every day?"

"Better than the cities. Can a woman walk down a street of any major city after dark without being attacked by some oversexed male driven by lust?"

"Oop. In my day some of us lusted in our hearts, but we didn't go spreading it around the city streets. I bet there are a lot more common muggings for money than rapes reported in any city."

"Of course. And how many sexual attacks go unreported because what comes after the report is almost worse than the attack itself?"

He'd tried to turn the conversation to calmer waters, but a glacial coldness had taken over her eyes and refused to be warmed. Her departure had been abrupt. Damn. Once they'd gotten onto lust, communication had disappeared. What had happened to the girl — she had become less woman and more girl in his mind — to provoke such a reaction?

Hudson shrugged. Her problems were no affair of his. But the odd combination of circumstances had nudged his interest. Puzzles were his business and a hobby. He and his partner, Don Gately, had built a small but successful company marketing puzzles and games. There'd been a chess board in his crib rather than stuffed animals. Ancient mysteries were early fascinations: the lost secret of swords bent in two without breaking; the fate of Atlantis; physical signs that might or might not indicate visits from other worlds. In languages it was their etymologies that most interested him. No, intrigued him. He smiled inwardly. Sylvia poked fun at her father for the time he spent researching a family tree, yet he, Hudson, could spend hours tracing a single word back to its original source.

John Fanstock was a large bluff redhead about fifty years old with a friendly smile and shrewd green eyes.

"I'd best tell you right up front that I'm not here to buy anything," said Hudson. Probably not the most captivating approach to a real estate broker, but it cut through small talk.

"Okay. What shall we talk about?"

"I'm interested in the background of the E. Wallace Carver property on Swallow Hill Road. Do you know it? It's right next to Augustus Mooney's."

"It happens I do. Carver built a four bedroom contemporary on it, didn't he? About...must be twenty years ago, right?"

"About then."

"Never been in the house, but a nice lot. Over ten acres. We sold it to him in the early seventies." He leaned forward in his chair. "Doesn't want to sell does he?"

"No. Mr. Carver died a few weeks ago. It belongs to me now and it isn't for sale. I'm trying to find the surveyor when he bought the land. Who might have information like that?"

"Let me look." Fanstock was back in less than two minutes with a folder. "Squires from Conway," he said reading from it. "I would have guessed him. He did most of the land east of the river."

Strike one. "Would Mr. Carver have needed a surveyor when the house was built?"

"Probably not, in those days. Long as he had a deed, the builder wouldn't have needed anything else."

Strike two. "Do you know a surveyor by the name of Wheaton?"

"Sure. Ben Wheaton. Up in Bartlett. Died a short while ago."

"What sort of man was he?"

"Thorough. Knew his work. Had a small office, just himself. Been in business a long time or he wouldn't have had any — business that is. Didn't keep up. Nowadays a surveyor has to be an engineer as well. The tree huggers have made life tough for us all. Can't build a driveway without a fistful of permits and an EIS."

"EIS?"

"Environmental impact study. Or survey, I never remember which. Got to be sure you're not wiping out a rare breed of ant. Then of course you need a hazardous waste study to be sure someone hasn't parked an old truck with a leaky oil tank on it. You planning to live here?"

"I'm recuperating from an accident and doing some hiking to get back in shape." He pulled out Wally's map from his breast pocket. "Came across a funny thing while on one...walk." Hudson swallowed the word. It had been a 'walk' like firemen 'walk' up ladders. He pointed to Owls Cliff. "I found a survey stake right where this X is. Can you think of any reason someone would be doing a survey out there?"

Fanstock studied the map. Then sat back in his chair. "What makes you think it was a survey stake?"

"It had some writing on it. I was told it belonged to Mr. Wheaton."

The smile was gone, and the green eyes were appraising. "By who? Who told you it was a Wheaton stake?"

"As a matter of fact it was his daughter."

"Silly Cilla? She's been in a nuthouse for a couple years. Someplace in New York state. Where'd you run into her?"

"She came home after her father died. And I think it was an ashram she was in."

"That's right." Fanstock bobbed his head. "One of those Jim Jones places where they sit around singing as they drink poison. Funny what happens to kids nowadays. Marge Tuttle's daughter. Good looking kid. Gone and buried herself in a woods shack. Dresses like a tramp. Family has bucks. Real bucks. And she lives out there on the edge of a swamp. We call 'em wetlands now. And God help you if you sink a shovel within a hundred feet of one. Probably genetic. Marge is a bit soft too."

"Too?"

"Cilla's mother." He thought a moment. "Strange woman. Smelled woodsy. She died"

Great obit. Cilla certainly fit the strange part. If the mother was anything like the daughter, how did anyone ever get close enough for a smell.

* * *

Though the ankle felt much better next morning, it wasn't ready for a climb. Hudson settled on an afternoon "gently ascending" trail — according to the Appalachian Mountain Club's hiking book — that brought him to Lost Pond, a tucked-away mountain pool across the narrow valley from the AMC's Pinkham Notch camp. A hazy sky leaked enough color for the water to reflect a pale blue and enough sun to glisten on it. He soaked his ankle in the cold water as he munched his sandwich. The conversation with Fanstock had never gotten back to the survey stake. As though a coin had been inserted, the real estate agent had rambled on about local gossip until Hudson had to announce another appointment to get away. There was no question the mood had suddenly changed. When? At the point of the stake, so to speak. Fanstock's eyes had narrowed, and his mouth had tightened. Maybe just indigestion.

He skipped a stone across the pond. Fourteen. Not bad. But then he was a self-confessed expert. One of his few outdoor adventures with Sylvia had been an afternoon canoeing down the Charles River. He'd rowed single sculls at Harvard, and the river was familiar territory. They'd picnicked under a large maple, and Sylvia had asked if Hudson believed George Washington had really thrown a silver dollar across the Potomac; wasn't it too far? He'd replied that it wasn't difficult for an expert dollar skipper — for obviously that's the way it was done. Those were days when a half dollar wasn't exotic currency, and he'd wasted five of them attempting to prove his point.

He roused himself and looked around. Mount Washington loomed at two o'clock with its top obscured by clouds. He pictured bear and deer grazing in the dark green forest that climbed as high as weather permitted. The rock face above treeline and under the clouds looked swept clean from the hurricane strength winds that were said to regularly appear. The pond had a swamp at one end and a beaver dam at the other. Across its narrow width was a steep banking with a mixture of hard and soft woods. Next to him was a large round boulder with an unusual vertical projection jutting from it. Like a closed fist with the middle digit extended — as though Mother Nature was giving him the finger. That about summed it up.

"Caught anything?" A heavy set middle-aged man with a red face leaned on a sturdy stick and, taking in air noisily, peered down on him.

Hudson pulled his foot out of the pond and examined his toe. "Not yet," he announced. "Guess they're not biting."

"Hmff." He lowered himself to a rock and studied Hudson with hands folded over his walking stick. "You're not from around here." It was an announcement, not a question.

"Living in Bartlett for a while. You know everybody in the White Mountains?"

"Know a flatlander when I see one."

"What gives me away?"

"You all give off a feeling you're uncomfortable here. As though you don't fit in. No offense. See it all the time."

Retired major or colonel, thought Hudson. Used to a command and at loose ends without it. "You a native?"

"No. Greenwich, Connecticut, but a long time ago. I've had the ski area west of town for many years." He blew noisily in a large handkerchief. "Great Haystack."

"Sure. I can almost see your mountain from where I'm staying."

"You've hurt your ankle." Under the major's heavy sweater Hudson could see a suit vest.

"Jumping rocks in the Saco. Started the day a young man; ended up middle aged. My name's Hudson Rogers." He reached a hand back.

"Floyd Carr," said the other grasping it. The grip was fleshy but like a vise. "Do you ski?"

"Used to. Hope to again some day. Maybe at your place."

"Sure. Come back in winter. Best time of year here."

"Might even take a look at it this summer if it's okay with you."

"We're closed. But occasionally someone climbs us for the blueberries on top. Hmff." With an effort Carr got to his feet. Hudson could almost hear a military band playing as he marched down the trail.

Hudson put his sock and shoe on and headed back. The mood of solitude had been broken beyond repair.

It was early evening and the car filled with groceries when Hudson turned off the gravel road and into Wally's driveway. Though meticulous in the ordering of his own life and affairs, Wally obviously felt nature should be allowed to do her own thing. The narrow driveway was as slight an intrusion into her kingdom as possible. Except where absolutely necessary for passage of a vehicle, trees were left undisturbed and, particularly in spots of deciduous growth, the forest seemed ready to reclaim its own. Hudson considered trimming it back whenever his Subaru squeezed under an especially flourishing beech which extended a stout limb to twang his antenna, but somehow couldn't bring himself to use a saw on what he still considered to be someone else's property.

As he was setting the groceries on the kitchen counter, his eye was caught by an open cupboard door. While not in Wally's class as a housekeeper, Hudson instinctively straightened chairs, smoothed covers and — invariably — closed cupboard doors. Leaving the groceries in their bag, he went back to the living room. A jacket he had placed over the back of a straight chair now hung from one side of it. Yesterday's newspaper had changed position from where he had left it at lunch. Assuming the house itself was not alive — a conclusion Hudson was as yet not ready for — someone else was making use of it along with himself. He mounted to his bedroom wondering if he'd find a little girl sleeping off a feast of porridge.

A bureau drawer stood open a full inch. Hudson opened it all the way. Nothing seemed to be missing. Nor was anything downstairs as far as he could tell. He put away the groceries, carefully relocked the front door — for all the good that did — and walked the gravel road to Augustus Mooney's. The geese tender was in his yard surrounded by his flock.

"I'm afraid I've had another visitor. Seen anyone on the road?"

"Anything stolen?"

"Not that I can tell. But I haven't counted the silver."

"Been afraid of this. There's been hooliganism in the village, but not on Swallow Hill. Think I'll give the police chief a ring."

"What's the point? There's no damage."

"*This* time. I'll get him to keep an eye out here."

Mooney went inside, and Hudson wandered home unsatisfied. He had no desire to cause a commotion. It was no hooligan who'd been in the house, but it wasn't until later as he planned his hike for the next day that he discovered the one item missing. An item he remembered deciding he didn't need for his short walk that afternoon and had thus left at home in his jacket pocket. The hiking map of the White Mountains with an X where a man had recently died.

Chapter 5

NUMBER ONE IT was definitely a survey stake. Number two it was Wheaton's. So much Cilla was certain of. Number three it was gone.

They'd searched the bushes around where it had been to see if by chance an animal had knocked it over. Nothing. Kids? Hudson's hooligan? The Wheaton-Carver affair was an unfamiliar jigsaw puzzle where pieces kept disappearing before they could be put together.

The second climb up Owls Cliff had been much worse than the first. Cilla had set a strong pace, her old red-checked shirt flapping over well worn corduroy jeans. Hudson, as the sole representative of the male race present, struggled to keep up. The announced need to rest his ankle — which surprisingly bothered him not at all — gained a little respite. Outside of that she was pitiless. The last stretch reduced him to a gasping blob, blood trickling from a barked shin as sweat did from every pore. Collapsed where the trail turned down again, it was several minutes before he could talk. When he tried, it came out squeezed. Cilla, showing no signs of strain, scampered on to look for the stake.

After Hudson had recounted the loss of the map and Fanstock's disbelief, he'd coaxed her into a return trip — feeling he might next be checked for suicidal tendencies. Cilla, strangely listless, had reluctantly agreed. The view was as striking as Hudson remembered. An enormous open valley with jutting cliffs and a tiny, deep blue wading pool in the distance.

"Beautiful, isn't it?" he wheezed.

"Hmm. Are you positive you didn't just misplace that map?"

"I'm sure." He gulped water. "What I don't know is where to go from here.."

"I know where I'm going."

That seemed to be the end of her statement. Like the first line of the song with the rest unimportant. "Where?"

"Back to Syracuse."

"You're giving up?"

"I'm going home. There's nothing more I can do here.

"And your father's...accident?"

"What of it? Nothing I do will bring him back." She looked into the distance as if for his spirit. "I miss my friends.

"When will you go?"

"Tomorrow. I made up my mind before you called."

"To spend the rest of your life there?" It sounded a bit dramatic, but Hudson was curious.

"Perhaps."

"Writing on papyrus by candlelight and slaughtering lambs?"

"Meditating." She eyed him. "Praying for those who need help."

"Appreciated." He studied her. "In a way I envy your beliefs."

"A few months in an ashram might do you some good."

"They wouldn't let me in."

"They let anyone in. Which reminds me. They don't allow pets. Would you take Juniper?"

"The kitten I saw the other day?"

"Yes. I've nowhere else to leave her."

"Well... I guess so." It was grudging. At this time in his life he didn't want to be tied down by anything. Even a cat.

"If you'd rather I didn't..."

"No, no. I'll take her."

At five o'clock the following morning Juniper had been delivered to her new landlord/housekeeper. As the days passed without incident, the map thief receded from Hudson's thoughts. In hopes that his mind would also release the pain of other memories, Hudson concentrated on his body. Each day he hiked a new trail. The first rainy day he took himself to Cranmore Sports Center, a tennis and fitness building at the base of that historic ski area. Nautilus equipment, looking like modern torture devices, sat with gaping mouths around a room open on all sides to Madame Defarges who could clack over one's suffering. A slim but strong-looking, young girl — undoubtedly related to the amazon of Black Cap Mountain — was assigned as his warder.

As they headed down the stairs a white haired man was coming up. He stopped. "Mr. Rogers. Decided to join us? Larry Cook from the bank."

They shook hands. He'd never have come up with the name. "Going to try it."

"You'll enjoy it. Don't forget chess some time." He continued on.

"Done Nautilus before?" The girl had her hand on a monster.

"No. I haven't really done much exercise in nearly twenty years. Thought it was about time to edge my way back into it." This last came out with a grin as if to say please note the word 'edge' and go easy on this aging body.

"That's okay. It's never too late to start." She scrutinized the bulge that hung over his gym shorts as though an exception might have to be made in his case, gave him a card to keep track of his progress and emphasized that he had to be regular in his workouts or progress wouldn't happen.

Each of the twelve machines worked a different set of muscles. They began on those for the legs.

"We'll start you off with a minimum weight."

"Sounds about my speed." Hudson was modesty itself, but was pleased when, after several exercises, she — who went by the unamazon-like name of Robin — added a little more poundage to each.

His confidence had risen a notch when she strapped him into the first of the upper body machines, only to be dampened by reminders from his ribs that they needed more time to heal. One machine worked just biceps. On this, at the end of several repetitions, he requested she add weights until his muscles were really pushed. She did so several times.

"I think that's enough. Are you all right?"

"Fine."

"You're at eighty pounds! That's a lot for someone in as lousy shape as you."

A mixed compliment — if one at all.

"You're actually very strong. Sometime in your life you must have worked those muscles."

"Wrestling and rowing in college."

"Let's leave it where it is for today. You can add more weight as you go along."

Hudson, feeling there might be hope for him yet, added Nautilus to his body salvage program.

That afternoon he received a call from Lander Margate, Wally's attorney, who had been guiding the Carver estate through probate and wanted to reassure himself about the condition of its sole heir.

"I'm physically better every day," Hudson admitted.

"How are you getting on at the Bartlett house?"

"Fine. It's a great section of the world. Are you familiar with it?"

"I've seen pictures. You found everything in order?"

"Oh yes. You know how meticulous Wally was. Only..."

"Only?"

"For a while I felt as though someone was in the house whenever

I left it."

"Things missing?"

"Nothing important. A map I was using for hiking. A curious story actually. Ran into a girl whose father fell off a cliff in the White Mountains last spring. That same cliff was marked on a map I found here in the house. And on the top of the cliff was a commercial survey stake — right in the middle of the National Forest. Her father was a surveyor, and she was certain the stake had been placed there by him."

"Interesting. What do you make of it?"

"The girl felt her father's death wasn't an accident. *Couldn't* have fallen without help. But when we went back to the cliff, the stake had disappeared. Then the map did."

"Was he alone?"

"The surveyor?"

"When he fell."

"Nobody's admitted to being with him."

"Would they?"

"Good point. Not if it wasn't an accident."

"So what now?"

"For the case of the fallen surveyor? Nothing. There's no proof, and not much hope of ever finding any. The girl's given up on it and gone back to her ashram...There *was* one thing that you might know something about. The surveyor's name was Ben Wheaton. Do you know if Wally ever had any dealings with a man by that name?"

"It is unfamiliar to me. Ought I know it?"

"Wheaton had a file with Wally's name on it. Also now among the missing."

"Wallace seldom confided his business dealings in me."

Hudson grinned into the phone. "Or in anyone else from what I gather. Secretive cuss. But I guess all you lawyers are. In any case it doesn't matter. The whole thing's a dead issue now."

Or was it. Hanging up the telephone, Hudson found himself thinking on Margate's question. Was he alone? Surveyors usually came in twos. Would Wheaton have set that survey stake all by himself? Could he? Didn't someone need to hold the pole, or whatever it was surveyors looked at?

The following morning Hudson approached a small ranch house on Bear Notch Road with an enormous willow tree in its front yard. It seemed to be a rule with willows. The bigger the tree, the smaller the house it sheltered. As though the more sunlight it blocked, the more stunted the house's growth. The door was answered by a short, stout, sixtyish woman, wiping her hands on her apron.

"Sorry to bother you. You knew Mr. Wheaton next door?"

"Yes. Who wants to know?"

"My name is Rogers. Hudson Rogers."

"Living in the Carver place on Swallow Hill."

Good God. Bartlett's a smaller town than I thought. "What did I have for breakfast?"

The woman threw back her head and roared. "I'm good but not that good. Emma Persons's my name. I'm the postmaster in Bartlett so I know everybody. Come in. You can help with the dishes."

Before he could get in another word, Hudson was in the kitchen with a dish towel in his hands and was listening to a story about somebody named Devereau who had a mail order business and whose catalogues kept getting heavier every year. The size of the house obviously had little relationship to the number of people using it, if the volume of dishes was any guide. Hudson counted twelve dinner plates he dried, plus an equal number of cups, saucers, salad and dessert plates.

"Well that's done. Now we can talk," the postmaster announced leading the way to a tiny living room, as though the dishes had been done in stoic silence. "What do you want to know about Ben?"

"Did he have a regular assistant? Someone who went out on jobs with him?"

"Little Tommy Cantring helped now and then. Rode his bike all the way from Albany every day."

"Albany...?"

"New Hampshire! Did you think I meant New York? Would that be a ride!"

"Of course. Just south of Conway. Do you know where in Albany?"

"Up near the Darby Field Inn I think. A nice place. He was the first one to climb Mount Washington, you know."

"Tommy...?"

"Darby Field!"

"Except for the Indians."

"Oh the Indians never climbed it. Thought the gods lived up there. Didn't pick a very comfortable home if you ask me. Worst weather on earth they say. Why are you interested in Ben?" Emma Persons' attitude made it plain that information wasn't going to travel in just one direction.

"His daughter felt the circumstances surrounding his death were...unusual."

"You met Cilla? She was here just a while ago. Had a bee in her bonnet about Ben's accident." Brown eyes suddenly held more shrewdness than her chatter had allowed to escape.

"It *was* an accident?"

"What else?"

"Cilla said her father wouldn't have fallen from where he did. Without help."

"Cilla was a sweet girl growing up. Right up till...Oh, look at the time! Grace filled in for me this morning only because of the lobster feed last night." She bustled out to the kitchen, as Hudson rose unwillingly to his feet. "You don't think I eat off all those dishes myself!" she called back. "There's just me, you know. Foster died three years ago. Men are so fragile." She came back with a handbag; paused to look him in the eye. "I do hope you take good care of yourself."

With these words Hudson found himself hustled out the door and onto the street. 'Right up till' what, he wondered. The ashram? Such places met more ready acceptance on the West Coast than in the east he knew. But does a 'sweet girl' become something else because she enters one?

'Little' Tommy Cantring's name owed more to his age than his size, being nearly as tall as Hudson himself. It wasn't until late in the afternoon when Hudson found him at home.

"Sure. Me and Ben went out lots a times." It came out 'shoo wa' in a high to low whine.

"Were you with him when he had his accident?"

"Nope. Neva called me." Little Tommy was aggrieved. "Neva called me fa two weeks befowa."

"Maybe he just didn't have any jobs for you."

"Had 'em fa somebuddy."

"How do you know?"

"Saw him."

"You saw him with someone during the weeks before he died?"

"Once. Neva saw him afta that."

"You don't remember what day, do you?"

Little Tommy scratched his head. "Hadda be a Thursday. That's my dump day. Here he come down the Kanc in his little van. I wave hello, but he din see me."

"And he had someone with him?"

"Yeah."

"Do you know who?"

"Couldn't see him. Cept a lotta hair. Goin on a job they was." The thought made Little Tommy unhappy.

"They were heading west?"

"Yeah."

"What kind of a job would they have been going to in the National Forest?"

Tommy wrinkled his forehead. "Maybe they was goin to Lincoln."

"Did Wheaton do survey work in Lincoln?"

"Not with me."

Back at the house, Hudson checked a calendar. May 1 was a Thursday.

Chapter 6

THE MAN IN the pine-paneled room dialed the telephone and sat back to listen. A scowl appeared with the speaker's final comment.

"You see the implications."

"Yes, yes. I understand. Hudson Rogers is on a course that can't be permitted to continue. I shall make sure he...gets the message." He hung up the telephone and gazed out the window at a June sky that had unexpectedly turned cloudy.

Chapter 7

· THE NEXT DAY dawned bright and clear, and Hudson was eager to get hiking but forced himself to visit the Sports Center's Nautilus equipment first. He did twelve repetitions of the lower body machines but skipped all the upper body exercises except the biceps.

Robin put it more bluntly. "You should be skipping a whole day. Didn't I tell you that?"

"But it will take twice as long that way."

"To do what?"

"To get back in condition."

"It will take twice as long if you don't. Your muscles need time to recover. If you just keep breaking them down they'll have no chance to develop."

Hudson wasn't at all sure about that. He couldn't remember following an every-other-day routine in college. Since then, though, sports had been taken over by the doctors. It had become a science rather than a game, and he didn't feel particularly confident taking on its practitioners in argument.

Though much too early for blueberries, Hudson decided to climb Great Haystack. How steep could a hill be that people came down on pieces of plastic. The answer appeared half-way up The Needle — an expert trail that connected top and bottom by the shortest possible route. Very. He sat panting on a rock and watched two workmen and a truck picking up debris under a chairlift, dropped by ascending skiers. It might be fun to ski again. He hadn't tried it since college when he'd been good enough to negotiate expert trails with ease. In those days it had been Vermont. He'd encouraged Sylvia to learn, but for her the outdoors was what one had walls to protect against, and he had little interest in going without her.

A third and fourth workers were gathering brush on the edge of the trail. It had been freshly cut back, he noticed with regret — making the trail wider. One of the delights of skiing for him had been the mystery of a narrow trail with unexpected turns and pitches, that kept you literally on your toes. The adventure of not knowing what was around the next bend. A straight, wide trail was merely speed. And the ability to see other skiers on it, even far off, took away the all-too-rare fantasy of being alone in winter wilderness.

He took a large gulp of water and trudged on. The view from the top was — he told himself — worth it. The Presidential Range lay before him like waves in a stormy sea. Even whitecaps on Washington, and was it Madison or Monroe? Jefferson and Clay he supposed were behind. How did Clay get in there anyway. There were lots of low bushes on top of Great Haystack that he decided were blueberry. He loved blueberries; at just that moment, though, the thought of climbing up again mid-summer to harvest them had little appeal.

The bulky frame of Floyd Carr was settled in a wooden chair on the base lodge deck, as Hudson reached the bottom of the slope. The ski area owner was in business attire, coat off, sleeves rolled up but tie firmly in place, leafing through a stack of papers. Other piles were placed on a bench in front of him, held in place by an assortment of round rocks.

"I see you haven't left yet."

"And you're hard at it. Isn't it too nice a day to work?"

"People think because you live in a resort area you're always on vacation. I work while others play."

"This time of year?"

"All twelve months. Takes a lot of planning and good Yankee sweat to run a ski area in New England."

"Harder than the Rockies or the Alps?"

"Damn right. It's the weather. The snow that falls isn't easy to work with. That's why we make it ourselves."

"You improve on Mother Nature?"

"We do. The surface under skis is now better here than anywhere in the world."

Hudson was certain if it wasn't, Carr would beat on it until it shaped up.

A little later, a bag of groceries in either hand, he mounted the steps to Wally's house. And stopped. On the front door, hanging from a nail, was a piece of paper. Before he drew close enough to read it, he knew it would have on it the one word:

STOP

With grocery bags on the floor in front of him, Hudson sat in the living room staring at the paper. After a moment he got up and looked for the notes he had found in Wally's books. He compared the printing. Certainly similar. Could be the same writer. A neighborhood joker? Wally seemed to have thought so, the casual way he had used them for bookmarks. The questions Hudson had been asking about Wheaton had alarmed someone? The helper with 'a lot of hair'? Was there a murderer out there?

Who the hell cares. It was none of his business anyway; people got murdered every hour. Come to that, what *was* his business. Any? An empty life stretching into what would be infinity, were it not for man's earthly time clock; a life without Sylvia, strung together with coffee spoon visits to grocery stores, for fuel to keep alive a flabby, aging body in a purposeless existence. He looked down at himself stretched out in the chair trying to picture a steely manhunter poised to pursue his prey. His legs still quivered from the short climb up The Needle. His sausage arms and overstuffed shoulders ached from muscles that of course didn't need a day off. Even his ribs gave periodic reminders not to be ignored. But the worst hurt was yet deeper inside. He hadn't realized how his life had come to revolve around Sylvia. He had cut off friends and other interests when they proved not to be hers. The closest they came to a circle of acquaintances was a Tuesday bridge group. Sylvia loved duplicate; Hudson enjoyed bridge, though, had he been asked, he would have preferred contract. But when the game was over, the other players went back to being strangers; fellow passengers on a weekly commute, with only the vehicle and the destination in common.

Who in the whole, wide world did he really give a damn about. A college roommate, Don Gately his former partner. Maybe one or two others...At 2 A.M. he woke to find himself still in the chair with the groceries on the floor in front of him and Juniper in his lap. He put her on the floor and them in the kitchen cupboards and took his tired body up to bed.

The sun was high in the sky when he next opened his eyes. No goal. No friends. STOP. A mawkish performance, full of self pity. He closed his eyes to shut out embarrassment. Over coffee he considered. In some ways he took after his mother. *Starry droog looche noviekh droog* — an old friend is better than two new ones. At seventy she complained that she had no friends, yet since college had made no attempt to make them, and the ones she had before that — those she considered her *real* friends — were starting to die off. At forty-one he was doing the same thing.

He needed a purpose. To find one, he first had to convince himself his was a life worth living. And right now he was finding that a little difficult. His body was mush and his brain flab. Or vice versa. To make anything of his life he had to do something about them. So let's start, Buster!

Immediately second thoughts crept in. He knew what he needed to do for his body. But his mind was set in reverse and would never shift into forward as long as it had Sylvia at the controls. Sylvia was the past, yet he quailed at the thought of losing precious memories of her. The books he'd recently read said time cures all. One called *Surviving A Lost Love* blurred his vision with tears, yet he was unable to put it down. That's it, he'd thought at the time, wallow in your grief and it will sooner be gone. His Irish streak admitted the utility of a wake, where feelings of loss were countered by laughter at the world we all find ourselves in. But his inheritance — or was it just his own reserved nature — permitted no such sharing of emotions.

All right. Let's take one step at a time. He hunted up a calendar. Was three months enough? During that time he'd work on his body and nothing else — build himself back to what he was, or as close as fortyish could get. And between now and September 29 he'd wear a blindfold on his brain. Sorry Cilla. Apologies Ben Wheaton. Thinking is out. Your puzzle will have to wait.

Juniper had climbed in his lap again. As he placed her gently but firmly on the floor and picked up his trail maps, he suddenly found his eyes filling with tears. In his mind a hand was waving as though in farewell — a hand whose touch he'd give anything for. No, no, Sylvia. It isn't goodbye. Just au revoir.

By mid-July Hudson had exhausted the White Mountains' supply of Class I trails and had started on those in Class II recommended by Augustus Mooney. His neighbor seemed to know them all from first hand experience. Robin at MCRC confessed she was surprised at Hudson's persistence. Most in his condition who came to build superbodies gave up on the super after only a few days; the body shortly after. Other priorities appeared in their lives and they'd *like* to stay with it but...Hudson added more weights.

One night, returning earlier than usual from the club, he was emptying his gym bag when there was a dull thump from somewhere in the house. He came out of the bedroom and listened. Nothing, yet he was sure he'd heard it, and it was *inside* the house. He went quietly down the stairs to the main floor. His tea water was boiling, steam spurting from the kettle spout. He turned it off and opened the door to the large dining room which had windows facing west. It was dusk; the sun had long since dropped behind the hemlocks. One twitched from a gust of wind. One? The other trees were unmoving. He went through to the living room and out on the deck. It was a hot night with not even the usual light breeze off the mountains he had come to expect. He ran down the stairs to pine-needled ground and raced to the tree he'd seen moving. Incautiously he dove into the thick stand of evergreens, receiving a branch in the eye for his efforts. But no hooligans. Or animals.

Back in the house, aided by Juniper, he went through Wally's "vacation home" from top to bottom. It was only his second visit to the finished basement. He'd had no reason to use its large family room. There was also a full bath and two other rooms, one of these set up as an office, though why Wally had needed an extra desk with the beautiful mahogany one upstairs...The furnace was quiet, only coming on when hot water was required. He tried to convince himself it had just been a branch falling on the roof, but wasn't quite successful.

He'd run into Larry Cook again at MCRC and felt it necessary to invite him over for chess.

"Great to find someone to play with. Almost nobody here knows what a chess board looks like." Cook rubbed his hands in anticipation.

"Did you used to play much?" asked Hudson.

"All the time. Was captain of the Bates team. You're warned."

It was an interesting match, but the conclusion was never in doubt. Cook was a good loser. "The last time I do any bragging before a match. You've played some."

Margate had called again. Hudson told him he expected to be back among the living come fall, and he, Margate, should make any decisions necessary concerning Wally's estate until then — which he was undoubtedly doing anyway. Gladys Swan, the librarian at North Conway library, had a nearly unlimited supply of novels that smothered Hudson's thoughts under a blanket of spies and detectives.

He made progress. Not since college had all his body parts seemed so connected. Sure, he thought, they all hurt together. But it was a good hurt. After early stiffness from yesterday's climb, they were eager for the day's adventure. His one irritation was the number of others who wanted to join in. He'd gotten accustomed to the feeling of aloneness, of never seeing another human on his hikes. With the arrival of summer, the sounds of the woods were no longer the splashing of a waterfall or the scurrying of a squirrel. The babbling was more apt to be a covey of campers than a mountain brook.

One day in late July he pulled the Subaru into a small, crowded parking lot off the Kancamagus Highway, ready to take the Greeley Ponds Trail to Waterville Valley. A stocky middle-aged woman climbed out of a Massachusetts plate Corvette and shrugged into a knapsack.

"Done this one before?" Her voice was raspy and Beacon Hill.

"First time. You?"

"Tenth or eleventh. You'll love it. Only problem's the people." She looked around at the other cars with a resigned smile.

"I was just thinking I'd even settle for the black flies."

"Relax and enjoy it. They're here 'till fall."

"Tenth or eleventh. Your favorite trail? Or do you climb them all that much?"

"The favorite...? Table Mountain on a sunny, fall day." She put on a wicked smile. "I take off all my clothes and lie naked looking at fifty miles of wilderness."

"Never been interrupted?"

"It would bother them more than me. Now twenty years ago..." She took a sip of water. "Well I'm off. Want to join me?"

"Sure. Lead on."

"Right. And I promise not to take anything off... today."

Hudson decided he liked this woman. Her name was Rita McGrath, and she lived by herself in a Commonwealth Avenue townhouse near the Public Gardens. She kept up a running commentary about the trail, the ponds, life and lust — all of which she loved and invited the world to share with her. Hudson envied her exuberance. With no more in life than he, she saw a full glass and intended to drink every drop. He was like the trail, he thought as they started the climb back after lunch at a Waterville Valley inn. He'd started life at the easy end, and half way through now had to work his way up just to get back where he'd been.

The first week in August he took a pail and again climbed Great Haystack. On the way down, the pail overflowing with blueberries, he stopped to watch workmen forking hay onto a trail.

"Why don't they build more trails instead of making these wider and less interesting?"

"No room."

"Looks to me like you've got enough land around to build forever." He waved a hand at the mountain behind him.

"Forest Service land. They're gettin' more touchy every year 'bout ski areas usin' it."

"Why? They let people hike it. Wouldn't think skiers would cause any more damage."

"Environmentalists. Snow makin' uses a lot a water. Too much they say."

"And sewage," chimed in the other leaning on his pitchfork. "Gave Loon a hell of a time."

"Not here though, Fred," said the first. "Got plenty of water and plans for a sewer system."

"So?" Hudson turned over a hand.

"Money, what else. Ski areas got none — leastwise what they tell us."

"Yeah," said Fred with disgust. "Used to be a full time job. Now they just call us at the last minute when they needs somethin' done. Lucky we got us regular jobs at the lumber company."

Hudson had developed the habit of stopping to chat with Augustus Mooney several times a week, and later that day asked him about Great Haystack.

"Seems to be doin' well whenever I'm by there," said the old gentleman, examining the ski area, visible through his westerly window. "Like any business nowadays they got to trim fat, though." He peered at Hudson. "You're trimmin' a little yourself."

"Thanks to your suggestions."

"Just bein' neighborly." Mooney had a friendly smile when he wanted to use it, which was seldom. And indeed, Hudson was beginning to feel a warm, neighborhood feeling toward Swallow Hill Road and its only other resident.

He soon moved on to Class lll trails. Here were college students instead of adolescents; backpacks instead of knapsacks. Several nights he stayed over at one of AMC's eight mountain huts. The half-day's hike in from any roadway to reach one, rewarded those who made it with a special feeling of comraderie. On his first stay he climbed apprehensively into a bunk, and had his best night's sleep yet.

A hike up Mount Tremont, next to Owls Cliff, brought the surveyor's accident to mind. With new perspective, what after all was there to it, except the understandable anguish of a daughter whose father had died before a reconciliation — anguish made doubly difficult by the possibility the father had taken his own life. The tie to Carver could have been anything. Wally had been an attorney, and attorneys hired surveyors for their real estate clients. Once in a while, though, Hudson had glanced again at the piece of paper — which for reasons he could not fathom he kept in his wallet — on which he had written the word K8EKK8AKKEK, if indeed it was a word, from the now missing map. Perhaps it was because he'd never conceded a problem as incapable of solution, and he told himself one day he'd uncover all the pieces.

One warm summer evening Larry Cook invited Hudson to join him and his wife at an open air concert in Schouler Park. North Conway's old railroad station with its Russian-like onion spires became a fitting backdrop to Tchaikovsky's 1812 Overture. The live fireworks that accompanied its climax had just begun when Hudson spotted a familiar face and towering figure in the audience. Trimble. George Trimble. The man whose confusion at a traffic signal had taken Sylvia from him. His home, Hudson remembered, was Lynn, Massachusetts. What was he doing in North Conway? When the music ended Hudson looked over again, but couldn't find Trimble in the crowd. A man of that size would be visible. Had he really seen him? Neither he nor later Margate could think of a reason why Trimble would pick North Conway for cultural entertainment.

Chapter 8

"AS YOU KNOW, I can be a patient person. I'm demonstrating that right now." The man in the pine-paneled room was speaking into the telephone.

"You mean the incident in the park."

"I hope he learns from it."

"Yes."

"Your medical friend. How are his nerves?"

"Better. You understand he isn't used to being connected with a murder."

"Who is? Do you still feel he can be trusted to keep his mouth shut?"

"I do. I've reminded him that if he doesn't, he and you and I are just as dead as the one he put in the ground."

"Good. I'm not proud of what I've done, but it had to be. Believe me, when I started this thing I had no idea it would result in murder."

"I know."

"Let alone three of them...But we are where we are. My scheme is long range. Although they sometimes don't seem to, events are now moving the way they must — as long as no one suspects I'm behind it."

"Then the fat would truly be in the fire."

He hung up and opened the window. It was a hot summer.

Chapter 9

AFTER LABOR DAY the hills were his again. As though someone had yelled 'fire', the human hordes had left the White Mountain theater with scarcely a trace. That hadn't always been true, thought Hudson, as he climbed the burnt slopes of Table Mountain the following Sunday. Some years before, a careless camper had torched hundreds of acres with a fire that had kept volunteers from all over eastern New Hampshire fighting towering forest flames for several days. The benefit: few trees to block a magnificent view. Hudson sat on a ledge munching a sandwich. The sweep of mountains from the southern tip of the Moats to the teat-like tip of Chocorua, past the Liberty Bell shape of Passaconaway to nearby Bear Mountain, with not a sign of humans. A delight, dampened only slightly by an occasional automobile on the Kancamagus Highway — parts of which could be seen far below and miles distant. At ten o'clock was the covered bridge that carried The Dugway road across the Swift River. He lay back on the rough rock with his hands behind his head. It was a beautiful, sunny day. He thought of Rita; this was her favorite mountain — with her clothes off. On impulse, he stood up, stripped and lay down on his towel naked. Shorts, socks and boots had been his usual attire during most of the summer, so his body was deeply tanned — except for a pale white band around a now flat middle and at the end of either strong-looking leg. His muscles had hardened, and rippled as he stretched out. He was down to his wrestling weight of 190, which for a six-foot-two height was right where he wanted it.

As a light breeze caressed him, he felt another part harden that hadn't for a long time. The suddenness and strength startled him. It hadn't happened like that since his teens. Well! he thought looking down at himself. There's life in you yet. He lay back, enjoying the sensation. Sex had not been a big item on his married agenda. Partly his fault. Maybe mostly. He thought with embarrassment of the early years when he had waited in vain for responses from Sylvia — responses, he'd later learned, hadn't been forthcoming partly because of his own lack of skill. He shook off the train of thought; it was not yet time. The slice of memory relaxed his groin, but he savored the feeling of renewed sexuality so much that he wore only socks and boots all the way to the car.

By mid-September he had climbed Mt. Washington three times, each by a different route. Twice the top had been buried in fog and rain, but today as he stood, looking down on the Lakes Of The Clouds, the air had a crisp, just-washed fragrance. To his right far below was the Mount Washington Hotel. To his left the Saco River cut its way through Crawford Notch, backdropped by the mountains of the Sandwich Range — a higher version of the view from Table Mountain. He thought back with amusement to his air-cooled performance there. Socks had gone on more slowly the next morning over sunburned feet. He shivered from the thought of being without clothes here. The temperature at the top was a good twenty degrees below that at the bottom, making removal of even sweater or windbreaker unacceptable. He bought a hot chocolate in the summit restaurant and brought it out to sit on the rocks looking south, feeling among friends. He had now reached the top of nearly every peak he could see, and he could see dozens. *His* favorite? He shook his head. There were too many. The view from each had its own appeal, but they all depicted sections of the same landscape. It was the unexpected brook or mountain pond that held the most charm. Arethusa Falls. Sawyer Pond with its little island. Nancy Cascade appearing suddenly through a tangle of trees. They were rooms in his home now, tapestries hung from his walls. How confined the suburban spirit, bottled up in tiny units, when the whole forest could be your mansion, there to live in idle splendor. But idleness was nearly over.

On the twenty-ninth of September, he sat down at his desk — no longer Wally's — with a fresh pad of paper and a pencil, ready to unchain his mind. It had never really been muffled, of course. Like not thinking of elephants, he hadn't been able to stop his brain from activity. But he had a well-organized mind and a reservoir of mental discipline that had sat untapped for years. He wrote the word 'Sylvia' on his pad. Then tore the paper off and started again. The future, not the past, Buster. The ache was still there, just writing the name. Had he expected it to disappear?

He got up and walked to the fireplace. Fieldstone, they called it, though he hadn't seen stones like those sitting in fields. Streaks of color ran through the rocks with odd whorls and twists. Unusual. Like Wally. The more he'd gotten to know his father-in-law, the more he'd realized what a complicated person he was. They were pretty even at chess, which said a lot for Wally's game as Hudson was a master at it. But Hudson was intrigued by the deviousness of the mind that had sat across the table from him.

The future, damn it. Why did his brain keep sliding backwards. He threw himself in a leather chair and looked at the ceiling. Okay. Maybe he had to sum up the past to escape from it. He had fled to New Hampshire on impulse, wounded in mind and body, seeking only an absence of things familiar. Returning to Massachusetts had no appeal. There was too much of Sylvia there. Yet none at all.

He'd established himself in New Hampshire. Though not yet a New Hampshirite, he'd rented his own box at the post office, argued with the local rubbish collection people and the telephone company over bills. The second gave him a momentary pause. He felt his mind was now clear and sharp; could he have miscounted the number of calls he'd made to Margate? Oh well, fit as he was, he was *still* in his forties. He'd discovered the joy of septic tanks to be pumped. There were two, he learned, and two leaching fields. He was a householder in Bartlett, New Hampshire. And here he had found a country that suited Hudson Rogers.

Middle aged or not, he had a lot of years coming to him. He couldn't spend every day with crossword puzzles and clipping coupons — or whatever Margate was doing for him. He thought of Cilla, seeking...what? A purpose to her life? What was his? Certainly seeking. That was part of it. The things he'd worked with — his puzzles, games, mysteries — always had a solution. Yet it was the pursuit of the answer that intrigued him. Obtaining it was almost anticlimactic.

For one who had gasped and struggled his way up minor hills in June, it was a slow awakening. The realization that true happiness was indeed in this struggle to the top, which became the substance of life long after the view from the peak was forgotten. For the human mind — was it selfish grasping? — wouldn't let it go at that. The satisfaction of a summit reached dissipated like morning fog in the valleys. And desire for a higher peak surged in. Could he apply this reasoning to the question of what next for him? Surely it was that he should seek. Not just solutions to games played for amusement, but as a way of life. To seek almost for its own sake. And where to start? Obviously with the ready-made mystery he'd put aside in June. He took the well worn piece of paper from his wallet. As he studied the jumble of letters and numbers, he could feel the turning over of a cold engine, one too long left unused. And as it caught, a glow came to his eyes. Life had returned to House Hudson.

* * *

He found the lead in a book of White Mountain history. A fragment of a map, purportedly drawn by Abenaki Indians with missionary help. Something about it caught his eye. With stirring excitement he studied a familiar looking series of letters and number:

PIG8AKET

There was the eight! Sitting there as though it wasn't completely out of place among the letters. The whole thing seemed to refer to an area. There were other such words — if words they were — but the others were composed entirely of letters. That implied the '8' was also a letter. In any case, the writing on Wally's map was pretty surely in Abenaki!

Gladys Swan had no books on the Abenaki language in her library. She doubted there would be anything anywhere in the state. Maybe the Huntington Free Library in the Bronx.

"But wait," she exclaimed. "What am I thinking of. We've got a real Abenaki right here in the Valley! Joseph Becancour. He's even a chief or something."

"Great! Where?"

"Bartlett village."

"Would he be there now?"

"It might be. He goes to Canada a lot. I can tell you where his house is."

It was a weathered colonial on one of the little side roads off Main Street. A cold wind down from the Presidentials set brown leaves whirling in eddies. A heavy, grey sky lowered itself on the village. Hudson's knock on the door was unanswered. He turned up his coat collar and looked around. There were two other houses on the dead end street. One had a retired tractor in the yard and a pickup truck out front. He crossed to it. The door opened before he could knock.

"Seen you lookin' at Joe's place. He ain't here." The speaker was a scrawny man of maybe eighty in grimy overalls with a stubbly, white beard.

"When will he be back?"

"Don't know. He never says when he comes or goes. Been gone a long time now."

"A day? A week?"

Watery grey eyes thought. "Been five months anyway."

"Any of his relatives around?"

"Nope. Not any more."

"What is it, Melvin? Don't leave the door open." A woman's voice came from inside. By the sound, about the same age as the man.

"I'm sorry," Hudson apologized. "I'm letting all the cold air in." He backed to leave.

"Come in and close the door." The voice belonged to an even scrawnier woman with iron grey hair, a long knit dress and a heavy sweater draped over her shoulders. "Come on," she ordered as Hudson hesitated.

"Well, just for a minute. I'm looking for someone who can read Abenaki. But I guess Mr. Becancour isn't around."

"He's gone," she announced, shutting the door firmly. "Probably to Canada."

"My name's Hudson Rogers. I was asking Melvin if there might be somebody else around here that could help."

"With Indian? Not since Ben's wife died." She looked at Melvin. "There aren't any others I know of." She turned back to Hudson. "Used to be a few around here. All died off." She shook her head. "Joe's the last," she gestured across the street.

"Ben's wife. You don't mean Ben Wheaton?"

"I do. Passed on maybe ten, twelve years ago. Then Ben went and fell off a cliff last spring." She eyed him. "You know Ben?"

"No. I've met his daughter. Is she...was Mrs. Wheaton her mother?"

"Yep."

"Kid's a half breed," guffawed Melvin.

"Nothing of the kind," the woman said sharply. "Words like that're what caused all the trouble. Martha Wheaton was only part Abenaki herself," she explained, "so Priscilla is certainly not half Indian. Martha could read Abenaki." She peered at Hudson. "You say you know Priscilla. Why don't you ask her? Maybe she can too."

"No. I'm sure she can't...though she did say it looked familiar..." Hudson was lost in thought. "You said 'trouble'."

"And that's all I'm going to say. Hush up, Melvin." She closed the subject as the old man started to speak. "Do you want some tea?"

Hudson had tea and a home baked cookie. The woman was Sarah and chatted pleasantly about the area, the weather and how nice it was when the tourists had gone, but not one further word from either of them about 'the trouble' that had been caused by a 'half breed.'

A boy in his teens and a girl in her twenties were behind the old front desk.

"Hi, there." It was the girl wearing a sari.

"Hi. I'm looking for Cilla Wheaton." He hadn't let Cilla know he was coming. The greeting from the ice maiden was not apt to be effusive. The ashram lay in the rolling hills of upper New York State. Formerly an Adirondack resort, it spread itself out in a manicured valley with open meadow on three sides. The chill of late September had brightened the leaves of an occasional stand of hardwood.

The boy and girl exchanged glances. "I don't know anyone by that name," said the girl.

"She's about twenty-five. Has black hair pulled back into a large bun." He gestured with his hands.

"Are you her father?" asked the boy.

College weight obviously didn't mean college face. "I'm a friend."

The girl hailed a passing woman, who was at least thirty. "Mrs. Glaume, do you know a girl named Cilla?"

That elder thought a moment. "Cilla...You must mean the Wheaton girl. She's in the gardens. Is there...something?"

"This gentleman's looking for her," replied the girl.

"A friend, not her father," said Hudson dryly.

"Go out this door and you'll see the Carriage House on your right. Our gardens are just beyond." She walked a few steps and stopped. "She's not Cilla any more you understand."

"She's not?" Hudson had a vision of her transformed into an oriental tiger, like something out of H. H. Monro.

"Her name is Muktabai," said Mrs. Glaume and continued on.

The Carriage House was several hundred feet from the main building and the gardens stretched as long as a football field behind it. Three figures were bent over rakes, looking like a scene from The Good Earth. Though two were rather obviously men, he still had trouble identifying the third as Cilla/Muktabai. Looking more like a humped-over bag lady, she was wearing a long denim skirt with a shawl draped over her shoulders. Afraid of startling her the way he had at the house in Bartlett, he spoke while some distance away.

"Hi. I guess I call you Muktabai here."

She turned a blank face; her eyes seeming to look right through him. "What?" Then they focused. "Oh, it's you." She went back to her rake. "What are you doing here?"

"I need to talk with you."

"I can't now. I have to finish my seva."

"Is that what you're doing?"

"Yes."

"Then when you're through."

She turned to look at him. "There's no purpose. The things of your world count for nothing here."

"It's about your father."

She shook her head tiredly. "Go away."

"I..." She turned her face to him suddenly, her eyes hard. Then without another word dropped her rake and walked toward the main building. The abruptness took Hudson by surprise. He considered going after her but rejected it and followed at a slower pace. He wasn't going to be put off so easily.

Cilla had disappeared when he reached the front desk. "You have a place for...someone my age here?"

"Oh sure," said the girl. "Some of the devotees are almost fifty." She pronounced it deVOtees. "Will you be joining us?"

"Just for tonight. Is that okay?"

"Of course. Janardan will show you the men's wing," she indicated the teen-age boy who stood waiting. "Dinner is at six o'clock."

The main course was a highly spiced dish served cafeteria style in the old hotel's zoo — help's dining room to the uninitiated. The guest dining room, he found later, was reserved for the after dinner program. Those around him at dinner assumed he would attend, and Hudson's curiosity prompted him to follow them in. The high ceilinged room was dimly lit by candles and crowded with devotees. Around an ornate chair at the front were grouped a half-dozen young men dressed in orange robes, whose morning shaving ritual apparently included all of their heads. This was a turn-off. Like Hari Krishnas on street corners.

The audience hushed, and a young woman in flowing robes quietly appeared and took the chair. As the lights dimmed still further, the orchestra — consisting of a drum and stringed instrument — began an oriental melody. The audience joined in with a long, slow chant. Though unable to see his watch, he figured it took over an hour. His legs that had carried him up nearly all the major White Mountain peaks began to quiver from the strain of just standing in one place. Attempting to divert his thoughts, he concentrated on the chanting, realizing with surprise that though the words to the chant were in a foreign language — and all different, not just a repetition of the same phrases over and over — no one had any books or scripts to go by. Yet everyone seemed to know them. To Hudson it was an effort like memorizing the entire Book of Psalms or — for all he knew — the collected works of Donald Duck.

Finally it was over, and with a sigh he sank to the floor, where he observed the others — who numbered in the hundreds — folding into lotus positions. After the remainder of the program, which included some thoughts from the chairlady and comments from a devotee, the huge crowd dispersed. He caught sight of Cilla, her arm linked with that of a slender man of about thirty in loose, bulky clothes.

"Why are you still here?"

"I told you. I need to talk with you."

"I suppose you'll hang around until you do." She sighed. "Oh all right. But not tonight. Tomorrow, after Guru Gita."

"That's the morning chant," said her companion with a smile.

"This is Kabir," she said diffidently.

Hudson shook hands. Kabir had brown eyes and dark brown, nearly black, hair; his quick smile revealed white, even teeth. Hudson was a little surprised Cilla still had her hand on Kabir's arm. Perhaps the security of the ashram let her open up more to others. "The men in orange. Are they hari krishnas?"

"Monks," said Kabir. He grinned "Want to be one?"

"No thanks. Do they go out on the street?"

"And beg?" asked Cilla dryly. "Not these. They stay with Swami. And you don't *decide* to be one. Some, a very few, are chosen."

"How about you, Kabir. Hope to be one?"

Kabir flashed his white teeth and shook his head. "I'm just a brahmacarya. A neophyte. I have...another role I hope to play in life."

A black girl joined them, introduced as Tanya Shaw. The three got into a metaphysical discussion. Hudson stifled a yawn and went up to his mattress — who needs a bed on a softwood floor. There was a boy named Haridas sorting keys. Something to do with *his* seva. The chinking sounds were the last he heard before sleep.

Breakfast at six was followed by a return to the already crowded hall for the Guru Gita. This chant went on for a full hour and a half. Hudson, who in his youth had found himself reaching the limits of boredom at a half hour church service, put his watch in his pocket after the tenth glance at it showed just an hour had passed. Good Lord, he thought, do we spend the entire day singing?

Suddenly there was silence in the large room. The chanting had stopped, all having reached the end at the same time. As the crowd dispersed, Hudson caught up with Cilla. The atmosphere in the ashram was oppressive to Hudson. He needed to smell something other than sandlewood. It was a golden fall day, and Cilla reluctantly agreed to a walk. There were the beginnings of reds, yellows and oranges spread throughout the valley like a patchwork quilt. Soon would come the bleakness of November, but now the world was becoming a candy store. Nature really goes out with a bang, thought Hudson. At least in vegetation.

The hills were not steep by White Mountain standards, and the two matched pace without difficulty. In June he would have been exhausted after ten minutes. Cilla too noticed the difference.

"You're not as noisy," she said as they sat on top of the ridge.

"Talking?" Hardly a word had been exchanged.

"Walking."

He grinned. "I wasn't always a blob. As a matter of fact I was pretty athletic in college."

"Way back when?" She made it sound like an eon.

"Even now." He stood. "Stand up a minute." She looked at him warily. "Come on. I won't hurt you."

She got to her feet facing him. Hudson wasn't too clear what happened after that. He intended to demonstrate how easily he could lift her 125 or so pounds — a little kid showing off — and put his hands on her waist. The next thing he knew he was doubled up on the ground in agony. There was an overwhelming pain in his crotch, and his throat felt as though someone had taken a hammer to it. He lay on the ground on his side with his hands between pressed-together legs drawn up to his chest, gasping for breath. After an hour of pain, a few minutes on his watch, his breath came more freely. He rolled on his back and tried to separate knees he had glued together.

Fully five minutes passed before he was able to sit up. Gingerly he looked about. Cilla was gone. What the hell had gotten into her. She had kneed him! Kneed him and hit him in the throat. Realtor Fanstock was right. The girl belonged in a nuthouse. Damn! Hadn't given him a chance to discuss what he'd found. Fruitcake!

Back at the ashram as he packed, he cooled a bit. At the front desk he got pen and paper and left a note.

Dear Cilla/Muktabai

    I wanted to talk to you because I had something to tell you. The word we found on my father-in-law's map is in Abenaki. I feel it is a lead worth exploring. I'm going back to do so.

                           Hudson Rogers

Back at Wally's house, with a feeling of relief shared by a pouncing Juniper, he picked up the telephone and dialed.

"Huntington Free Library."

"This is Hudson Rogers. I called the other day looking for someone familiar with Abenaki. They said a Mr. Kahn would be back this afternoon."

"I'll connect you."

It was a short wait. "This is Kahn."

"I'm calling from Bartlett, New Hampshire. I was told you might be able to help me with a word I think is in Abenaki?"

"Oh, yes. I don't read it, you understand. No one here does."

"A question. I'm not even sure it's a word. I've got some letters and a number mixed together. The number is always eight. Does that mean anything to you?"

A dry laugh. "Our state-of-the-art printing doesn't accommodate an ancient language. What looks like an eight is really the letter 'O' with the letter 'U' on top of it. It is pronounced 'W' before a vowel and as OU before a consonant. When written it comes out like an eight."

"So what I've got is really a word?"

"It certainly could be."

Armed with this information, Hudson returned to Gladys at the library, handing her a slip of paper with the eight changed to a 'W' so it now read:

PIGWAKET

"Of course," she exclaimed. "Pequawket is how we spell it now. That's a well-known name here."

"Name of what?"

"The Indian tribe that lived in this Valley."

He wrote on a piece of paper:

KWEKKWAKKEK

"How about that?"

She studied it and shook her head. "No. I'm sure I've never seen that word."

His next stop was John Fanstock.

"Sure. Some years ago there was talk of changing the name of one of our mountains to Pequawket. You know Kearsarge?"

Hudson nodded. He remembered the climb as ending in a fine westerly view of Moat and the Presidentials. "Why a name change?"

Fanstock leaned back in his chair. His well-rounded middle settled in comfortably. "Our Kearsarge is really Kearsarge North. There's another one in southwestern New Hampshire. I think Pequawket may have been the original name of the one here."

That didn't get him any further. Then the word from Wally's map may have just been the Abenaki word for Owls Cliff. He offered the paper with KWEKKWAKKEK.

"Does that mean anything to you?"

Fanstock read it, tried pronouncing it. "Nope. Not a thing. Doing historical research?"

"Sort of...Ben Wheaton, the surveyor who died last spring. Do you remember hearing about any trouble connected with him?"

"Trouble?" Fanstock sat forward.

"It would have been some years ago and maybe had something to do with his wife or daughter. The one in a nuthouse."

Fanstock relaxed. "Trouble was the name for that girl. She carried it with her. Too bad. Hurt a lot of people, including old Ben."

And Hudson. His groin still felt tender. Cilla certainly made her presence felt.

Larry Cook added the information that the local charitable foundation — of which he was the current president — was also named Pequawket.

"Pequawket's interested in land of any kind. I've some through the lumber company I'd turn over if I could afford to."

"Lumber company? You bankers own the whole town?"

"Small town. Everybody wears several hats. Bartlett Lumber. Not a biggie, but it has some nice land abutting National Forest. Bought it a few years back as an investment. Need to preserve whatever we can. The Weeks Act is what saved this area. Without the National Forest a country as beautiful as this would be overrun with people. Most of us are here to get away from that." Including me, thought Hudson.

It had started to rain as he drove up Swallow Hill; little puddles began to form at the end of the gravel driveway. His antenna made the familiar 'sprong' as he passed under the beech limb and drove up to the front door. He pulled in close to the steps. Close enough to see the white square on the door. And read the words that said:

STOP

OR

ELSE

Chapter 10

WHEN HUDSON WAS eleven, the boys in his neighborhood had been ruled by a tough Italian kid named Gino, whose lofty age of thirteen and bad temper made him admired by some and feared by most. Gino had a talent for organization, which resulted in successful raids on clubs — gangs were for the city — in other parts of a residential town unused to violence.

You didn't join Gino's club. You were told you were a part of it, or you were out completely. Hudson was big for his age, already with muscular shoulders, and Gino tapped him to serve as a soldier. At first Hudson was pleased, though acceptance by his peers had never been a high priority. But after the first raid on a local variety store — headquarters for a rival club — during which the proprietor suffered a broken arm, he told Gino this wasn't his idea of fun. Count him out. Gino did not take the news well. Once in one stayed in — like with the Big Guys. The following day, Hudson found a note shoved under his door advising him in blunt language he was no longer welcome in the neighborhood, and furthermore his mother was...

Brought up in the rather sedate atmosphere of an only child of older parents, Hudson had never before been threatened by anyone or anything. A quiet boy — bookish the neighbors said — but used to getting his own way, he discovered a strange, new feeling welling inside himself. He carefully took the note, folded it and went to his leader's house. Gino, though two years older, weighed less than Hudson, and before he knew what was happening, found himself on his back on the floor with the note shoved in his mouth. Hudson left without a word.

Gino's immediate impulse was to call out the troops, but the look he had seen in Hudson's eye stopped him. He considered. There were no witnesses to the incident. His reputation was not at stake. The matter was allowed to rest.

Had he been there, Gino would have recognized the look in Hudson's eye as he put down the groceries on the kitchen counter. He picked up the telephone and dialed Augustus Mooney.

"It's your neighbor wondering if you've seen anybody around the house here."

"Yep. One car. Bout three o'clock. You had another prowler?"

"No. Nothing's missing. Someone left me a note is all. Know the people in the car?"

"Stranger. Just the one. Thought he might be a friend of yours."

Hudson hung up the telephone, built a fire in the large fieldstone fireplace and sat down to think. He was a different person than the overweight, underwilled wreck in June when the first warning arrived. And it *was* a warning. Of what? Whatever it was had apparently happened since he returned from the ashram. He'd found the house as he left it; no sign of intruders.

What had he done since? He'd spoken with Gladys Swan and Larry Cook. In each case the subject had been the Abenaki language. He couldn't picture either of them tacking a note on his front door. And for what? Because he was asking about an Indian word?

John Fanstock. Now there was a different story. He thought back to their first conversation. Fanstock was affable enough, until Owls Cliff was mentioned. Owls Cliff and Ben Wheaton's stake. Then he changed the subject. Today his little green eyes had remained half closed as they'd discussed the Abenaki word. When had they opened? Ben Wheaton again. And the trouble! And Ben had married an Abenaki. It went in circles. Why did Wally get his warning notes? What was he doing to warrant them? The one item taken from the house had been the map with both the X where Wheaton had his accident, and the Abenaki writing. They tied together somehow. And Wally had died.

He drove to the Bartlett post office, getting there just as Emma Persons was closing the door.

"There's the lady who knows everybody in town."

"Not everyone," said Emma Persons with a pleased smile. "But there're not many I don't. It would be pretty hard not to after thirty years."

"In town?"

"With the post office," she remonstrated. "I've been in town all my life."

"At work thirty years! Didn't they have child labor laws?" he asked innocently.

"No, I was..." She tossed her head to one side. "You're after something."

"Joseph Becancour. Sarah and Melvin say he's been away five months. They think he goes somewhere in Canada, but they don't know where."

"You know I'm not allowed to give out forwarding addresses," she said sternly. "Now if you was to ask me if I knew any Indian reservations, I'd say...let's see...Odanak. That's what I'd say."

"Odanak. Is that a town?"

"That's the reservation. The town is Pierreville. It's all French up there you know."

Hudson tried five gas stations before finding a map of Canada. Pierreville was between Montreal and Quebec City, almost on the St. Lawrence River. How amused Sylvia would be, he thought. Here he was planning to drive four or five hours to find what one word meant — a word that might only be the name of a mountain. Hey Syl, he'd say, that's why they call them dead languages.

Figuring this was a good opportunity to get the house cleaned, he called Mary Walton, Wally's cleaning woman. She had her own key and said she'd be glad to come by, though busier than ever. Mr. Carver's house never needed much. He was such a tidy man. Hudson hung up with a shrug. She'd find more to do this time. He liked a clean house himself but wasn't obsessed with it.

He left at seven the next morning, planning to be at the reservation by noon. The road from the Canadian border ran through rolling countryside dotted with picturesque little villages. Much like Vermont, he thought. And quite different than the craggy look of New Hampshire.

He had just turned off Route 55 to 143 when the drive shaft let go. It happened without warning, fortunately at a slow speed. The Subaru garage was in St. Charles, a ten minute tow away. While Hudson considered himself reasonably fluent in french, he had to struggle to understand the harsh Canadian version, particularly of auto parts he wouldn't have known in English. Luckily the ones needed were on hand, but it was dark when he crossed the bridge over the St. Francis River between St. François du Lac and Pierreville. The sign said sharp left for Odanak.

If he'd thought of it, he would have expected an Indian Reservation to have a gate and perhaps a long gravel driveway into an encampment. This road seemed just a residential street, no different than any other. The administration building was mixed in with the houses. And was closed. He looked at his watch. Seven thirty. He drove down several side streets. The only clue that he was in Indian country was an occasional totem pole and a shop — also *fermé* — that advertised Abenaki products. On a street named Awassos he found a sign 'Abenaki Registraire.' It was *Ouvert Lundi et Mardi* 10:00-16:00. Since it was now a Wednesday and after 4 o'clock, Hudson felt he had two strikes against him as he knocked on the door. It was opened by a teen age girl.

"*Oui?*"

"*Excusez-moi. Je sais que vous n'êtes pas ouvert maintenant. Mais je suis ici seulement un nuit et je cherche un Monsieur Joseph Becancour.*"

"*Il est mort.*"

Great. A four hour drive and the man he'd come to see is dead. How long ago. "*Quand?*"

"*Il y a cinq ou six mois. Il etait un ami?*"

"*Non, non.*" Five or six months ago. He must have died soon after leaving Bartlett. "*Vous êtes la Registraire?*"

"*Non. Ma tante. Elle reviendra demain matin.*"

Her aunt's the one to talk to. She'd be back tomorrow, but maybe this girl would do. "*Mais vous êtes Abenaki?*"

"*Oui, comme tout le monde ici.*"

A real Abenaki. He pulled out his precious word he now knew was in that language. "*Vous pouvez lire ça?*"

She glanced at the paper. "*C'est Abenaki je crois, mais je ne connaissais pas le mot.*"

Damn. She didn't know it. For sure a dead language, when the descendants can't read it. Well, there was nothing for it. He'd visit the aunt — Madame La Registraire — when she returned in the morning. He'd better see about a place to stay.

"*Vous pouvez recommander un motel pour ce soir?*"

The girl looked at his clothes. "*Il y a un bon motel dans St. François mais c'est fermé maintenant.*"

Did everything close after the summer?

"*Un hôtel?*"

"*Pas pour vous, Monsieur.*"

Well, I don't really want a hotel anyway.

"*Je n'ai pas besoin d'un grand hôtel.*" Actually a cabin down by the river would be delightful. It wouldn't hurt to ask. "*Peut-être vous connaissez une cabine que je peux louer pour la nuit. Près de la rivière si possible?*"

She studied him. "*Mon fiancé a une petite maison sur la rivière qu'il loue en été.*"

Perfect. A little house on the river owned by her boyfriend. Worth whatever the price. "*Combien?*"

"*Cinquante.*"

He'd pay that for a motel. "*Je vous paye?*"

"*Oui.*"

He took out his wallet. "*Et la clef?*"

"Pas de clef. On n'en a pas besoin ici."

Well he had nothing of value with him. A key wasn't important. She wrote out directions, and he gave her his name, saying he'd be back the next morning.

The little house could not be classified higher than a one room cabin, but it was clean. It sat close enough to the river that flood season must be a worry. A cold Canadian wind had risen after dinner — the Montreal Express they called it in New Hampshire — and Hudson was gratified to see a substantial gas heater. He hadn't thought to ask if the summer rental was equipped for fall weather. He turned it up, climbed into bed and was soon asleep.

He was in a galaxy of pulsing, throbbing stars pressing in on him with enormous force. They emitted a horrifying buzzing sound like a hundred dentist drills boring into his head. He tried to put his hands over his ears, but couldn't get them to obey. The stars pressed in on his chest and mouth. He couldn't breathe, nor could he get any part of his body to respond. Then suddenly the pressure vanished, and the stars receded, leaving him gasping and cold. Cold. He opened his eyes. The stars were back where they should be and someone was bending over him. It was dark, too dark to make out features.

"Are you there?" A woman's voice.

"I think so." He rolled his head. "What am I doing outside?"

"Lie still. You've had an accident. I'll get blankets."

He looked down at his jockey shorts and bare chest. Christ! No wonder he was cold! He tried to get up, but his stomach turned on him, and he retched on the ground. A blanket was wrapped around his shoulders.

"There's help coming," said the woman, layering a second blanket on him.

"Can't I go inside?" He lay back gasping after the dry heaves diminished. The wind was like a knife, and he was shivering uncontrollably.

"Not yet," said the woman. "Damn, where are they."

He curled into a fetus position, hugging himself against the cold. Reality faded out. He was back in Cambridge in his old king size bed. Sylvia crawled in next to him. He put his arms around her and could feel the warmth of her body against his. Gradually the shivering stopped.

Oh Syl.

He slept.

A shaft of sunlight pried open an eye; a jolt of pain closed it. His head throbbed, and his tongue felt like old leather. He could still feel Sylvia next to him, her breasts against his chest. He groaned as awareness flooded in. The dream had been so real.

"All right?" A woman's voice, though hard to understand.

"No. I just lost my wife...again." He tried opening his eyes. A middle-aged woman with redder hair than nature provides was checking equipment next to his bed. Hospital. "Where?"

"Yujshdalitlasidon." It was American English, but so heavily accented he could make no sense of it.

"En français, je vous en prie." Even Canuck French would be easier to understand.

"Vous êtes a l'hôpital. Vous avez eu un petit accident."

"Quelle sorte?"

"Hôpital Sorel."

"Non, non. Quelle sorte d'accident?"

"Le docteur viendra tout de suite."

That bad? He'd had an accident so serious she wanted the doctor to tell him about it? He began an inventory. Both sets of toes wiggled. He could raise his head, which turned his stomach over...

"Visiteur!"

A slim figure was silhouetted by light from across the hall. Red Hair, having announced company, slid out of the room. The figure took shape.

"Kabir! What on earth are *you* doing here?"

"I live here."

"You're a doctor?"

"Lawyer, Indian Chief." An impish grin. "You sniffed a lot of that stuff, didn't you?"

"What stuff? Kabir, what's going on?"

The younger man sat at the foot of the bed. "They haven't told you?" Hudson shook his head. "You got gassed. The flame went out on your gas heater. A passing neighbor noticed the smell and got you out. How are you feeling?"

"Lousy. Why does my head hurt?"

"Maybe it got bumped as they pulled you out of the cabin. What do you remember?"

"Very little." He searched his mind. "I went to bed in that cabin and...horrible dreams...then I was outdoors and it was cold. Was it ever!...then it was warm...That's it. I woke up here.

"That's all?"

Hudson lay back. "Kabir, what in hell are you doing in this...godforsaken part of Canada?"

"I was brought up here. On the reservation." He flashed his infectious grin. "It's the one part of the world that isn't 'godforsaken' to me."

"You're an Abenaki?"

"By ancestry. Nobody's full-blooded any more." He noticed Hudson's look. "I know. Most of us don't look like Indians."

"But the name Kabir...?"

"Given me at the ashram. If you were named Zacheus, which would you use?"

"And Cilla's mother...

"Was my aunt."

"So you're cousins."

"He's quick."

Hudson tried raising up on an elbow. Decided against it. "Why are you here and not at the ashram?"

"Partly because of you."

"Me!"

"Cilla, actually."

"Cilla?"

"Are you up to a story?"

"Anything for a little light!"

Kabir settled himself on the bed. "Growing up, Cilla was a happy child, strong, athletic and confident. I didn't really know her then. I'm five years older. But I knew she had a good mind. And that was the problem. She was sensitive to what others were thinking, and how she was different. Bartlett, New Hampshire in the nineteen seventies — did you know it?" Hudson shook his head. "It was a town the rest of the world passed by. It seldom saw an hispanic or black. French-Canadians took the place of Polish in local jokes. And the low people on the totem pole — so to speak — were us Wabanakis: Cilla, her mother and my father's family."

"Joseph Becancour was your father!"

Kabir nodded.

"Maybe you know I came here looking for him."

"Suzanne told me. The girl at the Registraire's house. That's how I knew you were here."

"She was the one who told me he'd died. Had he been ill?"

"His heart was never strong."

"I'm sorry."

"Let me finish my story. I mentioned Cilla's mind. Kids don't start out prejudiced, but Cilla could see a change in her friends; that they treated her a little differently than each other. Instead of being cowed, Cilla went the opposite direction. She began to wear Indian clothes, and sometimes painted her face. The more Wabanaki Cilla became the less she was accepted in Bartlett."

"The 'trouble'," said Hudson. "It came from this?"

"You've heard about it?"

"Just people talking about the 'trouble' like a plague visitation. Bad?"

"The worst. Rape and murder." Kabir got up and walked to the window. "It happened when Cilla was fifteen. She and Aunt Martha went swimming on a hot June day at Second Iron — that's a favorite spot in the Saco where it's crossed by a railroad bridge. No one knows exactly what happened. Martha's body was found on the western bank. She'd been raped and strangled. Cilla was lying in some bushes a hundred feet away. She had also been raped and apparently left for dead. There were deep bruises on her throat. It was several days before she recovered consciousness. And then remembered almost nothing. She'd wandered away from Aunt Martha. The doctor said she'd been hit on the head. Cilla was barely conscious as her clothes were torn off — strangely her one thought was her Indian skirt was ruined. Then there were hands around her throat and she passed out." Kabir turned from the window, smiling eyes for once grim. "They never found who did it." His fingers tightened on the foot of the hospital bed. "The police say it must have been an outsider. We'd never had that kind of thing happen in Bartlett before."

"But you don't think so."

"Not many strangers know Second Iron. I think it was local."

"Does Cilla?"

Kabir nodded. "She thinks it was her fault. For being different."

Hudson looked at Kabir. "Why are you telling me this now?"

"I know what happened to you that day with Cilla when she...injured you. Since the age of fifteen she has never let a man touch her. She's gone to women's school, women's college, and when it came time to face the world of men, she couldn't. So she hid in the ashram. When you put your hands on her waist, her reaction was automatic. As a matter of fact, you're lucky she wasn't trying to seriously hurt you."

"Damn good imitation!"

"But only that. She's had training the equal of a black belt in tae kwon do. She was never going to let it happen again." Kabir grinned suddenly. "Hey, she told me yours' was just an easy tap." He grew serious. "But it upset her." He looked Hudson in the eye and nodded. "As much as it did you, Hudson. It also scared her. She knows she can't continue this way. I suggested she come visit me for a while."

"She's here?" asked Hudson with surprise.

"Back on the reservation."

"How did you know I was here in the hospital?"

"Suzanne again. The next door neighbor called her."

"Is he the one who pulled me out? I remember a woman..."

"*She's* the neighbor. The one who sounded the alarm."

"But this woman spoke English."

Kabir looked at him out of the corner of his eye. "I'll tell you a secret. Most people here do. They just don't want to."

Something was nagging at Hudson, but he couldn't push the mist away to bring it into focus. Then it parted a little. "I came up here to find the meaning of an Abenaki word." He made as if to get up. "In my pocket..."

Kabir eased him back. "I know. KWEKKWAKKEK. Cilla told me. It means 'on top of a mountain.'"

"That's all? Just on top of a mountain?" Hudson's disappointment was visible.

"Not on top of *any* mountain. On top of *the* mountain. On the map you had, it may have referred specifically to Owls Cliff. Where Uncle Ben died."

The fog was rolling in again. All Hudson could think of was rice. "So?"

"Let's talk when you're out of here." Kabir moved to the door. "The doctor said two or three days."

Hudson never heard the end of the sentence.

Chapter 11

SOMEONE HAD TRIED to kill him. There was no question in his mind. Hudson sat on the cabin's bed. He'd turned on the gas heater and tried to extinguish the flame. The chances of it happening by accident were next to zero. He looked around the room. The door had no key — a bracket for a padlock but no lock — so anyone could have entered. Why hadn't he awakened? Perhaps the tender spot on his head was the answer. It was on the rear, just above his neck. It might have occurred as Kabir said, when he was pulled from the cabin. But...

He walked to the next house a hundred yards away and knocked on the door. There was no response. He circled the one floor ranch, peering in windows; one had a broken pane which he called through. No one home. This had to be the neighbor who saved his life. There was no other house within half a mile.

He went back to the cabin and stood outside the door, trying to picture what had happened that night. The threshold was a foot from the ground, and there was as yet no frost in the soil underneath it.

He entered the cabin and looked at the bed. Really a cot. The mattress was perhaps a foot and a half above the floor. He slept on his stomach. If the good neighbor had dragged him out of bed by his feet, the bruises would be on his face and front of his head as it hit the floor. Could she have rolled him on his back first? The floor was carpeted and, though not a deep pile, ought to have cushioned the blow enough to avoid bruising. The one foot drop to soft soil outside also shouldn't have caused damage.

Sleeping on his stomach though left the back of his head exposed to a blow that would keep him out. He went outside and lay down on the ground outside the door, just far enough to get away from gas fumes. He looked up at the sky. There had been stars out then, not the bright October sun. What else. The river. He'd heard it on his right not his left. He changed position. There had been no moon, and it had been bitter cold. He remembered he'd just been wearing jockey shorts, and the wind had made his bones chatter.

Not like today, with a nice warm sun and practically no breeze at all. He unzipped his windbreaker. There were distant sounds of traffic and the murmuring of the river...and someone calling his name.

"Hunh?" He sat up. Kabir was standing over him.

"Waiting for the next ambulance?"

"Oh. Must have drifted off." He started to get up. "We elderly take naps during the day."

"Uh huh. My guess is you like it there," Kabir grinned impishly and offered a hand to pull him to his feet. Over Kabir's shoulder a girl in familiar red checked shirt and corduroy jeans appeared; her hand on Kabir's neck.

"Hi." Cilla's voice had a little more warmth than he could remember hearing in it. "The doctor said you'd feel sleepy for a while."

"You didn't call," said Kabir accusingly.

"No phone," Hudson gestured toward the cabin.

"No excuse. You were supposed to call us before you left the hospital. If it hadn't been for Suzanne we'd never have known."

"We didn't expect you out so soon." Cilla was looking at him closely, as though expecting him to pass out again.

"Come inside. I've something to show you." Hudson led the way. Cilla and Kabir sat on the bed as Hudson demonstrated the safety features of the heater."When I called Suzanne about moving back in, she said the gas heater is practically new. I don't think it could have caused a problem...without help."

"You're saying...." Kabir looked at Cilla

"That someone tried to kill me."

"We'd about arrived at the same conclusion," said Cilla softly.

It was one thing to arrive at a conclusion that someone wanted you dead. It was quite another to have the suspicion independently confirmed. He looked from one to the other. "You've talked about this? Between the two of you?" Kabir nodded. "But why? What on earth would anyone want me dead for?"

"Maybe your name," said Kabir.

"Because it's American?"

"Because it's Rogers." Hudson looked blank. "Robert Rogers pillaged Saint Francis — Odanak. In 1759."

"That's a long time to hold a grudge."

"It was quite a pillage. The whole settlement was burned flat, including the church. Many Indians killed."

"Kabir's not serious. There was a treaty soon after that." said Cilla.

"The one who pulled you out of the cabin said she had trouble getting the door open. A piece of wood was holding the padlock bracket closed."

"Then it's attempted murder!" Hudson thought about this. "The police. Hasn't anyone called them?"

Cilla looked at her cousin. "After the stick had been removed from the latch, there was no proof that anything had happened, except an accident," said Kabir.

"But that woman!" exclaimed Hudson. "The one who got me out. She can testify it was there."

"She had to leave town," said the Abenaki."

"Besides," said Cilla. "You don't really have Indians after you. Whatever is behind this has more to do with New Hampshire than it does Odanak."

I wonder, thought Hudson. The only witness someone who had to 'leave town?' And the police. Couldn't they at least have looked for clues? Perhaps there was something other than the stick. He studied the two. They certainly didn't look murderous. A slim, good looking Indian boy — it was only recently he had thought of thirty as being a boy — with a tan Hudson couldn't duplicate after a month in St. Martin, and a scruffy girl with an enormous bun. What possible reason would they have for doing him in. No. There was something else. Something...He turned to Cilla. "You remember those warning notes that my father-in-law received?"

"'Stop' and 'stop at once'?"

"'Stop or else,'" he corrected. "I got the second the other day."

"The same words?"

"Yes."

"Do you hear what you're saying?" exclaimed Cilla.

"Yes. That Wally's accident wasn't an accident." He shook his head. "And yet I was there! Nobody tries to kill someone by crashing his car into their's...unless he's either wacko or sure he'll come out of it okay." Suddenly grief flooded in. "If that bastard Trimble is a murderer, he killed my wife for no reason!" He paced the floor. "Is it possible?...He hit us broadside. Not as much danger to himself. And it was his big car against my little Toyota." He stopped. "Maybe that's it..." He turned to face them. "I've got to go to Massachusetts."

"What have you got?" Kabir asked.

"Maybe nothing. My memory of the accident is so vague. But if what I'm guessing is true, the odds on murder go up."

"Then I'm going with you," said Cilla.

Hudson stared at her.

"Think about it. If your father-in-law was murdered it was because of something he was working on with my father." Hudson started to interrupt but she overrode him. "The map with the X on Owls Cliff, the missing Carver file. Both houses searched. I know there's a connection. And I know my father didn't just fall off that cliff. Or jump," she looked sharply at Hudson.

"I don't know," he started slowly. "I may take several days. For one thing, I want to go through Wally's Marblehead house. And quick. If I'm annoying people this much...

"I have money. I can stay in a motel."

"There's no question of a motel. Wally's house has plenty of bedrooms," Hudson was half lost in thought. "When did your father die? When this spring."

"Early May. Why?"

"Could it have been the first?"

"Of May? They found him on the third. The doctor said he'd...had his accident about two days before. Is that important?"

"Wally died on the first. It was his birthday."

Kabir groaned. Cilla turned to him. "What?"

"Do you remember when my father died?"

"Sure. Just before they called me about *my* father. I remember you weren't there when I needed you." Her eyes widened. "Your..."

Kabir nodded. "My father was found dead the morning of May first. He'd died in his sleep. Or so they said."

The three looked at each other. It was Kabir who broke the silence. "I guess I'd better do a little detective work here."

"Dear God," breathed Hudson. Which said it for them all.

Chapter 12

WALLACE CARVER'S HOUSE sat on the ocean side of Marblehead Neck, a few doors down from Carcasson, a duplicate of a French mansion, called by one and all as just "the castle." The Neck was almost an island, connected to the rest of Marblehead by a narrow causeway. Marblehead Harbor, in summer festive with sailboats of all sizes, now lay bleak and grey in the early evening of mid-October, sandwiched between the old town and the peninsula, a few masts sticking up like dead trees in a burned forest. Wally's house, though no castle, had extensive landscaping and its own rocky piece of the Atlantic coastline. Hudson pointed it out to Cilla as they drove past.

"Why aren't we stopping? "she asked.

"Casing the joint."

"Is someone staying there?"

"Not legally."

"It looks quiet."

It was dusk, and the autumn surf pounded against the shore. Hudson parked the car around a curve in the road. "Let's see if it is."

They walked back. Though there were houses on either side of the road, there were few lights; as if most were unoccupied. "Where is everyone?" asked Cilla.

"I think many are summer homes. I'm not sure how many people are around this time of year."

The sound of rolling and crashing waves covered the small squeak of the iron gate across Wally's driveway. A semi-circular drive led to the front door. Hudson ignored this entrance and crossed a patch of lawn to a glass porch on the side of the building.

"Now very quietly..." He tried the porch door. It was open. The porch ran the width of the house toward the ocean. Halfway down it, was a door to the main building. This one was locked. Hudson pulled out the key ring given him by Wally's attorney. The door swung open. The two stood there, listening. From somewhere deep in the house came a scraping sound, as though furniture were being moved. They looked at each other. Hudson took Cilla's hand and silently entered. They were in a short hallway that ran to the center of the house and off of which were several open doors. They peeked in each room as they passed. All were empty. As they left the hall for a large open room, they heard the sound again. It was coming from someplace upstairs; this time followed by a loud slap. The stairway was on the far side of the room they were in. Its carpeting had a deep pile which emitted no sound as they mounted. Suddenly they stopped. Someone was speaking. The words were indistinct but the periodic silences indicated the speaker was on the telephone. The corridor at the head of the stairs ran both ways. To their right, there was light coming from one of the rooms that overlooked the ocean. They crept closer down the darkened hall, and soon they could make out words.

"I *am* upstairs. He has a desk up here."

Hudson froze, grasping Cilla's hand tightly.

"Nothing...Hey, you've been here, I haven't. Where the hell are his files?...Well why the hell didn't you tell me that in the first place!" There was a sound of a receiver being violently hung up. The light went out, and, before the two could move, a figure came out of the room and headed toward them. The man was a large bulky figure in the darkness and saw them at the same time they saw him. There was a flashlight in his hand. He gave a grunt, threw the flashlight at them and turning, ran in the opposite direction. The flashlight hit Hudson in the chest. Hudson went after him.

For a large man the intruder moved quickly, taking the hallway in giant strides and dashing into a bedroom at the far end of the hall, where he flung open a window and climbed out on the roof of the enclosed porch. Hudson got to the window and incautiously started to follow. The man had been waiting for him and delivered a hard punch to the right side of Hudson's jaw. Hudson sprawled on the roof for a moment, stunned. He shook his head and got to his feet in time to hear an "oof!" as the man landed on the lawn below. Hudson took the same route more slowly, hitting the grass on his toes and finishing with a shoulder roll. He bounced to his feet and stood listening. The roar of the surf drowned sounds of movement. He ran to the street and looked both ways. As he had remembered, there were no cars parked on either side. He paused, undecided. A car started up several yards down. He ran toward the sound. There! Lights came on in a driveway between high hedges. Clever fellow. No one would notice a vehicle between the hedges of a private yard. Knowing he would have little chance of stopping a moving automobile, he paused at the driveway entrance. As the car came roaring out, he focused on the rear. Honda, Massachusetts plate. It turned left, picking up speed and disappeared toward Marblehead.

Back in the house, Cilla had found lights. "He got away?"

"Not completely. I know who he is. His license number will confirm it."

"You know him?"

Hudson's face was grim. "George Trimble. The man who killed Sylvia and Wally."

"Then there's no question..."

Hudson nodded slowly. "They were murdered."

Cilla sank into an overstuffed chair. "And so was my father." She looked down at her hands. "Oh, Daddy!"

Neither one of them spoke for a few moments, each lost in thought. Finally Cilla raised her head. "What now?"

"Now we try to find whatever Trimble was looking for. Wally's files are in the den." He crossed the large living room and opened a door to the left. Cilla got up and followed him.

"Trimble mentioned files on the phone. Who do you think he was talking to?"

He turned on a light, revealing a dark paneled room with bookshelves from floor to ceiling. The sound of the ocean came through French doors at the far end. Along the left hand wall were three rows of filing cabinets. "I can't begin to guess. All we know is that Trimble isn't alone in this... Whatever this is. Why don't you start at that end, and I'll take this one." He pulled open the top drawer of a file.

"Looking for a mention of my father. What else?"

"Your uncle. Bartlett. The White Mountains. Maybe Odanak. I don't know. We need pieces that fit together. If anything looks familiar, pull it out."

Two hours later they had gone through two of the three cabinets, paper by paper. Hudson looked over at Cilla. She was sitting in lotus position on the floor with piles of folders around her. Her normally tight bun was leaking hair around the edges, which she absently brushed from her face. Odd. Despite the deep black color of the hair, neither she nor her cousin had the blunt features of an American Indian. More the sort of face one might find in an old family locket, thought Hudson. Though that was probably the effect of the bun. A rather pointed nose below grey eyes that glistened in the light from the floor lamp to her right, atop a long gawky neck. For once she looked like a normal person, dressed in light blue sweater and dark blue slacks. "Hungry?"

"Not very. Is there food here?"

"Maybe some canned stuff." Hudson rummaged through the kitchen cupboards and came up with sausages and tomatoes, even canned potatoes. Wally had cooked for himself. Cilla settled for asparagus which she ate right out of the can. They brought their food into the den, continuing to go through folders. By midnight they had finished with the files, gone through the bookshelves and searched the drawers in the tables. Hudson sat back in a chair. "Let's tackle the genealogy files tomorrow. My eyes are beginning to blur."

"Genealogy files? What would be there?"

"Let's hope more than we've found here." In all there had not been one paper of real interest. There was a folder on Wally's Bartlett house, filled with house plans and copies of bills, that Hudson put aside. But other than that the files contained mostly client folders. None of the names were familiar to Hudson. He yawned. "You take the bedroom at the west end of the hall."

"The one you ran through?"

"Yeah. That one has its own bath."

Wally's bedroom was in the northeast corner, overlooking the ocean. The sound of the waves and the smell of the sea were soporific, and Hudson was soon asleep.

He couldn't say what woke him. In his dream someone had been calling him urgently. As he opened his eyes, no one was there. But the ocean fragrance had turned acrid. He coughed. Smoke! He sat up and turned on the bedside lamp. The room was filled with wisps of white. He quickly pulled on his pants, pushed his feet in loafers and with shirt and jacket in a hand went to the door. Remembering lessons long ago taught but never employed, he felt the door. It was still cool to the touch. He wrenched it open and raced down the hall to Cilla's room. Mistake. Before he was half way there his lungs had filled with smoke and he was coughing with huge wrenching heaves of his chest. He turned back and ran to the bathroom that adjoined his room, soaked his shirt under the faucet, tied it around his face and tried the hall again. He could actually hear flames licking at some part of the house. Cilla's door was closed, which he gave thanks for as he opened it.

"Cilla! Cilla! Get up!!" No sound came from the bed. He stripped back the covers and put his arms under her shoulders, lifting her. Heavy smoke was pouring into the room from the hall, blocking exit in that direction. The window he had gone out before was partly open. He carried her over to it and, climbing out, lifted her over the sill. The heat here was intense despite the cool night. Suddenly he realized that the porch itself was ablaze; there were flames curling around the edge closest to the street. He lifted Cilla's limp body and carried it to the ocean end. At the edge he carefully lowered her toward the ground, lying on his stomach on the burning roof to get her as close as possible before letting her drop the remaining several feet. She landed in evergreen shrubs; Hudson rolled off after her.

Not having properly prepared himself for it, the fall took the wind out of him, so a few seconds passed before he was able to get to Cilla and pull her to an open patch of lawn. Laying her on her back he brushed hair from her face, opened her mouth and put his over it, blowing air into her lungs as he forced hers to work by pressing on her chest. Her long wool nightgown had ridden up to her thighs. He pulled it down, thinking that her modesty wouldn't be too important if...there! A spasm shook her body followed by coughing. He lifted her head up, cradling it on his legs. Her long black hair almost came to her waist, he noted. Which should be no surprise; something had to make up that enormous bun. She opened her eyes, at first just a fraction. Then as she became aware of Hudson, they opened wide.

"What..." She tried to sit up.

"Easy. We've had a fire. We're outside and safe."

She looked down at herself and put her arms around her chest. In one quick movement she rolled off his legs and sat up facing him. "An accident?" She looked back at the house. The porch was now gone, and flames were working toward the center of the house.

"Not likely." Hudson got to his feet. "You stay here. I'll see if the phone still works." He raced around to the front door. The fire had apparently started on the porch side. Maybe there was time before the east side went. He put his still damp shirt around his face and went in. The living room was full of smoke, but he found the telephone and punched 911. When they answered, he told the voice there was a fire and gave the address.

"And your name?"

"Hurry." He hung up and looked around the room. The lights still worked, but he could make out little in the smoke. He crossed to the den. All he could see was the file of Bartlett house papers he had left on a table near the door. He picked it up, feeling it a futile gesture. Flames were now visible in the room, and beginning to make a roaring sound.

"Hudson! Come out!" Cilla was at the front door. "There's nothing here worth risking your life!"

A burning timber crashing next to him decided it. "Head for the car," he shouted.

The Subaru was pointed away from the house, and that was the direction Hudson drove.

"Did you call the fire department?"

"Yes."

"Shouldn't we wait for them?"

"I think you and I had better be among the missing for a while. We're not very popular with some people. Trimble being the visible one. But I don't know who or where his friends are." He turned up the heater. "Would you give me a hand with my jacket?" Hudson threw the wet shirt in the back seat and with Cilla's help, shrugged into his coat. He looked over at her. "Are you warm enough?"

She hugged herself. "I will be in a minute. Where are we going?"

"You're going to get a chance to pay for a motel room after all."

"Not unless you rescued my money along with me."

Hudson felt in his pocket. "We're okay. I've got my wallet."

"We're going to check into a motel in the wee hours of the morning...what time is it anyway?"

"About three."

"I'm in a nightgown! And you say it's 'okay'?" There was panic in her voice.

He looked at her. "Could be an evening dress from what girls are wearing nowadays." She stiffened. "Okay, okay. I'll register. You can stay in the car." He still felt tension. "Two rooms. Keep an eye out behind. I doubt if anyone waited around to see us burned, but...We'd better find a place where the car doesn't show from the street." He circled around to the middle of the peninsula. The Eastern Yacht Club and its tennis courts passed to his right.

"And then what?"

"First we've got to get off the Neck. There's just the one road, and someone may be waiting." He slowed the car as they came upon the Causeway. No automobiles. Nor were there any on the far side. All the same, he breathed a little easier when he turned on to Route 114 and headed for Salem.

"What do we do tomorrow?" Cilla persisted. "All my clothes are back at the house."

"Someone's trying to kill us and you're worried about clothes?" She gave a quick nod. "First thing tomorrow I'll find a store and pick up some things for you. Okay?"

Her lips pressed tightly together. "I know you think I'm being silly. I...have a problem with some things."

Hudson was contrite. "I know. Kabir told me."

She turned quickly to him. "He...he didn't..."

"Only because I asked. I'm really sorry. You've had a rough time." He peeked at her slyly. "I needed to protect myself. Against another kneeing."

She lowered her head. "That was reflex. I didn't mean to hurt you." She looked up. "But when you put your hands on me..." She looked out the window. "No man touches me."

Hudson thought, it's a good thing she didn't come to when I had my mouth on hers. She'd have bitten my tongue off. "Anyone behind us?"

"Oh..." She turned and looked out the rear window. "No cars."

They entered the quiet center of Salem and continued through on Route 114. The streets were empty of cars. It would be difficult for anyone to follow at this time of night, thought Hudson. He rummaged through his memory. There were some motels on Route 1; sleazy looking. Maybe that was best. 'They' mightn't think to look there.

The one he picked at least appeared to be clean. Better still, cars parked behind the units — away from the street. He buttoned his jacket, turned the collar up and registered under the name Thomas Hayman, paying the clerk in cash for two adjoining rooms. Though the decor was fifties and the smell of disinfectant strong, they were adequate. When the car stopped next to them, Cilla looked around like a trapped bird before dashing into one. Hudson followed her. "Take a piece of paper from the drawer and write down what clothes you need. And the sizes."

He entered the next door unit, lay down on the bed and was nearly asleep when she brought him the list. After she had gone, he hung up his wet shirt and, on a separate hanger, his trousers. His shoes went next to the bed. In case of another fire, he thought. He looked at his sockless feet. First thing tomorrow. October was no month to be running around without clothes.

The 'first thing' was closer to ten o'clock when he woke. He got coffee at a fast food place and drove to Northshore Shopping Center. He bought clothes for himself, put them on in a men's room and started on Cilla's list. He could picture her struggling over writing the words 'bra' and 'panty hose'. The word 'dark' had obviously been added afterwards. Something tugged at his memory. He could picture her legs before he pulled down the nightdress. Good legs. Too good to hide under heavy stockings. But that wasn't it...They were shaved! Why would a girl who doesn't want a man anywhere near her and intends to hide her legs under dark material, go to the trouble to shave them?

He finished her list. What else? They might need more than one set of clothes...and now 'they' were aware of Cilla, they'd be looking for both of them. What would they know about her? That she dresses like a tramp? If they could track him to Odanak, they would. Might be a good idea to change that. He got her a suit and then high heel shoes the same size as her sneakers, wondering if she'd be able to stand in them.

Back at the motel Cilla nervously cracked her door open on chain before letting him in. "The maid has been here three times."

Hudson displayed his purchases. "I got you a few things I've never seen you wear. We're going to have to look like other people."

"What other people? Where are we going?"

"Wally's attorney. I called him from the store. He can see us at two o'clock. Let's both wear suits." He took out the high heels. "Can you manage these?"

She looked doubtful. "It will be an adventure. Why the attorney?"

"He was first on the list anyway. But now we need a place to start, finding out just why Mr. Trimble and company want to get rid of us."

"We were on the news, on television."

"Us specifically?"

"The fire. They didn't mention us. The E. Wallace Carver residence. Fire of unknown origin."

"Burned flat?"

"I guess. They didn't have pictures."

"Did they say anything about bodies not being found?"

"Nothing about bodies. The house was empty since Mr. Carver died. Now get out while I try to get into this stuff."

Hudson caught himself humming as he shaved with a throw-away razor. What in hell was he so cheery about. He'd been gassed and burned. Going to bed was becoming hazardous to his health. He'd have to get rid of the car. A pity. He liked the unobtrusive four-wheel drive.

The suit fit Cilla perfectly, but...the hair. "First stop a hairdresser."

"What's the matter with my hair?"

"You might as well be wearing a miner's flashlight as that bun. You'd be recognized from a hundred yards. If you're going to be with me, it's either lose some hair or your head."

"Cut it?" There was a startled look on her face.

"And style it."

Discussion began, heated at times, but finally the opinions of a hairdresser were sought. More discussion. A shoulder length was selected, and Hudson made himself scarce while surgery was in process. When he returned, Cilla was in post op, looking as though it had been her arm that had been taken. She needn't have worried. Or maybe she should. Cilla's problem — men — was going to be more of one now. The soft wave of the hair framed her face, smoothing the sharpness of her features and framing her long neck. It was quite a bright light she had hidden under that bushel of hair. She looked at him apprehensively. "Say something."

"I was just thinking we may be headed in the wrong direction."

"What do you mean?"

"For making you less noticeable."

She tottered over to a mirror, fingering her hair. "It took me years to grow that."

"Believe me, it's an improvement. Come on, let's go."

With some manoeuvering they got her back in the car where she promptly took off her shoes. "This is ridiculous. Why do I have to go around in this costume. It's you he's after. He never caught sight of me."

"He probably saw there was a woman with me. But our problem isn't just Trimble. Three men hundreds of miles apart may have been murdered on the same day. Murdered so expertly that there was no suspicion. Except yours. Someone knew enough about me to find me in a cabin a hundred miles into Canada. A cabin I'd not only never been in before but hadn't decided on until an hour before I went there. Pretty impressive organization. I was followed, by someone I never saw. Why are they after me? It must be because I've been asking questions."

"So there's someone in Bartlett..."

"Exactly. Now you come to town with questions too. Who did you talk to?"

"A lot of people. I was pretty upset...so if they really did murder my father..."

"They know just as much about you as me."

She sat back and looked out the window. They were retracing their route into Salem. Hudson watched her out of the corner of his eye. After a few minutes she put the shoes back on.

Lander Margate was waiting. His office was in the redeveloped section of town on the second floor of a new brick building built as though it was still the nineteenth century. Margate was in his middle seventies with a long face, rimless glasses and thinning hair that had gone completely white. He brought them into an interior room with an oriental rug on the floor, soft lighting and expensively framed pictures on the walls. They sat at a polished mahogany table in chairs with carved arms.

"Gotten bored with the role of country squire?" Pale blue eyes that looked at life with the amusement of one who is not involved in its difficulties, glanced at Cilla.

"This is Cilla Wheaton. Have you seen the news today?"

He nodded at her. "The Globe. Did I miss something?"

"Wally's house burned down last night."

"That's a shame. Beautiful spot. How did it happen?"

"First, two questions. The car that caused the accident last May. Was it rented, and what was its make?"

The pale blue eyes appraised him. "I think I have that information here. But..."

"Humor me."

Margate was back shortly with a legal folder. "A rental. Ninety-five Chrysler New Yorker, Avis rental by George Trimble, 147 Bassett Street, Lynn." He looked up. "So?"

"Rented heavy car. Air bag."

Margate looked blank. "Of course. That's why Trimble wasn't hurt."

"Why rented? The little I saw of Trimble he didn't seem to be the type to own a big, expensive car. He had to rent one. A perfect murder weapon. Take a big car with an air bag, you can ram a little Toyota as hard as you want without danger to yourself."

Margate sat forward. "You're saying the accident was really *murder*? Just because Trimble was driving a rented vehicle?"

"Plus a couple attempts on me. You'd better have the whole story." Hudson gave it all to him, starting right from the time in Bartlett he'd first walked through Wally's door and felt the house had been searched. Margate listened without comment, though his eyes widened a little when Hudson described their escape from the burning Marblehead house. When Hudson was done, the old attorney drummed his fingers on the table.

"You're sure it was Trimble you saw last night?"

"How are your connections in the motor vehicle department?" Hudson rummaged in his pockets. "I got a license number." He handed a paper to Margate. "Can we find out who owns this?"

The attorney reached for a phone on a table next to him and punched in a number. Hudson looked over at Cilla. "Have I missed anything?"

She shook her head. "How did you ...bring me around?"

"You mean from the smoke?"

She looked down at the table and nodded,

"The normal way. Mouth to mouth with pressure on your lungs."

"I see."

Margate hung up the phone and turned to them. "It's Trimble. A chancy way to do away with someone. The automobile crash I mean. In the first place, how did he know your car would be along at just that time and location?"

"I've thought about that. It's one of the things that indicate a well organized group. Most people take the same short cut coming back from Boston. He'd wait there. There must have been someone following us and communicating with Trimble's car by telephone. It's the only place where the stop sign is in my direction."

"And you were being a good driver. Stopped at the sign, so you were moving slowly through the intersection. But should have seen him coming. Did you look both ways?"

"Yes, I did. It had rained earlier and the streets were still wet. At that time of night you don't look for cars, you look for headlights. There weren't any." The attorney raised his eyebrows. "He must have kept his lights off until just before the crash."

"Why turn them on at all?"

"For just what happened. A survivor. A car without lights would have caused suspicion. As it was, I put it down to real bad luck."

"What about an absence of skid marks?" asked Cilla.

"Trimble said he hadn't had time to put on the brakes," said Margate. "We had no reason to question it at the time."

"And now?" she asked.

"Good question. I think I'll let you answer that, Lander." Hudson looked at the attorney.

"I wouldn't want to be in court with what we have now." Margate breathed on his glasses to polish them. "We still have nothing new on the accident." He peered at Hudson. "I'm right you were the only one to see the intruder? The young lady didn't get a look at his face?"

"Yes. But we have his license number."

"It's not illegal to be on Marblehead Neck. Again, you were the one who saw the number. She didn't."

"And I'm prejudiced."

"Certainly. Any action you brought against Trimble now would be open to question. Your revenge motive is strong."

"Damn right it is. And I'm going to get him, Lander. That's why we need help. The obvious course is to identify the others in this through Trimble. But we can't very well go sit on his doorstep to see who calls. Now if you were a private eye..."

Margate looked into the distance. "I'm a bit beyond the gumshoe role myself, but there is a firm I've done business with before. Patten and Plough. They have a Boston office. Neither is at all what you'd think of as a private detective. Horace Plough's an accountant. That's where most of the detecting is done nowadays. Came here a few years ago from Pennsylvania." He looked at his shoes. "He has some rather odd associates, not the least of whom is Patten." He glanced at Hudson. "I would think cost is not a factor."

"No. I can use some cash though."

Margate nodded. "Money isn't a problem. Wallace Carver was a very well-to-do man. Now you are. In addition to his stock portfolio, there are substantial investments in real estate, not the least of them being the house in Marblehead. Which reminds me. We'd better get word to the insurance company."

"Maybe not yet." The lawyer raised his eyebrows. "Let the enemy think we died in the fire. They'll know the truth soon enough. In the meantime they may not be looking for us. Your friend Plough. Could he put someone to follow Trimble? I don't suppose they tap phone lines?"

"I'll call him. Now cash. How much do you think you'll need?"

"Can you get me five thousand?" Margate gave a slight nod and spoke into the telephone. "We'd better find rooms someplace," he said to Cilla, "until Plough comes up with something."

She looked startled. "Why don't we go back to Odanak?"

Hudson thought about it. "If we do it right away, before they start looking for us again." He turned to the attorney. "Would you call Plough now? See how fast he can act?"

As Margate pushed a button on the phone, Cilla asked, "Is there a ladies room?"

"I'll show you," said Hudson. He walked her to it and returned to the office.

The lawyer was just finishing his call. "We're in luck. Mr. Plough will personally attend to it. He and two of his associates will be on the job by dinnertime."

"Good."

"Your friend is an attractive young lady."

"Yeah. It came as a bit of a surprise to me. You should have seen her when I first did." The attorney's smile was encouraging. "Oh, no. There's nothing more to it. She's only a kid. With some real hangups. The combination of her looks and feelings about men is someday going to give some poor infatuated kid a queen size problem."

"She seems to get along with you."

"She would with any man, who tiptoes around her on broken glass."

There was a sneeze at the door. Cilla entered with a handkerchief to her nose. "I think I caught a cold last night."

Hudson stood up. "Were you in touch with Wally at all before he died?"

he asked the attorney.

"About a month before. At a Bar Association dinner. Why?"

"Did he mention anything about what he was working on?"

"No. He talked a bit about his hobby. He'd come across a colorful family tree. What was it he said...something about a camera having been invented over two hundred years ago by an ancestor of this person. I think he was just pulling my leg. He had that sly look he often got."

"Can you remember exactly what he said? We're grasping at straws I know."

"Let's see...he used the word 'Kodak'." The attorney frowned. "I'm afraid I wasn't paying that much attention. In any case, I doubt if it has much relevance."

"Kodak. Any more?"

"He started to say something else, but the main course arrived."

"Can you remember what?"

"He was about to ask a question...he said, 'what's so...' and that was all." He smiled wryly at Hudson. "There. Perfectly clear?"

Hudson was rueful. "As day. In Mexico City."

The door opened, and an elderly woman came in with an envelope, which Margate handed to Hudson. He put it in his coat pocket.

"Tomorrow about four?"

"You'll call, yes."

Said just as though he'd still be alive then.

Chapter 13

IT WAS WELL after midnight, and the streets of St. François du Lac were empty as they drove slowly over the bridge to Odanak. At Drummondville Hudson had decided to change cars, but it being after 10 PM the rental car offices were closed.

"I don't feel I'm a desperate enough brigand to steal one. A stupid one though. I perhaps should have rented a car while we were in Salem."

"Why didn't you?"

"I don't know what we're dealing with." He shook his head. "The North Shore is Trimble's home ground. I felt we needed to get away from there before we made changes." They had traveled the length of Boulevard Saint Joseph. At Route 20 Hudson turned the car around and drove back to a gas station he'd noticed was open. The attendant's memory, aided by a few American dollars, recalled the name of a person who might be willing to rent them a vehicle. The prospective renter lived on Rue Saint Alfred which ran parallel to Rue Saint Pierre and thus, Hudson felt, must be doubly blessed. Even just awakened from sound sleep, the French-Canadian is a tough bargainer, and an hour passed before a deal was struck. Hudson and Cilla drove off in a white Toyota, leaving the Subaru in the care of one M. Levesque — who pronounced his name 'Levike.' They headed north again, through the darkened farmland of the 'heart of Quebec'.

"You must be familiar with the accent. I'm pretty comfortable in French, but what's spoken here might as well be Chinese."

"Mother used to speak it sometimes. She was brought up with it."

"Not Abenaki?"

"She wouldn't allow Indian spoken in the house. She wanted us to be like everyone else." She looked out the window. "We weren't."

"Weren't there other people in Bartlett who were part Indian — should I be saying 'Native American?'"

"There were no 'Native Americans' growing up in Bartlett, New Hampshire. We were Indian then, American Indians," her tone was as flat as the land they were passing through. Cilla had changed out of her new suit the first gas station they came to. Now jeans and sweater. Had she also changed out of her attitude — slipped back into the bottled up character she had been — or was it just the subject?

"Your uncle, Joseph. He had a house there. I visited it."

"He was there summers. He went back to Odanak after the tourists left."

"Was he in a tourist business?"

"He had an Abenaki museum. I helped him once in a while. When mother let me. It closed in nineteen eighty-five."

"What happened to it?"

She shrugged. "People stopped coming. The second home owners had all seen it. Those who wanted to anyway... There was a lot of interest in Indians during the seventies. The Mashpees and the Passamaquoddies were trying to get back some of their land. People from Maine and Cape Cod particularly were upset about it. Wanted to know what basis Indians had for their claims; and if they might be after *their* land next."

"I read a little about that. The Indians in Maine actually got something out of it, didn't they?"

"Both the Passamaquoddies and the Penobscots did. The Mashpees didn't."

"What was the basis they won on?"

"That they were right."

"Okay. I guess I'm asking what the legal basis was. I don't think it's happened anywhere else that native people have won anything back, without taking it by force."

"They had the force of being right."

"Which isn't always enough."

Some silence. "In seventeen-ninety they passed a law — Congress did — protecting Indians from people who wanted to steal their land. In Maine and Massachusetts there was some legal stuff about whether or not the Indians were a tribe — the ones who went to court — and if they had a treaty. In Maine they were, they did and they won."

"I'm tempted to say 'only in America', but I guess we've really treated the Indians pretty poorly in general."

"That was about the only time Indians ever won anything."

Hudson decided on a truce if not a treaty, and they drove in silence to St. Francois, turning right on its main street. Hudson slowed as they approached the bridge. There were no cars moving or parked. Nor were there any as he turned into Odanak. Kabir's house sat back from the road. With him was an elderly Indian he introduced as Azo. Over tea and toast they told Kabir what had happened.

As he listened, a rare serious look pulled Kabir's face into unaccustomed lines. "People don't go around burning down houses with other people in them. Do you have the mob after you?"

"No, but it isn't Publishers Clearing House either," said Hudson.

"Azo was just telling me he saw my father the night he died. He'd met someone in Sorel for dinner. You tell them, Azo."

"He was angry. Joseph not a man of emotions, but he was very upset."

"Tell them what he said."

"No better stock than Abenaki. That's what he said."

"Azo thinks he must have been with an Iroquois."

"Them savages."

"Why is it important who he was with?"

"Father fell down twice on his way to bed. Azo had to pick him up the second time. He didn't drink."

"A stroke?"

"Perhaps. That's what the doctor said, and what I thought at the time. But he was an active man; didn't have high blood pressure. And with what's happened since..."

"Yes...?"

"I think he was poisoned."

The room was quiet. Perhaps they had become hardened to violence with all that had happened the last — was it only two days? It almost seemed a matter of course that Joseph Becancour would have been assisted from this world by human hands. No one died of 'natural' causes any more.

"By the Iroquois, or whoever he had dinner with?"

"It wasn't an Iroquois." Cilla entered the conversation. "I know you have your beliefs, Azo, but that feeling between tribes ended long ago. It only exists in the minds of a few old Indians."

"Huh." Azo was unconvinced.

"They can still do tests, Kabir," said Hudson. "To see if there's poison in the body." Kabir hesitated. "I know it's not pleasant to think about."

"I put the idea to the doctor. It wouldn't have his approval. The question is do we want to go around him and try to get a court order."

"How about the days just before he died?" asked Hudson. "Was he doing or thinking anything unusual?"

"That's the other thing," replied Kabir. "There's an old tribal fable that the Abenakis own a lot of land somewhere. Land that was deeded to them by treaty. I'd heard the story growing up. But I also heard about spirits living in rivers and on top of mountains."

"Even I heard about the mysterious Indian land," said Cilla

"Joseph find a paper saying it true," Azo said firmly.

"Azo never actually saw the paper, but he says father got it just a few weeks before. From a friend. And it describes the land. Father was pretty excited about it, but I've gone though all his things and can't find even a mention of it."

"Where is the land supposed to be," asked Hudson.

"And there's the rub," said Kabir. "Near the Hidden Mountain."

"And that is...?"

"Obviously hidden."

"That's it? That's all that's known? That it's near a mountain but nobody knows which one?"

"Of course," said Cilla. "That's why it's a fable."

"I don't think so," said Kabir. "That it is necessarily just a story. Father was pretty hard headed. You remember, Muktabai. He used to tell some fantastic tales to tourists; supposedly Indian lore. And then he'd chuckle over them when the people left."

"It was Uncle Joe that told me about the lost land," said Cilla. "But I don't think he believed it any more than he did his other stories."

Hudson leaned forward in his chair. "Hey, folks. Do you realize what we have here? A missing parcel of land... How much land, do we know?"

"Unknown. I've pictured it as being in the thousands of acres."

"So, several thousand acres of land, deeded when? Must have been a long time ago if it's in Indian folklore. An attorney whose hobby is going over old records, and a surveyor who's put a stake in the middle of the White Mountain National Forest. That tell you anything?"

Cilla's eyes opened wide. "Owls Cliff? That's Hidden Mountain? But it sits right out in the open."

"Try to picture a mountain that doesn't." Hudson got up to pace. "Maybe 'hidden' means behind other peaks."

"It does tie things together," Cilla said slowly.

"Are we ready for me to plant our totem?" Kabir's dark eyes were only partly joking.

"Of course," answered Hudson, "aside from a few details such as a deed and a description. What's your totem?"

"The bear," said Azo, whose native tongue was French, and who had desperately been trying to follow the English conversation.

"Is that what you do? Go put a totem on land to claim it?"

Kabir shook his head. "It's been so long since we've had a chance to claim anything I don't think anyone would know how to go about it. You got nothing from the Marblehead house?"

"Ourselves out. At the time that seemed enough...There was one folder. It's in the car." Tea cups were refilled while Hudson found the file and brought it into the house. He rummaged through its contents. "It's mostly bills. I'm not sure why I took it...Here's some plans of the Swallow Hill house...seems to be the house he built...Wait. What's this?...There's an enclosure behind the living room wall. Look at this, Cilla. Do you remember seeing anything like this?"

She came over and studied the plan. "It's in the wall next to the fireplace... That's the bookcase. Where I picked up the *Bhagavad Gita*." She shook her head. "There was nothing there."

"Not visible anyway. Could be a wall safe...a place to put private papers anyway. If it ever actually got built." He looked at Cilla. "You know what this means."

"We go to Bartlett."

"Someone goes to Bartlett."

"We."

"Is it worth the risk?" asked Kabir earnestly. "They'll certainly be watching that house."

"Not as easy as it sounds," said Hudson. It's on a dead end road with only one other house on it. Mooney would notice any cars hanging around."

"They could come through the woods," Cilla put in.

"They better have their long johns if they're going to spend October nights in the forest. But look. There's no need of both of us going."

"And afterward? After you've finished at the Carver house. Where do you go?"

"A point. The Trimble Tribe seems to know all our hideouts."

"Maybe not." She looked at Kabir.

He stared blankly at her. Then grinned. "Niagara."

"It's not even in father's name." She turned to Hudson. "In the early seventies my father did a survey in Hart's Location. The customer couldn't come up with the money and offered a little cottage he had there in payment."

"Shack."

"Shack. It's not much. Kabir and I used to play there as kids."

"But your father never got a deed to it?"

"He got a deed. Just never bothered to record it."

"So it's still in someone else's name. Who pays the taxes?"

"No town taxes. Hart's Location is unincorporated."

"I guess I knew that. Neighbors?"

"None. Well, one at the foot of the hill. But they're never home."

"How long is it since you've seen it?"

"Ten years."

"It could be downtown Chelsea by now."

"Not likely. Behind the house on the highway, it's all father's land. And it abuts National Forest in back. Did you ever take Nancy Brook Trail?" Hudson nodded. "It runs near the back of the property."

"And how about you, Kabir?" questioned Hudson.

"I'm OK. No danger here. At least until I push for an autopsy."

"Which may be reason enough not to. At least right now."

"The conclusion I'm coming to. I'll play simple Indian. That's a role I know well." He paused. "Can't appear to be too simple though. I'm running for Chief next month."

"Running? Isn't it hereditary?"

"Nope, we're almost civilized. Two year term."

"How's the opposition?"

Kabir shrugged. "My disadvantage is I haven't been around lately."

"And your age?" Hudson smiled an apology. "Sorry but I think of Indian Chiefs as old men — looking like the pictures of Sitting Bull."

"So do our voters." said Kabir.

Hudson glanced at Cilla. "Maybe we'd better get some sleep."

Cilla nodded. There had been no further argument on her going.

It was after eleven when he cautiously turned the white Toyota into Swallow Hill Road. It had turned warm for October. Camping out wouldn't be all that bad, he thought. He pulled to the edge of the road and shut off the engine.

"Let's walk from here."

There were still reds and yellows deepening on the hillsides, waiting for a strong wind to scatter them. Nowhere in the world is the sky bluer than New England in autumn. Or maybe it's just New Hampshire, he mused. They had both put on jeans and sweaters over heavy shirts. A suit would have been the only one visible in town.

Augustus Mooney was coming out of his house rake in hand, taking advantage of the still air to organize his leaves.

"Pity. Don't let you burn anymore." was his greeting. "Nothing like the smell of burnin' leaves. Probably before your time."

Hudson smiled. "Cilla Wheaton, Augustus Mooney."

He leaned on his rake. "Ben Wheaton's daughter. Grown some. Still live on Bear Notch Road?"

"Sometimes." She turned to Hudson. "Where I need to stop. I want my own clothes."

"Okay. Anyone come by looking for me, Augustus? Any cars?"

"Not even yours."

"We...decided to walk. Such a beautiful day."

They continued on, as Mooney started stuffing large bags with leaves. An army could have been encamped in back of the house unseen, but they could do nothing about that. No sound was heard as Hudson opened the front door and entered a living room that seemed undisturbed from when he'd last seen it — was it less than a week ago? Juniper pounced from behind a chair, and Cilla picked her up with a squeal of delight.

"She must be starved!"

"No way," called Hudson from the kitchen. "She's still got a week's supply of food."

"Let's let her out. Just while we're here."

"Can't. Don't forget, this is a quick in and out." He picked up the kitchen phone and called Mary Walton. No, she'd had no trouble getting in. Did she find anything disturbed? No. As a matter of fact it was very tidy. Just the way Mr. Carver kept it. All she had to do was dust and vacuum. Hudson hung up with a bemused look. Had single status turned him into a neatness freak? From the kitchen door he watched Cilla stroking the cat and purring along with it. There *is* affection there.

He crossed to the bookcase and studied it. Then stacked books on a side table. While the exterior of the house was contemporary, on the inside Wally had become more traditional. Hudson ran his fingers over the paneled surface. "If there's anything here, I don't see it... On the other hand, if there's a wall safe here, Wally wouldn't have wanted it seen...He had a secretive streak." He tried pressure on the shelf and on the wall itself; stepped back and studied the wall. It was good quality paneling, as it was throughout the house — here a deep mahogany. Anything that slid back would have to do so vertically. Which meant that it would have to slide into someplace. He knelt down and examined the floor. The baseboards were about five inches high and seemed solid. But even if the whole panel moved down, that would only leave an opening at the ceiling. He went back to the shelf, pulling it. Then to the kitchen where he took a hammer and screwdriver from a drawer. Using the hammer as a fulcrum, he inserted the screwdriver behind the shelf and pried it an inch away from the wall. Behind it was a horizontal break in the paneling about six inches long.

"Gotcha! Now for the 'open sesame'." He walked the length of the bookcase, stopping in front of the fireplace.

"Why don't you just pry it open?"

"Union rules. The Professional Puzzle Piercers." She looked at him. "The more practical reason is I can't cut through metal." He inserted the screwdriver in the thin line and used the hammer on it. There was a muffled 'clunk', and the screwdriver vibrated in Hudson's hand. "Good solid stuff. Doubt if Wally used a blowtorch every time he wanted to get in...He loved a gimmick, but he'd never have put up with an *ordinary* wall safe." Hudson contemplated the fireplace. "In most movies I've seen — and probably that Wally saw — if there's a fireplace next to a secret compartment, that's where the key is." He stepped back a pace. "Notice anything unusual about this one?"

"Good work. When was the house built?"

"Early seventies."

"There weren't many around here who would have tackled a fieldstone fireplace in those days."

"There's more variety of color than in brick. For example, most of the stones are grey. But see here. There's a group with a brownish tinge." He pointed to the left side.

"There's one on the right, too." Cilla's interest was growing.

"Let's step back a little further," said Hudson. "Now what do you see?"

"A curving line on the left and two curving the opposite way on the right. It could almost be an 'S' on the left."

"How about a '5'?"

"Not a very clear one."

"Our mason was working with stones. It may be a bit much to expect graphic precision. Could the ones on the right be 'twos'?"

She looked at him curiously. "What are you after?"

Hudson grinned. "Let's say we have a '5' and two 'twos'. Take a look on the left side of the opening."

"A straight line."

"Could that be a '1'?"

"It could also be a toy soldier holding up the mantle." Her tone was not kindly.

"Good. We'll explore that next. If by chance they happen to be numbers, we might have a '5', a '1', and two '2s'."

"Five thousand, one hundred and twenty-two. About the year B.C. when the city of Jarmo, Mesopotamia was flourishing. Or almost the number of feet in a mile."

"Or the number of angels who can dance on the head of a pin."

"Or the number of bricks you're missing from a load."

"Or Wally Carver's birthday."

She exhaled slowly. "May one, nineteen twenty-two." She turned to him accusingly. "You knew that all the time."

"I was *looking* for that all the time. Nine times out of ten people use their birthdays for combination locks or ATMs. Wally was a genius for some things, but his creativity was only average."

"So what next? We call out the numbers in Carver's voice?"

"I think we use manual labor, or digital, if you prefer." He approached the fireplace and explored the stones with his fingers. "There should be...Yes, here. A smooth spot." He applied pressure. Then moved to his right, feeling each number and pressing the two smooth spots he found. "Now, with any luck, the last 'two' should..." There was a 'thunk' as the panel slid down, revealing an opening behind it. Hudson reached in and pulled out a folder. The tab read, "Becancour, Joseph".

"Let me see!" She took the folder from him.

Hudson did not deny his own exhilaration, but was amused at Cilla's reaction. The kid was really excited.

There was only one document in the folder. Cilla scanned it. "It's not signed! Look." She turned it toward Hudson. "It describes an area...just like a deed...but there are no signatures." She dropped into a chair, deflated. "What good is that?"

"It's an indication that a signed copy was planned." He stopped. The sound of automobile tires on gravel. Hudson moved quickly to a front window. "Two people. A couple in a Lincoln. The man's getting out." He stepped back from the window. A knock came at the door. Hudson picked up a poker from the fireplace and, holding it behind his back, opened the door.

"Yes?"

"I'm dreadfully sorry to bother you. We seem to have gone astray somewhere." The somewhat patronizing tones of an educated Englishman. A strong, warm-for-fall wind had come up, scurrying leaves and bending branches. A fusillade of acorns rattled onto the Lincoln. "We're looking for Stillings Grant. Can you help us?"

Both of the man's hands were in evidence and empty. The woman remained in the automobile, examining her face in the car mirror. Hudson gave instructions. The Englishman thanked him profusely and left. Hudson watched the big car squeeze under the low hanging beech limb and disappear around the bend.

"Enemy?" Cilla joined him at the window.

"If they aren't, why didn't they ask Mooney?"

"Maybe he'd gone in."

"Whatever. We'd better get moving."

"Food. Do you have any? There's nothing at the cabin."

"Bread in the freezer. PB and J on the shelf and in the fridge. Just take it all — and anything else you can find .

"I'll see if I can close up the vault."

"Juniper!"

"We can't take her. There's cat food next to the peanut butter. Put some more in her bowl."

The aperture closed with a reverse pressing of the numbers. Hudson found a box and helped Cilla stuff it with the few groceries the kitchen held. Cilla gave Juniper a last stroking and closed the door quietly. There was no sign of the Lincoln as they made their way back to the Toyota. Mooney waved and went on struggling with blowing leaves.

The house on Bear Notch Road sat on its foundation like an old hen sitting on a nest, its siding bulging over the foundation. Hudson drove in the driveway and parked out of sight behind the house. Cilla ran up the steps to the back door as Hudson drummed his fingers on the steering wheel. She had barely closed the door when Hudson heard a thump and a muffled shout. In an instant he was out of the car, bounding up the steps and inside the door. He had a quick glimpse in the darkened room of Cilla's back and a man beyond her on the floor, then an arm encircled his neck and a cloth was forced over his nose. He choked on harsh fumes, but ancient instinct from wrestling days took over. He reached behind him, grabbed at cloth and, dropping down, threw the body over his head. As it crashed to the floor he was up again, starting to go down to it when he was knocked off his feet by a falling body. Cilla. Hudson rolled and got a choke hold on his attacker, as, out of the corner of his eye, he saw Cilla scrambling to her feet to confront hers — her slim body challenging a strong looking male who topped her by several inches. He doesn't stand a chance, was the thought in one part of Hudson's mind as he applied more pressure to the violently struggling body beside him. Cilla's right leg came up as the stocky man rushed her and, grasping his sweater with both hands, she put her foot in his stomach and fell on her back, sending his body pinwheeling over her head. Maintaining her hold on him, she flipped her body over his to land astride him. A sharp stab to the throat with stiffened fingers made Hudson wince. He had first hand knowledge how that felt. An edge-of-hand blow to the neck ended the misery.

Next to Hudson the struggles grew less and less, and finally the body went limp. He stood up. Cilla was rubbing her jaw. Both men were unconscious, breathing with loud rasping sounds.

"Very nice," he complimented. "All the same, I'd rather have a house with mice. Are you hurt?"

"I'm stupid. I should have finished him off before he got a swing at me." She gently moved her jaw. "I'll have a bruise, that's all. What should we do with these?" She nudged the sleepers with her foot. "They won't be out for long."

"They'll be out a while. Get your clothes. I'll slow them down."

Cilla ran up the stairs, returning with a small bag, as Hudson finished tying wrists together with some clothes-line and the two bodies back to back.

Hudson turned left out of the driveway saying, "We'll take the long way around. There may be reserves around."

"I suppose there's no question they're part of the enemy."

"The average householder doesn't come home to thugs with chloroform."

"Is that what was on those rags?"

"Or something like it. Never smelled the stuff before."

"What were they doing in my house?"

"The really interesting thing is why they were there and not at Wally's. Anyone behind us?"

"Clear. You taking the Kanc?"

"And ninety-three through Franconia. A long way — for a couple of miles."

The Kancamagus highway runs between Conway and Lincoln, a distance of over thirty miles, with National Forest on either side. Until the nineteen-sixties it was a gravel road — dirt it would have been called then — that didn't quite make it across the mountains. In the nineties it could never have gotten built, such was the change in environmental thinking. Bear Notch Road, that Hudson took, connects Bartlett with the Kanc, joining it at the thirteen mile mark.

For all the casualness Hudson displayed, he was shaken by the encounter at the Wheaton house. It had been many years since he had been in a fight, and never one where the other side played for keeps. He had little question that the attackers intended to arrange another 'accident' for them. He and Cilla hadn't just been shot or knifed. Trimble and company were careful people. Their bodies would have been found in a lake. A boating accident. Or in the wreck of the white Toyota. He looked over at Cilla. She, on the other hand, seemed to be taking the whole thing in stride. The blow on her jaw must have been a powerful one; it had thrown her hard enough into Hudson to knock him off his feet.

"We'll get some ice for that in Lincoln.

"Okay."

"You're pretty good with the karate."

"Tae kwon do."

"I don't think Theodore the Thug much cared what it was called. You must practice a lot."

"Three or four times a week. There's a group of us at the ashram."

"Going at it pretty hard, I'd guess. That punch you got didn't slow you down at all."

"We take practice seriously." She was quiet for a minute. "Tanya, my friend, was also...abused when she was young." She looked out the window. "We sometimes hurt each other."

"Really hurt?"

"I broke her leg once. She dislocated my shoulder."

"Are there — God help them — men in your group?"

"Not any more. We killed them all."

Hudson thought to himself, I almost believe that. These are people working out *heavy* problems.

"Read our find."

"The treaty? What's the use. It's unsigned."

"People have been murdered for it. That makes it important."

"You think this is what they're after?"

"Must be."

"Why? It's just some notes, with no legal value."

"Think a minute. If it's a draft of a treaty that actually exists and that deeds land to Indians, it takes land from people who now think they own it. Maybe the description will tell us who."

"Hmm." She opened the folder and took out the single sheet it contained. "It's going to be guesswork. Much of it has been crossed out or written over. After the preamble...some stuff about the promotion of peace...Here's the deed part. 'That land encompassed by the Chataguay River to the south, the Pemijawsitts River to the west, and the Saco River to the north. The boundary to the east shall be a line from the Chataguay to the Saco as follows: from the Chataguay on a straight line that passes through head and foot of Wabanaki Awiben, then turning to the right and easterly to the peak directly behind and thence continuing to the Saco on the same course and direction as before.'"

"Pemijawsitts must be the Pemigewasset River. Chataguay... Where have I seen that name before?"

"There's a building — a house — in Conway Village called something like that. Right where the Saco and the Swift Rivers join."

"Sure! Chataguay was the original name for Conway. It must have been the name for the Swift." Hudson took a New Hampshire map from the glove compartment. "That gives us three sides. Any thoughts on what an Awiben is?"

Cilla shook her head, studying the map. "The rest is all National Forest. We're right on the southern boundary now."

"Depending on where the eastern end is, that could take in most of Bartlett and a large chunk of North Conway."

"Certainly narrows down the suspects."

"In fact, it does. Instead of the whole world being out to get us, it's probably only a few thousand residents of Mt. Washington Valley. Who are the signatories?"

"Written over...The only word I can make out is Wentworth. We had a Governor Wentworth."

"Three of them I think. All during the eighteenth century. They were Royal Governors. Appointed by the King of England."

"With the right to deed land."

"And probably negotiate with Indians in the King's name."

They read the surmise in each other's eyes.

Chapter 14

IN LINCOLN CILLA bought ice as Hudson looked for a telephone. They met back at the car and headed north on route 93.

"Margate?" Cilla fashioned an ice pack from Hudson's handkerchief.

"Some information. Not a lot yet. Trimble lives with his parents, Paul and Marie. Flunked out of B.C. after Lynn English High School. Bartends in Saugus — out where we stayed on Route One. Has a checking account at Essexbank under four figures. No unusual deposits, as there might be with a payoff. Credit cards have small balances. Ordinary guy and no connection with Wally."

"Telephone calls?"

"He got one at one o'clock, but they hadn't the capability to hear what was said. Trimble was still at home so they had no opportunity to plant a bug, or whatever they do. Maybe they have by now. Trimble went out right after the call."

"How did they know he got a call if they couldn't listen?"

Hudson grinned. "I asked that too. They heard the phone ring. I guess they were right outside a window." He looked at her. "He's going north on ninety-five."

"Our way."

Hudson nodded.

The cottage/cabin/shack was up a winding dirt road — definitely not gravel. There were no signs of life in the house on the highway. Several turns up the hill and the — yes, shack was the right word — appeared. The door creaked open to an L shaped room with a rusty sink leaning tiredly against one wall. Two sagging cots, a well-worn but sturdy table and two rickety chairs that wobbled when touched comprised the furniture. Bottlecaps, torn pieces of newspaper and old tin can labels littered a floor whose boards had turned nearly black from ground-in grime. Wisps of cobwebs hung between walls and low beamed roof, and years of dust and dead bugs sat on all flat surfaces.

Cilla put down the box of foodstuffs. "I'm taking a shower."

Hudson looked around in some surprise. "Where?"

"The falls. Can't you hear them?"

As he stopped to listen, Hudson heard the splash of falling water. "Next you'll tell me there's hot water."

"It's cold. But I'm feeling really dirty. Those men. In *my* house." She shuddered. "If you want to try it, I'll show you the best spot when I'm done."

"Thanks. I may just stay dirty. I'll ring for the maid to tidy up the room though."

He found a broom with a few bristles remaining and went to work on the larger cobwebs, as Cilla went out. This is a fine kettle of fish you've got me into, Ollie. There had been no cars following them, and no one as they turned into the cabin's driveway, or climbing its half mile length. They were safe here — at least for a while. But what then? The unseen enemy seemed to have little difficulty seeing them, wherever they popped up. Yet they couldn't stay here forever. He had to get back to a normal life...And do what? The thought stopped him. He took his metaphysical pulse. It had a stronger beat than he could ever remember. He smiled wryly. At a time when numerous people were doing their best to end it, he was savoring his life most fully. Perhaps that's just what happens. Life isn't really appreciated until someone tries to take it from you. A hell of a note.

He swept a pile of dust out the door and stood a moment on the sagging, narrow porch looking over the valley below. They might be hundreds of miles from civilization. He found some empty cans in back of the cabin and string from between two of its beams — perhaps used as clothesline. He threaded the cans onto the string and walked a hundred feet down the road to where two trees bowed to each other from opposite sides. He tied the cord between the two, put pebbles in the cans and stood back to inspect his work. Perhaps a car or even walkers at night coming up the road wouldn't notice it, until they'd made enough noise to carry to the cabin. He shrugged. In any case, it was the best he could do.

He wiped perspiration from his face. Here the road swung close to the brook. He pushed through the trees and heavy undergrowth along its edge, cupping his hands to scoop water to splash on his cheeks and forehead. As he rose, he stopped transfixed. The falls were a hundred feet upstream, a delicate, fifty foot cascade glinting in the late afternoon sun. In front of the falls, silhouetted by that sun stood Cilla, on a rock by the pool formed by the falling waters. Her wet, naked body glistened, poised with arms over her head in a long stretch, her face to the sky as though in obeisance to the sun god. This was a Maxfield Parrish painting to be seen only by the deer that romped through the woods. Or the raccoons that drank from the stream. He had come upon a woods nymph bathing, and any movement would surely break the spell. He held his breath. Muscles rippled ever so gently beneath the surface of her long, slim body. Firm breasts reached skyward. Enough, voyeur, he scolded himself. He edged quietly back toward the road, feeling a little guilty, as though he had in some way been untrue to Sylvia, but more over invading the girl's privacy. And all too aware of her reaction had she been aware of it.

Dinner was tuna fish, fresh from a 3 Diamonds can. There was hamburg from the Carver freezer, but they didn't want to risk a fire.

"Feel like a visit to beautiful, downtown Bartlett?"

"Uncle Joe's house? I thought of that too."

"It's the one place we haven't looked. May have to break in."

"Not necessary." Cilla produced a key. "I got this from Kabir, before we left Odanak."

"Way ahead of me. It will be dark enough when we get there. Let's go."

The white Toyota bumped its way down the hill — Hudson stopping to disengage his warning system. Clouds had moved in blocking whatever moonlight might have brightened the night. Hudson parked the car just before the railroad tracks that formed the village boundary, and they went ahead on foot. As they crossed the tracks, Cilla gestured for him to follow her. She led him behind several houses, staying clear of the wash of lights from interior rooms. They came across no people outdoors, though the night was still mild. The sounds of television came from Melvin and Sarah's as they crept through their backyard. There Hudson stopped Cilla. From behind Melvin's pick-up he surveyed the street. A car was pulling into a driveway at its end. As he watched, it stopped and a man and a woman got out. He looked at Cilla in the darkness. She shrugged. The couple entered the house, and the street was quiet. They waited five minutes. Nothing. The Becancour house was dark and still. They crossed the road to it at a trot. Cilla had the key out and the front door open in seconds. From inside Hudson scanned the street again. Still no sign of any interest in their arrival.

Cilla felt her way to the kitchen and returned with two candles, as Hudson drew the shades in each of the ground floor rooms. Cilla went upstairs, and he started on the living room. It had wide-board floors that gleamed from the light in his hand. Dark walnut furniture, braided rugs and a roll top desk. He pounced on this, taking papers from each cubbyhole and drawer, and returning them carefully when they had been inspected. He could hear

Cilla going through the rooms above. Bills paid and unpaid, grocery lists, bank statements. He started to go through each check and deposit. He shook his head. The enemy must have already done this. If there was anything there then it wouldn't be now. Had they found what they wanted? If so, would they be trying so hard to get rid of them? Then, if there was a clue anywhere here, it was either hidden or, like the Purloined Letter, invisible in plain sight.

He moved to the bookcases. They extended from chair rail to ceiling on two sides of the room. Where to start. He held the candle to several rows. There. A thick book titled *Indian Treaties Of The United States*. He took it from the shelf and thumbed through the pages. A compilation of documents. If *their* treaty were in this book, nobody would be searching for anything. He started to put it back; then thought better of it and sat it on a side table next to another. His eye caught the book already out. A recent publication...a biography of his namesake, Robert Rogers, famous, or infamous depending which side you were on, for Rogers' Rangers. He put that on top of the treaty book.

The steps creaked as Cilla tiptoed down.

"There's someone outside," she whispered. "A car. Across the street."

"Damn. I've just started on the books." Hudson snuffed his candle and lifted the corner of a window shade. The driver's side window of a dark colored automobile framed the faint glow of a cigarette. "A watcher." He released the shade. "Find anything?"

"No. You?"

"Not sure. Some bedtime reading anyway. We'd better move. Where's the back door?"

A car door closed.

"Damn. He's noticed the shades."

Cilla led the way as they scrambled through the kitchen. The door squeaked open to a dimly visible yard of scraggly hay. They inched their way down creaking steps, and Hudson peered around the southerly corner of the house. There was someone coming cautiously along the side.

He motioned to Cilla. "The other way."

They ran as fast as they dared in the darkness toward the house to the north. A fence came on them suddenly. As they clambered over, a voice from behind. "Hold it!"

"Keep going," Hudson whispered urgently.

"The river," Cilla sprinted back out onto the road and turned right toward its dead end.

Hudson could hear the "Oof" as the fence surprised their pursuer. The woods got thick at the end of the road. He lost sight of Cilla, then picked up sounds in the brush, and pushed after. Hudson could hear crashing in the woods behind him. If he had a gun, Hudson was pretty sure he wouldn't use it. So far, there had only been "accidents". This man would have instructions to keep it that way. Maybe Hudson could make him less enthusiastic. Suddenly he could hear no sounds, the pursuer had stopped. Hudson dropped to a knee and peered around the oak. A blob of white hung just beyond the tree, listening. Slowly it moved toward him. Behind him he could hear Cilla. Cilla! Good God, she was coming back! He rose. As the man drew level with the tree, Hudson, using his arm with heavy book as a club, swung from his heels — feeling the book mush into a cheek. He hadn't caught him straight on. The pursuer must have been looking away, but the body fell with a crash.

He turned. Cilla was at his shoulder.

"Go!" Hudson gave her a shove, and they rushed toward the river. "Are we going to swim for it?"

"No." Hudson could hear the water as they ran through the trees. "I hope your rock jumping has improved though."

The beach was mostly large stones. Cilla turned upstream. After a hundred yards, they stopped to listen. No sounds of pursuit. Hudson thought he heard a car start up.

"We'll cut through here," whispered Cilla, moving across a well-mowed and still soft lawn. Another hundred yards and the road became visible. They crouched behind a house that fronted on it. A car was on the same street as the Becancour house, pointed toward Main Street.

"He knows we've got a car here someplace; he's just going to sit and watch the only road out until we make a move," said Hudson.

"The car's on the other side of the road. He'll see us as we cross." They could see the Toyota two blocks away. Three other cars were visible.

"He doesn't know which is ours. We'll go opposite it and wait for a diversion."

Staying behind houses they worked their way to some bushes across from the Toyota. There they crouched again, watching the watcher who watched the highway. After what Hudson's knees said was an hour but was no more than ten minutes, automobile headlights appeared from the west. "Just after it passes we'll go."

As oncoming headlights went by, blinding the hunter car, they scurried across the street and climbed quickly into the Toyota. Hudson clicked off the ceiling light. "Don't close the door hard....Now quietly..." He started the engine. "Hold tight."

Cilla was watching the rear window. "Here he comes."

The speedometer read 70 as they rounded a curve and headed north. Hudson kept his foot to the floor.

Cilla plucked at his sleeve. "Turn right when I say...Now!"

With a squeal of brakes and tires, suddenly they were on a dirt road. Hudson wrestled the car to a stop, quickly switching off the engine. Within seconds the follower sped by. Hudson started the engine and backed up. The road crested just beyond them, so their lights weren't visible to the car in front as they turned to follow it.

"He won't expect us behind him." Hudson leveled off at fifty.

"There aren't many others on the road — and he knows us."

"He can't see the color behind our headlights."

They kept their eyes on the road. The other car was far ahead. After a mile or so, they came to a gravel road on their left. Hudson turned into it, parked the Toyota well off the road several hundred feet in, and shut off the engine. They walked back to the main highway and hid in some trees. Five minutes later the dark car came back, moving slowly without headlights. Hudson wondered for a moment if he had driven far enough in, but the car stopped only briefly at their road and continued on.

He let out a breath as it disappeared over a small bridge and around a curve. "Let's go before his next trip."

As they continued north, Cilla said, "On the left there'll be a For Sale sign. We can park at the house there and walk the rest."

"Empty?"

"Yes. Mrs. Thompson's. She died last summer."

"Relatives?"

"None that can use it. It used to be on the Thank-You-Ma'ams." Hudson looked blank. "The old road; it had lots of bumps."

Hudson was forming a mental picture of the name's origin as he turned off at the sign. The house was an elderly cape set well back. The driveway curved around it, and Hudson followed it to its end next to a sagging shed.

"Let's hope the broker doesn't have an early showing."

They walked back along the highway. The new section was wide and straight, and Hudson felt confident they'd have plenty of warning — even of a car without headlights. The temperature was beginning to drop to a more seasonal level, and a cold northerly breeze was in their faces. No car had passed them from either direction as they climbed the driveway to the shack Cilla and her cousin called Niagara. Hudson re-attached his warning system. The cabin, without benefit of the sun, was cold. He found two candles, lit them, and by their flickering light, arranged the cots so Cilla and he were at opposite ends of the L. All the clothes they weren't wearing were piled on top of the thin blankets. Hudson climbed into bed fully clothed, minus only shoes, and studied the book he'd taken. Rogers Rangers and treaties. War and peace. The raid on St. Francis had been in 1759, killing many of the Indians. Hudson noted with relief that the Rangers had also found hundreds of white men's scalps in the village. His namesake had at least *some* justification. In a margin someone — Becancour presumably — had written, "By then the document had gone." Document could mean the treaty — the draft of which they now had. What had happened to the original? What were the chances of it still being in existence? Not many, he thought. But then why were people being murdered? Were Wally and Joseph Becancour running a giant bluff; hoping to win an enormous chunk of land with a busted straight? They had been called, and lost more than the pot. Now Hudson had been dealt a hand. And had to play it face down.

Chapter 15

"YOU GOING TO sleep all day?" Cilla was closing the door behind her.

"I'd like to. But in a nice warm bed." This one was an icy cocoon.

"A couple of laps up and down the hill will warm you."

"It did you, I take it."

"Yes."

"How's your jaw?"

"How does it look?" She tilted her head.

He threw back covers and got up. "Bruised. Hurt?"

"Not much. Take your run and I'll make breakfast."

"Wonderful. I'll have Eggs Benedict."

"You'll have PB and Js Wheaton."

He looked at her curiously. "You're enjoying this, aren't you?"

She turned away. "What do you mean?"

"Just that. We're being hunted and chased by people who've shown no particular reverence for life and are right now probably poking through the backyards of Bartlett for us, and I almost saw a smile on your face."

She kept her back turned. "I feel safe here...not just in the cabin. I grew up in this valley."

"And know it well. That first road we turned off on, on the way back? Trees and underbrush make it invisible until you're right on it. I turned the steering wheel completely on faith. Going close to seventy. You had to time that to the second; I saw no opening in the woods."

"That's a road I won't forget," she replied in a flat voice.

"Oh?"

She turned back abruptly. "I don't want to talk about it, okay?"

"Sure. Sorry. I don't know what things bother you."

"It goes to Second Iron," she flung out.

"Where...?"

"Kabir told you. Where I found out what people are really like."

"Men, you mean."

"All right, men."

"One man, anyway. They never caught him?"

"No."

"Would you recognize him?"

"No. I never saw him! Why are you asking these questions? I told you I didn't want to talk about it!"

"I guess you've become more of a friend than I've had in a long time, and I don't like to see a friend suffering — as you obviously are."

"There's nothing you can do." Her words were harsh, but her face softened a little, and there was a glistening in her eyes.

"I can listen."

She nodded abstractedly, as to her own thoughts rather than his words. "Now get out of here."

On his second run to the bottom of the hill, he thought he saw the car from the night before disappearing around a curve on Route 302, but wasn't sure. There were few houses in Hart's Location. If they had decided their prey was still in the area, they were bound to find the cabin sooner or later. When they did, he and Cilla couldn't be there. He stumbled over a half-hidden branch. Damn. That was their problem; stubbing their toes on enemies who seemed to know all about them, while remaining hidden themselves. They had to find a way to stay safe until Margate's people turned up what the hell was going on.

Cilla had set the cabin table with the two candles, paper towel napkins and sandwiches on paper plates.

"And I'd heard they'd stopped serving luncheons at the Ritz."

"Eat. They may still be searching this area."

"My guess is they'll find the cabin sometime today."

"And the car."

"They may not know it's ours."

"If they find nobody here, won't they just go away? They can't watch every place in Hart's Location."

"They obviously haven't tied the cabin to you or they'd be here. We'd better clear out for a night anyway. Maybe two,"

"Where?"

"We've run out of houses."

"A...motel?" The word came hard.

"No. We'd stand out."

She let out her breath. "Right. There aren't many visitors this time of year."

"Look. It can't be any colder in the woods than in this cabin. Let's get warm sleeping bags, a winter tent and make camp in the high country near here. We'll come back when they've checked this place out."

"Above Nancy Falls," Cilla got enthusiastic. "In the spruce and fir forest."

"With mossy carpeting that looks like it would make a nice mattress."

"Yes!...Eastern Mountain Sports?"

"North Conway may be risky, but they'll have what we want."

"Let's do it!"

The trip back to the Toyota was uneventful. They bushwhacked fifty feet off the highway rather than walk along it, which took three times as long, but felt more secure. They scouted the woods around the car before approaching it. We may need another vehicle, thought Hudson, as he unlocked the door. He tried to picture how much of it the enemy had seen in the dark. They must know it's white, but probably didn't see the license, so a Quebec plate might throw them off.

They took the long way around again, through Twin Mountain, Franconia and the Kancamagus Highway, this time not turning off at Bear Notch Road, but continuing on through Conway. He parked the car behind Eastern Slope Inn. Between EMS and International Mountain Equipment across Main Street they purchased — cash, no credit cards — frame hiking packs, self-inflating camping mattresses, a compass, knife, a small folding shovel, water resistant matches, Head ski jackets, Europa lined warm-up pants, long underwear, warm hats and gloves as well as extra warm sleeping bags made for — the literature said — Arctic use. The latter might be overkill, but Hudson had a strong memory of the previous night's cold. The two person tent seemed adequate until he pictured how they'd fit in it, and bought the three person. He'd handle two pounds more. A small stove, cooking pot, water purifying tablets and dehydrated food came last. They split up to make the purchases, buying the items in several trips, alternating stores and buyers, so the quantity of their purchases wouldn't be noticed. When done, Hudson felt ready for Everest — or at least K2.

He telephoned Margate from Lincoln. The attorney was in and had news.

"Trimble's in your area. Stopped at the bank, then checked into a motel. Came running out several hours later, jumped in his car and went off at high speed. Plough's man couldn't follow closely going so fast and lost him in Glen. He believes Trimble must have taken Route 302, since he himself followed Route 16."

"He's right. Trimble came to Bartlett to supervise the search for us."

Hudson told him about their visit to the Becancour house.

"Good Lord! You must keep yourself and the girl safe until we get to the bottom of this."

Hudson assured him they would not be taking callers and hung up. He related the conversation to Cilla as they sped north on Route 93. Cannon Mountain Ski Area appeared on their left as the road turned eastward.

"Ever skied?" Hudson asked.

"Since I was three. I worked at Great Haystack one winter when I was fourteen."

"What did you do there?"

"Ski patrol."

"A girl of fourteen. Young for that job, weren't you?"

"I can ski better than any man." A pronouncement that brooked no argument.

"Do you know Floyd Carr well?"

"No. I grew up skiing there, but only worked for him one winter...then went away to school." She noted Hudson's glance. "It didn't snow the next winter anyway...it was before they had snowmaking." Hudson was silent. "All right! That was the summer my mother...died... And I..."

"And you were raped. At fifteen. Why does that sound so much worse than your poor mother being killed? Murder is the most heinous of crimes. Maybe because he stole the rest of your childhood. And more." He looked over at her. Her head was bowed, eyes tightly closed. Her hands clutched together as though restraining each other from covering her ears. His impulse was to put his hand over hers. It lasted only a second; just long enough for the picture of her reaction to flash on. If he survived — and the chances were in his favor only because her range of motion was limited — the car would be in a ditch. How do you give comfort to someone who can't accept it? In Cilla's case, very carefully. If at all.

"Tell me some Abenaki history. What was their connection to this area? A connection strong enough to pry a large chunk of land out of New Hampshire."

"They were Pigwakets and Sokokis here."

"Not Abenakis?"

"The white man always wants everything in neatly labeled boxes. The Indian doesn't see things that way. Abenakis were Algonquins, just as Sokokis and Pigwakets were. And also Wabanakis."

"Who are they?"

"Original name for Abenakis. Wabanaki means those of the East or rising sun."

"So they were also Japanese."

She looked at him and chewed a lip. "Do you want to hear this or not?"

"Sorry. I *am* interested."

She watched the road ahead. "The Indians used rivers as roads. So they mostly didn't settle upstream any further than the water was deep enough for their canoes."

"Which means not in Bartlett."

"They probably didn't have settlements that far north. Though they hunted all over this area."

"What happened to them? Seems to me I read about a battle in the Fryeburg area."

"They were just about wiped out there. A gang led by a man named Lovewell."

"When was this?"

"Seventeen twenty-five."

"Some years before the raid on St. Francis."

She looked at him curiously. "What are you getting at?"

"A note in the Robert Rogers book I took from your Uncle Joe's house. That the document had gone by the time of the raid. I'm guessing he meant the treaty. So the important period for us is before seventeen fifty-nine. Something happened then that caused it to get lost. Or hidden."

She pulled her lip. "Maybe there isn't one. Despite what we've found, it's just an old tribal fable that a treaty exists."

"People don't get murdered over old tribal fables. Unless there's some truth to them."

"Or maybe we're looking in the wrong place. Maybe it has nothing to do with treaties or history or anything. Maybe it has only to do with *now*."

"Can you think of another possible connection between your father, your uncle and my father-in-law?"

She smoothed a wrinkle in her jeans. "What are we going to do with the car?"

"Hide it in the woods."

"At the cabin?"

"Don't think so. Any other ideas?"

She rested her chin on folded hands. "There's an island in the Saco. It isn't really an island. But there's water all around it, and a road to it over a little bridge. Guys used to drive through the island for a party. When the river was low, like now, they'd take their cars right through the Saco to the far shore. There used to be a little clearing on the other side where the cars couldn't be seen by...anyone."

"Like the cops."

She nodded. "If it hasn't grown up too much we might still be able to do it. You'd have to know it was there to find it."

"Tell me where to turn."

It was a very narrow road over a small brook that lead to the river. Cilla got out and walked the shore.

"I think it's over here," she called.

Hudson maneuvered the Toyota over rough ground to where the river bank wasn't quite as steep. Cilla supervised from the outside as he lowered the front wheels into the water. The river bed was large round rocks, and the car weaved from side to side as it entered. There was the uncomfortable sensation of water flowing over the hubcaps. Then a wide beach of more stones that jarred the Toyota with each revolution of the wheels. Hudson wished he had his four wheel drive Subaru. Cilla rolled up her jeans, took off shoes and socks and waded behind.

"To your right," she directed.

Hudson could see an opening in the trees, with long grass and bushes. He tried to go right for it, but the bank was too steep, and his wheels spun futilely. He backed up and approached at a different angle. On the third try the wheels found a grip and, with a lurch, the Toyota climbed the bank. Its momentum carried it through some bushes to settle against a double birch. With some work Hudson got the car turned around so that it faced the way it had come. He got out.

"Good," Cilla called from the rocky beach. "You wouldn't know it was there."

"We're not very smart."

"Why?"

"Should have left the tent and supplies on the island. Save carrying them back. Oh well. I'm not trying that river again until we leave. Let's load up."

They separated the equipment and supplies into two equal — Cilla would have it no other way — loads. Hudson followed Cilla's example, rolling up his jeans and taking off boots and socks before taking on the river. He was in immediate agony crossing the rocky beach. Though months of strenuous hiking had toughened his legs, the bottoms of his feet had been cushioned by heavy socks and boots, and were in the same suburban-soft condition as when he arrived in Bartlett four months before. Cilla was amused as he tottered painfully toward the water. The river, when his bruised feet reached it, was no better. Here the rocks were bigger but slipperier, and the water felt like melting glacier. On his third step he went down on a knee, soaking one jeans' leg and a sleeve where he put out a hand to get his balance.

"I'm okay," he gasped.

"I wasn't worried. I have the food."

"Great. I could be swept downstream. But as long as you have the food..."

"In three feet of water?"

"Just get over to the bank. I'll be right there." The shoes tied around his neck banging against his jaws didn't improve his mood. He reached the bank wet but thankful.

They trotted across the highway opposite the entrance to the island, and bushwhacked down to Nancy Pond Trail where it crossed the first of several brooks. What a shame, Hudson thought. Beautiful mountain streams all over, and here we are lugging in bottled water. Actually, the water in the brooks was probably perfectly good. Few hikers were on the trails at this time of year to pollute them. But a case of the gallops would be inconvenient. To say the least.

The trail followed an old logging road and, in a half mile, entered National Forest. As they passed the red painted cairn which marked the boundary, Hudson could still hear sounds of trucks on the highway far below. Two thirds of the way to Nancy Cascade, the trail crossed Nancy Brook itself; then a somewhat steeper climb to the falls. No, cascade was the right word. The water coursed down the mountainside, seldom leaving the rocky surface but falling almost vertically.

They sat on chilly boulders — the weak, October sun had already disappeared behind the cliffs — and ate sandwiches to the tunes played by the falling waters. Cilla took off her shoes and socks and dangled her feet in the cold pond at the bottom. Hudson stuck in a hand and quickly withdrew it. The girl's feet must be made of leather.

After lunch they went on. The trail wound steeply through the woods next to the cascade, emerging in the flatland at the top. Along the way, Hudson could see there were actually a series of cascades where the water paused at pools before continuing its rush down the mountainside.

"Beautiful, isn't it?"

Hudson leaned against a tree. "Better when the leaves are on the trees. Have you been up here often?"

"Three or four times. I never get tired of it."

On the right further on was a hidden pool with its own tiny waterfall. "Like a little fantasy world," said Cilla.

"That we'd all like to live in."

"Why can't we? People used to live in these mountains years ago. Why do they have to live jammed up against each other in squalid cities."

"The question is, how much longer can the earth continue to absorb geometric increases in human population."

Soon there was a series of thirty rock steps, thoughtfully set in place by a long-ago trail builder, and then Nancy Pond. Nancy Swamp would be more appropriate, thought Hudson. Listed on the map as four acres, the open water covered barely one. The rest was wetland, the water hidden under long swamp grass and bushes. Here he and Cilla left the path and struck off through the woods — away from the pond and toward the river. Finding a dry patch of the soft, bright green moss that Hudson remembered from his one previous visit as looking so comfortable, they set up the tent.

"Do we dare build a fire?" Cilla asked.

"Better not. We've got the gas stove for cooking and warm sleeping bags." He unrolled the latter and stretched them out inside the tent. Cilla examined them and reversed their positions. Hudson saw their zippers now faced away from each other and grinned to himself.

Dinner was spaghetti with a packaged sauce. Afterwards it was too cold to sit out without a fire, so they crawled into their sleeping bags. Even fully clothed, it was a while before Hudson felt warm.

"Do you know a man named Larry Cook?"

"The banker? No."

"Tell me about Carr. He doesn't seem the type to be running a ski area."

"Why?"

Hudson thought a minute. "I suppose because he seems more like a city businessman. A man should get enjoyment from managing a ski area."

"You don't think a woman could run a ski area?"

"I didn't say that."

"What did you say."

"I can't picture Carr on skis. Or running a business for outdoor-type athletic men and women.

"Do you ski?"

"Did. Years ago. I don't know about now."

"Once you learn it you don't forget. You should get back to it this winter...if we make it that long."

"We will. Don't ever question that."

They became silent, each with own thoughts. Despite his words Hudson knew there were people out there ready to make sure he never skied or anything else again. What kind of motivation would bring people to killing not one but three men. And one woman, thought Hudson. The unkindest cut of all: Sylvia, who never had a harsh word for anyone. The others were all well along in years. Sylvia... He turned his body in the sleeping bag. He was going to have to act a lot more intelligently in the future. The enemy had proven their deadliness. And his narrow escapes owed more to luck than planning.

Why were they after him so urgently anyway. As though they had to get him before...before what? What did he have or know that made him the object of such an intense pursuit, where every place he went there was someone waiting to remove him from whatever game they were playing. Sure he'd asked some questions about Wheaton's death, but what he had learned could easily fit in an ant's pillow. Someone had accompanied the surveyor on the day he died. A: that's hardly a crime and B: there's no evidence there *was* a crime. Wally's death was now definitely not an accident. Again, no proof. Joe Becancour the same.

Okay, so what did he *have* that made him a threat. An almost illegible draft of a treaty that may never have been executed. Sort of like the draft of Lincoln's Gettysburg address. Not worth a damn thing until the speech was actually given...No, even scribblings by a President of the United States would have value. Because of the person who wrote them. Did *his* piece of paper have value because of its writer? It had to have been Benning Wentworth — New Hampshire's governor during the 1750s — if anything tied together. Where had Wally gotten it. Margate said something about a client's...estate was it? The draft had presumably sat in a file or safe deposit box for many years. Perhaps even unknown to the owner — like great grandmother's diary. Not of much interest, unless in it she confessed to an indiscretion that substantially changed what you'd thought was your genetic make-up.

He was trying to picture what it must have felt like to be brought up Indian...when he slept.

The next morning they explored Norcross Pond — here at least was some open water, not completely a swamp — and the sweeping view of the Pemigewasset Wilderness from its western end, the Franconia Range stretching from left to right. Then down past the junction with Carrigain Notch Trail to Desolation Shelter. Here there were many options: the Wilderness Trail along the East Branch of the Pemigewasset River, the Shoal Pond Trail toward Zealand Hut or Desolation and Signal Ridge Trails up over Mt. Carrigain and down to Sawyer River Road. Drops of approaching rain decided a return to the tent.

After scrambled eggs and hashed brown potatoes, Hudson put on rain gear and hiked down to telephone Margate. Cilla's objections were muted.

One hiker was less conspicuous than two.

"Plough's man in New Hampshire located the Becancour house," said the attorney. "He went on foot the last few blocks. A wise move. There is somebody in a car watching it. But it's not Trimble. He's back in Massachusetts. They picked him up again at his house this morning. Would you like to hazard a guess as to where he is this afternoon?"

"In church, praying for our souls?"

"At the Japanese Consulate in Boston."

"Christ! Don't tell me we're up against a *yakuza*."

"International overtones are now a possibility."

"Anything else?"

"Not yet. These things take time."

On the trail back to the tent he suddenly stopped. 'These things take time.' Yet everything the enemy had done demonstrated urgency. It was obviously important he and Cilla be put out of action. Quickly. And wasn't that just what had happened? Hadn't they politely obliged; taken themselves out of the 'game', even though only for a matter of days? Something was going on — maybe even with international implications — and he and Cilla were off enjoying a camping trip in the White Mountains.

He kicked a stone into the woods. If time was a factor, they had no more of it than the enemy, before whatever needed to get done got done. Plough's people were just watching; he and Cilla were the ones feared, thus the ones with stopping power. But what? And how?

"It all has to do with that treaty," he said to Cilla as he threw clothes in his backpack.

"Why? Where are we going?"

"Something happened to the original in the seventeen-fifties. We've got to look for it there."

"Time travel?"

"In a sense. How much of Odanak dates back to then?"

"Not much I'd guess. Your ancestor pretty well wiped it out. Is that where we're going?"

"And fast. I've been asleep; it's time I woke up."

Chapter 16

"WABANAKI AWIBEN," READ Kabir. "Wabanaki of course is Abenaki. ...Awiben?...Let's ask Azo." He glanced at a clock. "He's probably still up."

M. Levesque's Toyota had been returned to him in Drummondville, with thanks and an extra large tip to cover certain mysterious dents and scratches that had appeared on the vehicle. The second crossing of the Saco River had gone even less smoothly than the first. They'd left the tent hurriedly wrapped around the sleeping bags and buried under brush. It was as good a place as any to store it.

"Awiben mean calm. Like when no wind," Azo had no difficulty recognizing the word, even as pronounced by Kabir over the telephone.

Kabir hung up. "A calm Abenaki. A quiet Indian?"

"They were *all* calm until the white man appeared," asserted Cilla.

"If he's out of the wind, perhaps he's hidden. Like the mountain," said Hudson.

"Maybe he's calm like at rest," said Kabir, bouncing from his chair. "How about some geologic feature that looks like an Indian lying down?"

"Some people have called Moat Mountain 'The Sleeping Indian'," said Cilla. "Moat is really a range. Not one peak."

Hudson looked at the map of the White Mountains he had spread out on the table. "As I picture Moat, it does look like a man lying on his back. His head would be North Moat and the feet, South Moat. If it's the eastern boundary of the treaty, all of Bartlett village would be included as Indian land."

Kabir whistled. Then leaned forward. "Could Moat be the Hidden Mountain?"

"If there's one thing Moat isn't, is hidden. It's the most prominent feature in the North Conway area."

"But before there was a North Conway it was just another mountain."

"Hudson's right. Moat stands out no matter where you see it from."

Cilla was deflated. "And there's no peak behind it."

"There's Kearsarge, which was originally Pequawket," Hudson said. "There's no reason why the hidden mountain and Wabanaki Awiben have to be the same place. We're talking about two different things now. Moat could still be just a boundary used for the treaty." He paused, musing. "How glibly I say 'just' a boundary, having thus transferred ownership of an entire town. Maybe two."

"Not until there's a *real* treaty. With actual signatures."

"Right," Hudson came back to earth. "Tell us about Odanak, Kabir. What here dates back to the Rogers Raid?"

"Almost nothing survived that. You think the treaty was drawn before then?"

"On the slimmest of evidence. A sentence written in the margin of one of your father's books. I wish I'd had time to really go through his library in Bartlett." He sighed. "Everything's happened so fast lately." He looked at Kabir. "Ever since the night I spent in that cabin here and got gassed."

"Not very hospitable of us."

"No."

Kabir felt Hudson's eyes on him and shifted uncomfortably. "Next time we'll have a welcoming dance." He said lightly. Hudson said nothing. "Hey, I don't mean to make a joke of it. You're lucky to be alive."

"Maybe."

Kabir was troubled. "Something's bugging you."

"Yeah. When you came to the hospital to tell me the story of what happened, I felt something was wrong but couldn't put a finger on it. Now I have. You said that a neighbor — the mysterious neighbor that 'went away' suddenly — had pulled me out of the cabin. I told you it was a woman, and I was surprised she spoke English."

"As most do here. I think I told you that."

"Yes. But when they're talking to themselves, as this woman did, they don't. More to the point, people almost never swear in a foreign language."

Kabir and Cilla looked at each other. "And this one did?" The Indian drew his legs underneath him.

"Unless you can convince me 'damn' is either french or abenaki."

"I'll make tea." Cilla was out of her chair, color rising in her cheeks.

"You've been my friend, Cilla. Don't run out now."

"Let her go," said Kabir as the girl disappeared into the kitchen. "She *is* your friend. More than you've realized. Muktabai — Cilla — was the 'neighbor next door.' She saved your life."

Hudson sat back. "Then why the mystery? God knows I don't often get a chance to thank someone for it."

"It was the *way* she saved you."

Hudson looked blank.

"You remember how cold it was that night?"

"I still shiver thinking of it."

"Cilla learned from Suzanne that you had been at Odanak and went to the cabin to apologize for what took place at the ashram; found you out cold with gas pouring into the cabin, shut off the heater and dragged you outside. You were breathing okay, so she ran to the house next door, broke a window to get in and telephoned me to hurry over."

"The empty house with a broken window!"

"When she got back you were just coming around. But it was very cold, and you don't wear much to bed."

"Just jockeys." Hudson could feel himself getting a little warm.

"She couldn't pull you back in the cabin with it still full of gas. She got the two thin blankets from the bed and wrapped you in them. You were still shaking with the cold, so she did the only thing she could."

Understanding flooded in. "She warmed me with her own body."

"To do so she had to take off her clothes."

There was a far-away look in Hudson's eyes. "I dreamt it was Sylvia."

"Can you imagine how difficult that was for a girl who's revolted by the touch of a man's hand?"

"Whew! I can remember bare breasts..."

"Don't out loud, when she's around. That's why she wouldn't let me report it to the police. She didn't want anyone to know what she'd done."

Hudson ran a hand through his hair. "Um...she say any more about it? About...how it affected me?"

Kabir grinned. "You got warm. You also got hard."

"Oh shit."

The grin widened. "I was kind of surprised she told me about it."

"Why am I still alive?"

"Because you were already unconscious. No threat to her. As a matter of fact, it may have been the best thing that could have happened."

"How in hell do you figure that?"

"Try to picture another situation where she would — or even could — get close enough to a man to discover that we can have male reactions without necessarily being beasts."

"Therapy by Rogers ...but, hey, I *was* reacting like a beast. Isn't that what she'd think?"

"It isn't what she *did* think. She knows how much in love you were in your marriage. She even told me your response was not to her but to your wife."

"And you think that experience alone will change her feelings about men?"

"Probably not. It's a start though. And I do know you are now the only male besides myself she isn't uncomfortable with."

"I make a great role model. I've almost gotten her killed several times."

Cilla sneezed to announce her entrance and brought in a tray with tea which she placed next to Kabir. She put plates with brownies in front of all three. She didn't look at Hudson.

"I guess I had things wrong..." he started. She sat and looked out the window. "I need to say thanks for saving my life."

"You saved mine. In Marblehead."

"I know how difficult..."

"Shut up and eat your brownie."

It was a little stale. But the tea was good.

The next morning Kabir and Cilla divided up the list of Abenakis obtained from the Registraire's office and started calling on their houses. Azo went along as interpreter, in case needed for the older people, some of whom spoke a mixture of French and Abenaki. Each one would be asked if they knew of anything that had come down from the 1759 raid or from any time during the eighteenth century.

Hudson took a table at the musée and began going over the many books and documents the museum had accumulated. At four o'clock he called Margate.

"It would seem the Japanese interest has a business basis," said the attorney. "At least the gentleman Trimble spoke with in the Consulate is their Commercial Attache."

"Plough's man follow him right in?"

"Plough himself. Showed a bit of initiative. Presented himself as interested in a Japanese business connection. Got to wander around a bit."

"Any indication as to what kind of business Trimble discussed?"

"No. A bit more on him though. Trimble's father, Paul, is his stepfather. Second marriage for Mrs. T. Maiden name Delacroix. Her first was to a Rene Gagnon also of Lynn, three months before young Georges with an 's' appeared."

Hudson hung up the telephone. So George Trimble was really Georges Gagnon. Certainly not Japanese.

The three met over dinner.

"Any luck?" asked Hudson.

Kabir shook his head. "It's a great excuse to politic, though".

"What *could* have come down from Rogers Raid. The village was burned flat." Cilla had put last night's discussion behind her. "They spared three houses that had stocks of grain, but I think all of them have since disappeared."

"I saw a photograph of one in the musée. Taken in nineteen-fifteen."

"Since torn down," said Kabir.

Azo came in. He didn't understand why they had been interviewing the tribe. "You don't need talk with people. They not the answer."

"What is?" asked Hudson.

"*Kodaak wajo.* You find that, you find answer."

Hudson sat back. "Say that again, Azo. The first words you said."

"*Kodaak wajo?*"

"Yes." He turned to the other two. "The last words Margate could remember Wally saying were something about Kodak and then he started to say 'what's so' which is the same way you pronounced it, Azo. What does it mean? Is it Abenaki?"

"Yes. It mean 'hidden mountain'. Where Abenaki land is."

The three looked at each other. "I wonder if Wally found it," said Hudson softly.

"If there was a question before what the three men were looking for, it's just been answered," said Kabir.

"And if they could find it, so can we," said Cilla.

"Let's try a different tack," said Hudson as Azo left. "A treaty in the seventeen-fifties, who would have signed for the Abenakis?"

Kabir thought a minute. "Probably a man named Gill. I'm sure the musée would have something on him. Does it have to be the seventeen-fifties? Or why even the eighteenth century?"

"Only because of Governor Wentworth's name on the document we found in Wally's safe. He was appointed by the English crown. After seventeen seventy-six that didn't count for much in the U.S. Then there's the note in the Rogers Rangers book your father had in his library. The raid in seventeen fifty-nine seems to put a cap on the date."

"It also puts a cap on our chances of finding anything," said Cilla. "In *Northwest Passage* Kenneth Roberts wrote that even the church was burned."

"But that was fiction."

"He did a lot of research. The major facts are probably accurate."

That evening, Hudson started on some of the history books in the musée. He'd picked up a French-English dictionary since most histories of that period were written by French missionaries, and nobody had felt them important enough — nobody who spoke English anyway — to translate them into the latter language. He'd expected it to be a lengthy job working with hundred year old syntax. But the absence of idiom made it easier to follow than a current newspaper.

He tried to form a picture of what life had been like in the Northeast before the American Revolution. Uncertain, for sure. The St. Francis Indians constantly sent raiding parties into New England. They would pick a house or settlement at random, usually one easily accessible by river, and kill or capture the inhabitants. Those taken prisoner, if they survived the long trek back, were usually treated well. Often held for ransom.

Hudson had pictured hordes of Indians plaguing the colonists, but their numbers were apparently very few. The English army had pretty well decimated them in 1679, with only the Mohawks — who were their allies — spared. A *Histoire Des Abenakis* written by the Abbot J. A. Maurault in 1866 estimated a total of only seven hundred Abenakis at St. Francis at the time of Rogers Raid, down from two thousand in 1700. The book actually said 1760, and it took Hudson a while to figure out the misprint. Of course, there weren't a lot of other people on the continent then either. For all of its dangers and uncertainty, what a time to be living here! An entire continent to roam on. How we should have stayed, thought Hudson. We're breeding ourselves out of existence.

And then he found the first clue. Nowhere in any of the books he read was there a statement as to who was the chief at St. Francis back then. But a footnote in the Maurault book revealed that one Joseph-Louis Gill was "*grand Chef des Abenakis pendant plus de cinquante ans*" If that didn't say he cooked the meals, he was the top gun for over half a century. Since he died in 1798, he was surely the Chief in 1759.

At breakfast he expressed his surprise at the real shocker. "He was a white man!"

Kabir nodded. "That's right."

"What the heck was he doing running an Indian tribe?"

"The Gill family is perhaps the most famous in Abenaki history. Like the name Neptune among the Passamaquoddies. There are those still living in Odanak who can trace their ancestry back to Gill."

Cilla was also incredulous. "They're *proud* of their white blood?"

"Why not? It's a common misconception that the Indian valued his genes so highly that he refused to taint them. He took life pretty much as it was given him."

"Wasn't hung up on racial issues," Hudson grinned.

Cilla looked at him sourly.

"Sorry. But this puts a different light on things."

"Why?"

"Maybe you know the story, Kabir. These two white kids, Samuel Gill and a girl whose last name was James but whose first name is unknown, at the age of fourteen and twelve were kidnapped from their homes in New England in seventeen-eleven. Brought to St. Francis, they were married to each other four years later. Their second child was Joseph-Louis who later became Chief."

"How come?" Cilla wasn't accepting the situation. "Why would the Abenakis allow him to be Chief?"

"Unknown. Probably because he was a good looking, full blooded white." Hudson moved his chair further away from her.

She glared at him.

"How does that change things?" asked Kabir. "What's the difference white or red?"

"All along I've had a problem picturing an Indian Chief in Canada making a deal with a royal governor for a hunk of land in New Hampshire. If the Chief was white and *from* New England, or his father and mother were, maybe there's the connection."

Mid-morning he found what he was looking for. In another Maurault footnote — all the important stuff was down there at the bottom of the page. Why did they bother with the main text? — the statement that the only item saved from the burning of the church by Rogers' men was an altar front, embroidered by the French royal family. It further had survived a second fire in the early nineteenth century. He went in search of Kabir and Cilla, finding them interviewing an elderly resident.

"Where's the church?" he asked.

"A sudden need for penitence?" asked Cilla.

"No, a lead. Let's go look."

The altar front at the church was new. They consulted the priest.

"Yes indeed," said the father. "Made by ladies at the court of Louis the Fourteenth of France. It's in the Rectory Archives. Much too ancient to leave unprotected."

The embroidery was in wool and indeed looked old. Hudson examined it in detail, but could find nothing unusual. "Let's turn it over."

"Carefully!" said the priest. "It hasn't been touched in years."

On the back was woven a strange pattern of lines.

"What on earth's that?" asked Cilla.

"Mean anything to you, Kabir?"

"Looks like a one-eyed sea creature. A jellyfish type." Kabir studied it. "Maybe someone just practicing."

"Or the logo of the maker."

"They took pains with it." Cilla ran her fingers over the lines. "It's tightly woven. As though they knew exactly what they wanted to do."

"I'll sketch it." Hudson rummaged through his pockets and found a scrap of paper and a pencil. Carefully he reproduced the "creature."

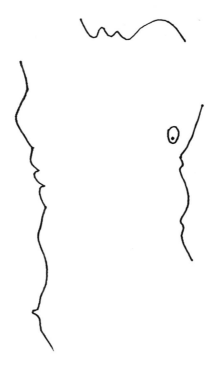

"It isn't much, is it," sighed Hudson as they sat around the table at Kabir's house.

"It isn't a treaty for sure."

"Let's see where we're at. Three men were murdered because they were investigating the possibility of a treaty that would turn over thousands of acres of National Forest and perhaps some privately owned land...Definitely some private land, unless the U.S. government is killing off people. What private land? Depends on the easterly line of the draft document from Wally's."

"If private property was determined to be Indian land, wouldn't the U.S. government make it up?" asked Kabir.

"Doubt it. Why should they?"

"When the Mashpee Indians began their claim, everything stopped in the town of Mashpee," said Cilla. "Banks wouldn't finance there, so business couldn't continue. That wouldn't have happened if the government was standing behind property."

"There's the answer." Hudson leaned on the table. "Someone wants — maybe needs — to sell. Someone else — an international firm? — wants to buy. Our seller got wind of what your fathers and my father-in-law were up to. He finds *his* property is part of a potential Indian claim. If even a *rumor* starts that a treaty exists he's done. Nobody will touch it until the problem is cleared up."

"That took years in the case of the Mashpees. Decades for the Passamaquoddies."

"The seller can't hang on that long. How do we know? Because he's murdering to protect his deal."

"All we have to do is find out who it is."

"And prove it."

"Maybe it's Trimble," suggested Kabir.

"No. Remember at the Marblehead Neck house, Cilla? He was taking orders from someone on the telephone...Trimble's just a big dumb cluck. *Couillon.* All his head is good for is holding his hair together." He stopped.

"What is it?" asked Cilla studying him.

"His hair. Trimble has a big mop, usually sticking up in all directions." He turned to Cilla. "Like the man Little Tommy saw driving off with your father the day he died."

Her eyes widened. "Trimble killed my father too?"

He nodded. "It's possible."

"But on the same day?"

"He was seen with your father in the morning. Wally's accident was late at night — just two and a half hours away."

Her lips tightened. "How do we get him." She turned to face Hudson.

There was a force to Cilla that always seemed to lie just beneath the surface. At times like this it emerged as though she had donned a suit of armor and picked up a lance. This was not a girl to be trifled with. He took the sketch from the altar cloth in his hands. "We attack. Finding the treaty will tell us what land is involved, and who has enough at stake to send Trimble out to murder. We now have two clues, the treaty copy from Wally's and this. Whatever it is. The place we started to look but got chased out of is your father's house in Bartlett, Kabir."

"Which is probably still being watched."

"Maybe. But they also may feel we won't chance going back there. I'm feeling like a yo-yo myself with this back and forth between here and Bartlett. But if we're going to stay on the offensive it's where we've got to look next."

"I'll pack." Cilla was out of her chair.

"Hold on people." Kabir raised his hands. "Aren't we being a bit hasty? Hudson, you hired someone to do the job. Why not give him a chance? He's only had a few days."

"Cilla?" Hudson queried.

"Get your stuff. I'm not going to sit around here while your... hairy monster goes free." She sat down and put a hand to her forehead.

"Cilla?" This time it was Kabir.

She shook him off. "I'm all right. I get these migraine attacks every now and then." She saw Hudson looking at her with concern. "I'm really fine. It's gone now." Impulsively she put a hand over his. "Thank you." She went upstairs.

The touch of her hand lingered on Hudson's.

Chapter 17

IT WAS NEARLY dark when they parked Hudson's Subaru behind the house for sale, and night when they reached Niagara. They'd decided to visit the Becancour house late in the evening, and lay down on the top of their bunks. Cilla dropped off immediately. Hudson dozed but couldn't sleep.

At eleven o'clock they put on dark clothes they'd brought with them. 'Burglar uniforms' Cilla said. Sneakers, heavy shirt and sweater. They'd considered parkas, since the night was cold, but felt their shiny surface might reflect light. Flashlights and a fresh copy of the Odanak sketch.

As they stepped off the little porch, Cilla gave a cry and fell to the ground. Hudson reached down for her as he heard a whirring sound over his head and a' thunk' against the cabin wall. In the darkness Hudson could barely make her out. She was lying on her side with something protruding from her leg. Hudson reached for it. It was an arrow! Another had just missed him as he bent over. Someone was shooting at them!

He dropped to the ground, attempting to shelter Cilla's body. She was writhing in pain. At least her twisting seemed at first to be only from pain. Then she cried out as though she had just lifted a thousand pounds. Her hands went in the air, and something clattered against the building. She had pulled the arrow out of her leg herself! Another arrow thudded into the cabin and decided Hudson. He scooped Cilla in his arms and in a crouch scuttled to the back of the shack. How many were there? No way to find out. And no weapons. Retreat.

"Can you stand?"

She got on one foot, but when she put weight on the injured leg it collapsed. "Damn!"

"We've got to move."

"You go ahead. I'll crawl."

"Too slow." He picked her up in his arms again and climbed uphill through the brush and trees behind the cabin. Another arrow twanged into a tree as he passed. He put on a burst of speed and crested the little hill. He put her down for a minute.

"Are you bleeding much?"

"I think so. Better get further away before we check."

"You won't make it if I do." He took out his handkerchief. "Here. Hold that tight against it." As she did, he picked her up again and took off up the higher hill behind the first. After a hundred yards, he turned left and waded through the brook above the waterfall, wishing he'd not left his hiking boots sitting in the cabin.

There was no path to follow, and his progress was a series of stops and starts, blundering into trees and stumbling over dead branches. Bushes pulled at his clothes. His sneakers squished with every step. Cilla gave not a sound, though he knew she must be in a lot of pain. Periodically he stopped to listen for pursuit. He knew he was making an awful racket with his bush-whacking and wouldn't be difficult to follow. He could hear crashings in the woods behind him that stopped shortly after he did. They need the sound to follow me, thought Hudson. *We* need a quiet path. Nancy Pond Trail wasn't far. He'd go for that.

He checked the sky for something to keep him on the same course, but it had clouded over. He figured if he went along the hillside rather than up it he'd have to come across the trail. Whether he'd know when he reached it was another matter. And he had to do something about Cilla's leg.

He figured he'd gone ten minutes when he reached a clearing next to a brook. The noise from the pursuers — loud enough to seem like more than one — seemed to come from more downhill than it had. The sound of the brook might muffle their own noise. He laid Cilla against a smooth rock.

"They were waiting for us!" she gasped.

"I know." Hudson was contrite. "It must have been the book. The one on Indian treaties. I should have brought them both with us. Here. Hold this flashlight while I take a look at your leg. Keep your fingers over the lens and just let a little light through."

"You think they searched *all* the houses in the area?"

His handkerchief was soaked with blood, and the wound was still seeping. He started a tear at the hole in her jeans and with an effort ripped it down the side.

"Sorry." he muttered. "Sure. What are there, a dozen or two in Harts Location. But arrows!"

"They're quiet, and it's hunting season for them right now."

"Another 'accident'."

"Yes."

The wound was high up on the inside of her right thigh, barely leaving room for a tourniquet. He tore off the pant leg at the crotch and split it into several strips. One of these he wrapped around her thigh above the wound, and with a stick, wound it tightly. Then with another strip he bound his handkerchief directly on it.

"Hurt?"

"Damn right. Think I'm a store dummy?"

Her voice had more strength than he'd expected. "They seem to be heading for the highway. My guess is that they'll cover that, figuring we've got to show somewhere on it."

"So let's go up instead of down."

"Could you stand a fireman carry? I'll go a lot faster that way."

"Do it."

It didn't prove completely successful as the stick kept jabbing him in the face, but he moved much more easily. He was almost feeling cheerful, when it started to rain. At first it was just mist sifting through the woods. Then it became torrents; cold, hard rain with drops that stung his face and blurred his eyes. All thought of their plan to explore Chief Becancour's library had disappeared — along with his ability to see the terrain he was blundering through. His vision was so poor that he almost fell crossing what must be Nancy Brook. Sure enough the trail, which he could only recognize by the empty space between woods, was a hundred yards on the other side — but atop a steep banking that he struggled up with his burden.

He put Cilla down and took in some deep breaths. Water got down his throat and he coughed.

"Maybe if I had a stick I could walk..."

"No way. Our first job is to stop that bleeding. We'll never do it with you gimping on it."

"What's our plan?"

"The tent."

"And warm sleeping bags." Cilla's teeth had begun to chatter and as he picked her up again could feel her shivering.

"Shine the flashlight ahead of me to be sure I stay on the trail."

It was slow going and became slower when they reached Nancy Cascade. He didn't relish the thought of the steep climb up it, but felt a twinge of pride that Cilla hadn't questioned his ability to make it carrying her. He scarcely recognized the soft, mushy suburbanite who'd fled to New Hampshire four months ago barely able to mount a set of stairs without puffing. He stopped just twice, once to check Cilla's wound — the bleeding seemed to have stopped — and once to catch his breath. A cold wind had risen that made even his hard working muscles shiver. Cilla's whole body was shaking. He hurried on as fast as tired legs would take him.

It took a while to locate the tent, since he hadn't thought he'd be looking for it after dark. While Cilla hugged her trembling body under a tree which provided next to no protection, he scouted the area with the flashlight. Once found it went up quickly.

"Crawl in, take off those wet clothes and climb into a sleeping bag."

A few minutes later he heard her groan from inside. "What's the matter?"

"I can't get my jeans over the stick."

"It's time we got rid of that anyway. Let me look at it." He crawled into the tent and unwound the stick, examining the wound by flashlight. The bleeding had stopped. "It looks okay. Just move slowly getting into the bag." He went out.

After allowing what he thought was enough time, he went back in the tent. Cilla was in her sleeping bag but shivering almost uncontrollably, her clothes next to her.

"Is the bag dry inside?"

"Ye..es," she chattered. "I just can't get wa...rm."

"Damn! I can't build a fire in this deluge. What the hell can I do?"

"The sa..ame thing I di...id when yo...u were..."

"Get in beside you?" With *her*? "The bag's not big enough."

"J...erk. Put the b...ags to...gether."

He shined the flashlight on the two bags. Sure, they could be zipped together to make one big bag. With shivering fingers he attached the two. He peeled to his damp shorts, for an instant contemplated taking them off, but quickly decided against and climbed in. She lay on her right side; he was careful not to touch the wound as he stretched his feet out to the bottom of the bag. Her body felt like ice. Tentatively he put his arms around her; hers were folded tightly across her chest. Her face pressed into his shoulder, her breathing a shuddering. He held her tighter. Ever so slowly the tautly strung body eased, and her breathing became more regular. And as it did, the urgency of rescue disappeared, and something else moved in. He felt himself start to get hard and desperately tried to get his mind elsewhere. He shifted his body so it was more sideways to her.

"D...on't move a...way."

Shit. He rolled back. Any minute now she'd notice, and then...

"I kn...ow. Its o...kay."

Sometime during the night her shivering stopped; her arms had come away from her chest and around him. In the morning when he woke, her eyes were already open, and she was watching him; the grey eyes calm, and the ghost of a smile on her lips. Full lips. If he hadn't been half asleep it wouldn't have happened. He was. She didn't resist the kiss. But while her lips were soft, they were passive. Her eyes slowly closed.

Time vanished for Hudson. After a year, he raised his head and looked down at her. When she opened her eyes, he saw they had become smokey, but the half smile on her lips remained.

"I..."he started.

She put a finger over his lips. With the other hand behind his head she gently pulled him down to her. The second kiss was longer. Hudson relaxed and let the full weight of his body rest on her.

"Ouch!"

"Damn! I forgot!" He rolled off her. "I'm sorry. Are you okay?"

"Sore."

"The rain's stopped. I'll build a fire." He crawled out of the sleeping bag. It was cold, and their clothes hadn't dried out from the rain. He put on wet sneakers and went looking for fire material. In a pocket of the tent he found the box of waterproof matches he'd left from the last trip. It took nearly a half hour but he got a sustainable fire going, and spread out their clothes on a branch next to it to dry. Her underwear was practical rather than frilly, and her socks were big and heavy — a man's size.

Cilla had watched from the sleeping bag. He must be a show, thought Hudson, jumping around in shorts and sneakers. "If I were a real woodsman I'd hunt you up a rabbit for breakfast."

"Snowshoe hare."

"If that's your taste."

"It's what's here."

"Hare it is."

"You'll have to be quick to stay ahead of the fisher cats."

"Hunger will lend me speed."

Her eyes closed and she slept.

Later, the clothes dry and stiff, Hudson put on his and went inside the tent.

"Your attire, Ma'mselle." There was no response from the sleeping bag. Hudson knelt and felt her forehead. Fever.

"Cilla?" Still nothing. Crap. A doctor. And fast. Her wound wasn't bleeding but didn't look healthy. He tied his undershirt around it loosely. Then separated his sleeping bag and zipped her up in hers, carrying her outside next to the fire while he collapsed the tent. Her dry clothes he stuffed into the bag with her, buried the fire in dirt and with Cilla's cocoon over his shoulder started down the mountain as fast as he dared.

His thoughts were jumbled; the dominant one was apprehension. He knew little about injuries — nothing about someone being unconscious from one. It couldn't be a good sign and was likely very bad. He *did* know what it was to lose someone he cared deeply about. And in an all-too-brief moment that morning he'd discovered Cilla had entered that category.

Faster. He tripped over a root and nearly lost his burden down an embankment. The word was surely not 'burden'. He felt her lips on his and remembered the smokey look in her eyes. A look of...caring? Maybe that was too strong. Certainly acceptance. He contrasted that with the hard, cold creature who seemed repulsed by his presence — to the point of nearly crippling him with a knee-hand combination at the ashram. He smiled at the memory of the way she disposed of the thug at her house. He'd looked somehow familiar in the dim light. Were they the ones shooting arrows?

Damn. Just when he had found someone to fill the void that had existed inside him for so many empty weeks. Or was it *because* of the constant life-threatening danger that they'd become close. And they *were* close. Even before this morning's revelation there had been a growing warmth between them. Kabir felt Cilla's saving him had broken the bars of the self-imposed prison. What was the old theory? A woman who saves a man's life feels bound to him? Something like that. But Cilla?

Again he nearly dropped her as his feet slipped crossing Nancy Brook. From here on the footing was better, he remembered. He increased his speed. What would he do when he reached the bottom? He must use the car. He couldn't stand out on the road hitchhiking. Even if it were safe, who would pick him up looking as crumpled and dirty as he was. And if the enemy had the car watched? The hell with it. There *was* no other choice.

And then where? The hospital? The enemy would surely be there, knowing Cilla was wounded. Where else? He knew no doctors in the area, let alone one who could be counted on to ask no questions about a mysterious thigh wound. Who could he contact? Larry Cook? Mooney? They'd help. They were the closest thing to friends Hudson had made in Bartlett. Maybe it was time for allies. He and Cilla couldn't take on this ubiquitous army all by themselves, particularly with her helpless.

Outside of a single groan when he'd almost dropped her, it might have been a corpse he was carrying. The thought chilled him. Though his concern at the time had been only the wound, his mind had retained a mental picture of her naked body as he had examined it. How could he have thought it ungainly. It was nearly perfect. Slim and firm with long well-shaped legs, marred only by the blood-clotted stain on her right thigh. She was damn well *not* going to die.

He laid her behind some bushes a distance from the car and went cautiously on to reconnoiter. His body urged speed, but his mind told him this was a time for patience. A hundred feet from the Subaru he stopped and knelt, waiting. After five minutes of no noise or movement he moved closer. The car was sitting behind the FOR SALE house where they'd left it the night before. There was no one visible. Again he waited. There! A curtain moved in one of the house windows. Someone was making this a comfortable surveillance from inside the house. He waited some more. Another ten minutes and a Honda drove up, and a man got out and went inside the house. It was Trimble. The big man was carrying a grocery bag, his mop of hair flopping from side to side as he walked.

His muscles quivering with impatience, Hudson forced himself to sit and watch. Shortly Trimble came out again, climbed in the Honda and drove away. No car other than the Subaru was visible. Perhaps the watcher or watchers had none. But he couldn't be sure. In any case, it was time to move.

Staying well clear of the house, he manoeuvered to the chimney end which had no windows. Then, with a quick sprint, he reached the structure and flattened himself against it. He edged his way around a corner of the house to the side away from the Subaru. The first window was locked. The second responded to a gentle jiggling. Gritting his teeth he slowly raised it. It made a small scraping sound but no loud squeak. He leaned his head in and paused, listening. The curtain that moved had been in an upstairs window. He crawled through the opening and out on top of a well-padded couch, then onto a wide board floor. His sneakers he'd regretted wearing during the climb the night before now snuck silently, making not a sound as he crept toward the staircase. He stopped. Was there one or more. He could hear slight movements from upstairs that sounded like just one.

He went back to the room he'd entered and to the fireplace, picking up a fire iron. He then took a small framed photograph, silently apologizing to its subject, and silently mounted the stairs. At their head were two rooms, one to the left and one to the right. Straight ahead was a bathroom. The room on the right was the one occupied. Hudson scaled the frame to land at the bottom of the stairs with a small crash, and ducked into the bathroom.

"George? That you?" Sounds of a body raising itself from a chair. "George?" From the bathroom Hudson could hear the man crossing the floor. As the footsteps reached the head of the stairs, Hudson leaped out and swung the poker against the exposed back. The man fell heavily down the stairs and lay still. Hudson looked into the room he had vacated. Empty.

But as he started to turn, a body landed on his back knocking him to the floor. Even as he fell, he instinctively reached behind him, and as they landed the attacker's head hit the floor first. Hudson took advantage of the man temporarily stunned to get a grip around his neck.

It was soon over. Hudson got to his feet and listened. Nothing. He dusted himself off. Then dragged the unconscious man into the bathroom, which he'd noted had a key. As he came out, the first man was reaching the top of the stairs. Both of the enemy were young men in apparent good condition. Why don't I get any feeble old farts, thought Hudson as he squared off against man number one. The fireplace poker lay inside the room beyond the stairs where it had fallen when he'd been attacked. The other man also saw it and turned that way. Hudson was on him before he reached it. Coupling his hands together, he brought them down with force on the back of the man's neck. With a groan thug #1 stretched out on the floor.

More? The room to the left revealed a bed that one apparently used while the other kept watch. But no reinforcements. The cellar had promise. It was a small dug area entirely below ground; thus no windows. He lugged both inert forms down the stairs and with considerable hefting and hauling got them tied back to back and to the bottom of the riser-less cellar stairs. The door had no key, but he figured he'd won enough of a head start.

Cilla hadn't moved. He lifted her gently and carried her to the Subaru, laying her on the rear seat with seat belts around her. The car started without complaint. As he drove out of the driveway he could see no other automobile. They depended on Trimble for transportation. He'd like to wait for that one, he thought, but his present errand was more important.

Hurry. No, *teeshee yedyesh dalshe boodesh,* make haste slowly. Larry would be at work by now. So Mooney. He cruised slowly through Bartlett village; no sign of Mophead. He turned into Swallow Hill Road and pulled up in Mooney's driveway. He left the engine running to keep the car warm and bounded up the front steps to pound at the front door.

"Hold on," the voice came from inside. "Don't break it down."

"It's Hudson Rogers, Augustus. I need help."

The door swung open. "So you do. Hot water?"

"How did you...?"

"Must of run out of it looks of you."

"Cilla, my friend, has had an accident. Long story. We need a doctor who isn't a gossip. And maybe will make a house call."

Mooney looked around him. "She in the car?"

"Yes."

"Well bring her in! What did she hurt?"

"Her leg. She got hit by an arrow."

"An *arrow*?" It took a bit to surprise his neighbor. He bustled to the telephone. "I'll get Jim Evans. Doctor Evans. He'll come over."

Hudson carried Cilla into the house and laid her, still in her sleeping bag, on a large leather sofa. Her breathing was irregular, and Hudson felt his heart sink. Hurry.

"He'll be here in five minutes. He's just around the corner. Let's take a look at the wound."

"Ah...if the doctor will be here soon, why don't we wait for him."

Mooney looked at him curiously.

"She hasn't any clothes on, Augustus."

"Oh...She warm enough?"

"I think so. She's been unconscious for several hours. Ah, I'd like to get my car out of sight. Can I drive it around back?"

"This is goin' to be quite a story, time I get to hear it. I'll open the shed." He went out. Hudson took a long look at Cilla and followed him.

By the time they had the Subaru closed in the shed, an elderly Cadillac was pulling into the driveway. Dr. Evans was only a little younger than Mooney but he mounted the steps with energy.

"Where's my patient?"

Hudson led him inside. "Did Mr. Mooney tell you the problem?"

"An arrow, if I heard right. Now let's see." He dumped an old black bag on a chair and bent over Cilla. He straightened up and looked around. "I'll work better with the two of you out of here."

Mooney led a reluctant Hudson Rogers into the kitchen and closed the door. "Now. You been out huntin'?"

"Someone's hunting us."

"With bow and arrow? Rough game."

"It's not a game." Hudson sighed. "I thought it was at first. Or at least acted that way — as though it was just another puzzle to solve. So I blundered my way around looking for solutions, not realizing what danger I was putting her in."

"And yourself?"

"Particularly me. She was just the one who happened to get hurt. Did Wally ever discuss things he was working on with you?"

Mooney considered, "Not much. He dealt in lawyer stuff, you know. They never talk about anythin' that means anythin'. This got to do with him?"

"Augustus, there's a possibility he was murdered. In an awkward, amateur way I've been investigating it."

The grey head nodded slowly. "Wasn't just a hooligan."

"No. It was someone warning me. That the same thing would happen to me if I didn't stop asking questions."

"And the girl? She mixed up in it too?"

"We think her father was murdered by the same people."

"What do the police think?"

"We haven't told them."

"For heaven's sakes, man!"

"And we can't, Augustus. Not yet. We just don't have the evidence."

"You got somebody shootin' arrows at you. That girl lying in the other room ought to be evidence enough for anyone that somethin's mighty wrong. Let me get the Chief in on it. Where'd this happen?"

"Up in Hart's Location."

"Then it'd have to be the State boys. Wilbur Eastman lives in Conway. Let me..."

He lost Hudson, for the door opened and Doctor Evans bustled in. "Okay, the wound is closed. She's got to go to the hospital, though. I'll call in." He started back to the other room.

"Why hospital? What caused her to pass out?" Hudson grabbed his arm. "What else is wrong?"

The doctor looked at him with suspicion. "I'm out of my depth. She's lost some blood but not enough for this." He studied the younger man. "If I had to make a wild guess, I'd say she was poisoned. Maybe on the arrow. But..."

"Poisoned!" Hudson and Mooney were a chorus.

"I had a 'but'. Tell me exactly how it happened."

"It was last night. We were coming out the door of a cabin when out of the dark came this arrow. Cilla pulled it out herself almost immediately. It couldn't have been easy."

"It probably saved her life. That might explain it. With most of the arrow poisons I've read about she'd be dead now. That is if it *was* something on the arrow."

"You're not sure?"

"She shouldn't still be unconscious. That's all I can tell you. She needs someone more worldly than this old country doctor."

"You've got such a person at the hospital?"

"We can all put our heads together. Usually that works."

Hudson turned to Mooney. "May I use your phone?" Then to Dr. Evans. "I'm going to try one other possibility." He went into the room where Cilla was lying, closing the door. She looked pale even for her, and nervous fingers snatched the telephone from its cradle to dial Margate. After a few impatient seconds the lawyer came on the line.

"Early for you. Problem?"

"The enemy got to us. Cilla's hurt; she's unconscious. The local doctor thinks it was a poisoned arrow. He's not sure. Wants to take her to the hospital and play guessing games. Question: have you got..."

"Can she be moved?"

"She'll have to be. In any case."

"Bring her right down here. I've just the doctor for her. He has his own private clinic so no one need know she's there. I'll...hold on a minute." There was silence. Margate was back in just over that. "All arranged. An ambulance will meet you at the toll booth on the Spaulding Turnpike in Dover. You know where that is? They tell me it's about half way."

"Yes."

"They'll take her the rest of the trip. There'll be a medic aboard who'll start her on IV. Leaving in ten minutes. Can you?"

"Yes. Thanks, Lander. I..."

"Get moving. We'll talk later."

Hudson hung up with a sigh of relief and went back to the kitchen. "I'm going to take her to Massachusetts. No knock on you, Doctor. I've been ordered to practically."

"No, no. They're more used to weird cases down there. Think it's something in the water." He gave a perfunctory grin. "Leaving right now?"

"Soon as I can get her in the car."

Mooney got to his feet. "Food. Had any?"

"No time."

"Well take an apple anyway." He gestured toward a bowl of fruit on the kitchen table.

Hudson put two apples and a banana in his pocket. It might be a while before he had another chance. With help from the other two, Cilla was settled again in the rear seat with belts around her. She had not regained consciousness and was still in her sleeping bag. No one came up with a better way to transport her.

The trip down was a blur. With nothing but the reflex actions of driving a car to occupy his mind, he went over and over what had happened. Something was wrong with this latest incident. What? Of course! All the other attacks had been made to look like accidents. Sure, accidents happen during hunting season. But how could the enemy expect a *poisoned* arrow to pass for one. Had it been successful in killing them — as it still might be with Cilla, he thought with a chill — an autopsy would reveal the intent. Or would it? Might they have obtained a poison that didn't show up? Nonsense. Would there even be an autopsy. Of course. They'd hit Cilla in the leg. Probably as accurate as they could expect in the dark. No one would accept a wound such as that as fatal.

As fast as he had driven, the ambulance was waiting for him at the Dover toll booth. The medic was young, bearded and seemed competent.

"Do you want to leave your car here and ride with us?"

"No, I'll follow you."

"We discourage that. Besides, we're going to go right along."

"I'll keep up."

"Right." The medic climbed in back of the ambulance with Cilla; the driver flicked on flashing lights, and off they went.

Hudson turned his headlights on and stayed right behind the ambulance so as not to get stopped. In Danvers they took Route 114. Last time they'd been down this road Cilla was wearing what seemed to be her first pair of high heels. Or deciding whether or not to put up with them. She was just a girl then, Hudson reflected wryly. A rather seedy looking old pants and lumberjack shirt girl who'd pulled a Cinderella.

The clinic was in a Salem residential neighborhood near the Marblehead line. Though unassuming in appearance, inside it was new, clean and high tech. Unfamiliar machines dwelt in brightly lit rooms, into one of which Cilla's stretcher was wheeled. Klaus Wendt was the doctor's name. A small, broad man in his mid fifties with wire-rimmed glasses, he greeted Hudson cordially, suggested he take a seat and disappeared. Sitting was what Hudson had done too much of recently, so he wandered around looking in open doors and through enormous glass windows into rooms of mysterious usage.

Hudson was not a hospital freak. Some of his old Cambridge friends knew every disease doctors did and all its symptoms — which they seemed to acquire with great regularity. Hudson's hospital experience from the accident did not create a desire for more. In hospitals you lost people. As he had Sylvia. He paused in mid thought. For the first time since that horrifying day she had not entered his mind for an entire twenty-four hour period. Hard as he had tried to numb his brain over the summer, her face would always be at the edges of his consciousness. Her smile following him up trails that would have been empty without it. And now?

He gazed out a window at the bare trees of late autumn. No. There was no change. His love for Sylvia was intact. And always would be, he thought. There might be additions, but she would never leave the place he had built for her in his heart.

"Mr. Rogers." The doctor was approaching. "She's resting. I know you'd like an immediate answer to the problem. I believe Dr...Evans, was it? was correct; she's been poisoned. I've given her an antidote for some of the possibilities. We have a very complete lab here. It shouldn't take us long to identify the one used."

"How long? And will she make it that long?"

The doctor looked into his eyes. "The next twelve to twenty-four hours should tell us more."

"Can I stay here? I'll pay patient rates, of course."

A smile played around Wendt's lips. "As a matter of fact, they are preparing Room Two C for you right now, anticipating your request."

"Two C."

"Yes. It's...ah, fitting. One we have made available for Lander Margate's... clients in the past."

Hudson looked down at his clothes.

The doctor nodded. "You'll have time to increase your wardrobe. And acquire toilet articles. The earliest we'll know anything will be late this evening."

Hudson got good vibes from the little man, so with a feeling of relief he telephoned Kabir. The Indian's first reaction was to jump in a car and rush down. Further conversation convinced him everything was being done that could be, and he could add little by his presence. He reluctantly agreed to stay at Odanak. And soon his normal optimism asserted itself.

"Muktabai has a strong constitution. She'll be okay."

Hudson hung up. He could certainly vouch for Cilla's physical condition. If anyone could make it through this she would. He went shopping. Northshore Shopping Center was going to think him a clothes freak. He again bought for Cilla as well as himself. Then lunch filled some of the void the apples hadn't been able to.

He next called on Lander Margate.

"What do you think of Wendt?"

"Seems competent. I'm not on the Medical Board."

"I've had excellent success with him."

"In the room where he put me, Two C. Who else has used it?"

The attorney looked at him. "Clients. Tell me, how is the girl?"

"Twelve to twenty-four hours. Maybe as early as this evening. Anything new from your detective?"

"Nothing of importance. They've lost Trimble again."

"He was in Bartlett this morning." Hudson brought the lawyer up to date.

"I'm inclined to agree with you. The poisoned arrow doesn't fit their modus operandi. Joseph Becancour's death — if it was indeed by poison — was orchestrated as natural causes." He thought a moment. "Desperation?"

"Why? If I'm getting close to something I sure as hell don't know it."

The lawyer gazed into the distance. "Does it seem to you that this man Trimble has some sort of personal vendetta against you?"

"I can't think of a reason. It should be the other way around. It was my family he killed."

"Never met him before the accident? — I should amend that to 'crash.' Had any dealings of any sort with him?"

"None. Our first meeting was at fifty miles an hour."

"Poison. By arrow. It seems so...vengeful."

"I've never had anybody go unconscious on me like that before."

"The girl isn't just a girl anymore, is she?

"No. We've become...a little closer."

"No longer 'a kid'?"

"Rub it in...Lander, I can't lose her."

"It sounds to me you got her to Wendt in time. If anything needs to be done, he'll do it."

"And then what. Some other 'accident'. One of these days they'll kill her. If it were just me, it would be another story. What's the point of trying to solve some puzzle created hundreds of years ago that could probably sit for another couple hundred without anyone caring, and having Cilla die in the process."

"Wally. Sylvia. They paid a high price for this puzzle."

"So enough. I can't bring them back, but I can certainly protect the living."

"By giving up?"

"By backing off. I'll go live in the Tyrol for a year and work on my skiing."

"With your young lady?"

"Lander, the first thing you must know about Cilla is that she isn't *anybody's* young lady. Just her own. And I'd better get back to Wendt's."

The older man had speculation in his eyes as he watched him go.

Chapter 18

THE MAN IN the pine-paneled room had been listening intently to what he was hearing on the telephone. The voice continued...

"But before that he crept up on the two, knocked them both out and took the wounded girl away. He has great intensity when he's after something."

"Yes. He can be a weapon, that man. And not just physically; I've had occasion to test his mind. What you say disturbs me. It's time we took more drastic action."

"More...?"

"More. Here's what I want you to do..."

Chapter 19

HUDSON GOT LITTLE sleep. He kept expecting — hoping — Wendt would knock on the door to tell him Cilla was out of danger. But the long night passed without interruption. He tossed in the narrow bed trying to get comfortable. He'd had no difficulty the night before in an even more confined space. The thought brought a grin.

Though the clinic was well screened from the main road, he could still hear the sounds of an occasional automobile. Gotten used to the quiet of New Hampshire's woods, he thought. Twice he heard vehicles coming in to the little hospital. Illness keeps no office hours. Toward dawn he slept.

A ray of sunlight through venetian blinds awakened him. He had his feet on the floor in an instant. He glanced at his watch as he pulled on clothes. Eight. He made his way swiftly to the reception area. The woman on duty said Dr. Wendt had been in the hospital most of the night and only gone to his own bed a few hours ago.

"Did he say when he'll be in this morning?"

"Nine o'clock."

"Cilla Wheaton. Can you tell me how she is?"

"I'm sorry. We don't have information on patients at this desk."

"Someone else who would know?"

"I'm the only one here right now. Except the food service people."

"What room is she in?"

"Why don't you take a seat. Dr. Wendt will be here in just... fifty minutes."

In the small kitchen Hudson found coffee and a roll. And patience.

Shortly before nine he went back to the reception area. The woman beckoned to him.

"Dr. Wendt just came in. He's taking care of an emergency and told me to tell you he'll be with you in a few minutes."

Hudson picked up a magazine and had turned a dozen pages before realizing he could remember nothing of their content.

"Mr. Rogers?" A woman in a nurse's cap stood before him.

"I'm Rogers." He rose from his seat.

"Come with me please." She led him down several halls to what was obviously an office and motioned him to a chair. "I have something to tell you."

Hudson caught his breath. "Cilla?"

"She's gone."

His heart dropped to his shoes. "Gone."

"Yes. We can't find her anywhere."

"You *what*!"

"She must have wandered off during the night."

"You mean she's missing. She's not dead. Just not here at the clinic?"

"Dr. Wendt is calling the police right now."

"Where's his office." Hudson was on his feet.

"Two doors down. But..."

Several strides took him to a door marked 'Klaus Wendt M.D.' He entered without knocking. Wendt was standing looking out the window. He turned as Hudson burst in.

"They should be here any minute." The doctor was quite upset, running his hands through his hair. "We'll find her, I'm sure." He saw the fierce look on Hudson's face and stepped back a pace. "I can't tell you how..."

"That's the word. How. How in hell could this have happened? Don't you have someone supervising during the night?"

"We..."

"And how could an unconscious girl have...did you find out what it was? Have you given her an antidote?"

"We think we know. The tests aren't complete, but we have administered what we feel will do the trick."

"Where's her room?"

"Fourteen A. I'll show you."

It was a second floor room with a single bed, which had obviously been used. It was bare of all personal articles. There was no sign of the bloody sleeping bag.

"Would what you gave her have acted this fast? For her to have regained consciousness and left the room?"

"It's possible." Wendt didn't seem too certain.

"You've searched the rest of the clinic?"

"Yes. We..."

The door opened and a uniformed policeman entered. "Dr. Wendt?"

"I'm Wendt. Thank you for responding so quickly, officer. We have a missing girl. Sometime during the night she apparently left this room and may now be wandering the streets, not knowing where she is."

"Amnesia?"

"No. You see she was unconscious when she was brought in here. Her last memory would be of New Hampshire." He looked at Hudson. "She's not familiar with this area is she?"

"No. Where are her clothes?"

The doctor glanced at the corner of the room. "Gone. They were hanging on that pole. She must have gotten dressed."

"What was she wearing in bed? A johnny?" The doctor nodded. "Then where is it?"

The three searched the room and its adjoining bathroom. There were no articles of clothing.

"Why would she take the johnny with her?"

"Maybe we're wasting time. Shouldn't we be out searching the neighborhood? She can't have gone far on foot." The doctor's eyelid had developed a twitch.

"I'll call for back-up," said the policeman. "They'll cover the streets while we talk with the neighbors. Let's have a description."

"She's tall — about five foot nine — slim, dark hair down to her shoulders. But you won't need that. She's wearing a dark blue heavy sweater and a pair of bloody jeans with the right leg missing and a bandage on the thigh of her bare leg. She'll be limping not walking. Or collapsed someplace."

While the officer went to his car, Hudson telephoned Margate. He wasn't in yet. His secretary didn't seem surprised.

"He's getting his boat ready for winter. He'll be calling in soon."

Then Kabir. The Abenaki was all but uncontrollable. He was unused to being this far out of the action. Hudson surely needed help with the search?

"You're more help there," urged Hudson. "If she gets to a telephone, you're the only one she can reach." He hung up.

They started with the neighbor next door to the clinic. Then down one street and up the other. Nothing. No one had seen Cilla. The police radio told them no one else was any more successful. It was mid afternoon when Hudson and the policeman — whose name was Marston — returned to the clinic, pulling up to the emergency entrance. Hudson kicked a trash barrel outside the door in disgust. His eye caught something white with brown stains that had been under it. He picked it up. It was a sock. He turned to Marston.

"This is her sock!"

"How do you know?' He examined it. "Looks like a man's sock."

"She has big feet. I know it's hers. The blood is from her wound."

"That means she came out this way."

"It means a lot more than that. If she was going to the trouble of dressing, she wouldn't have discarded a sock."

"So? You saying she's still wearing the johnny?"

"She didn't walk out of here. She was taken!"

"By who?"

Hudson shook his head. "If it wasn't Wendt, she's been kidnapped."

"Oh for Christ sake. What for? People don't get kidnapped out of hospitals."

Hudson tried patience. "If she put on her own clothes, where's the johnny? Her clothes were in her room. Why put them all on except one sock which she carries out here and throws away."

"It could have gotten uncomfortable to wear with all the blood caked on it. She might have gotten this far and decided to take it off. We can't call the FBI every time someone's missing just on the chance they've been kidnapped."

But *he* could, thought Hudson, after further argument proved futile. From Room Two C he telephoned information and got the number of the FBI regional office.

"John Krestinski." After two low key operators, the voice was strong and solid. Just the way the FBI should sound, thought Hudson.

"My name is Hudson Rogers. A friend of mine, Cilla Wheaton is missing from Doctor Wendt's clinic here in Salem. There's evidence that she was taken without her consent."

"You're saying she was kidnapped?"

"Yes. I'm certain of it."

"Just a minute." He was gone for longer. "We've nothing on it from the Salem Police."

"You wouldn't. They think she just wandered off. But she's injured. She couldn't have gotten far by herself, and we've been searching all day."

"We'd have to hear it from them."

"Look, I know you must get a lot of crank calls, and it's tough to tell if this is one or not. Lander Margate. He's a respected attorney here in Salem. Would you call him and ask him about me? My name is Hudson Rogers."

"I hear you Mr. Rogers. Right now we can't get involved."

There was more, but none of it useful. Hudson hung up the phone and telephoned Margate. He still hadn't come in. Nor had he called. His secretary actually showed some surprise. Hudson went back to Room fourteen A. It was on the second floor rear and, in fact, overlooked the emergency entrance. The bed had been made up fresh, and there was nothing to show that Cilla had ever been there. He lay down on the bed — making a concession to the next patient by taking off his shoes — and tried to picture Cilla waking up there. What would she think? Had she regained consciousness at any time between Nancy Pond and here? He thought not. If he was right, she would be completely disoriented on awakening. If she *had* awakened. If she had been taken, how was it done? He had already checked that a nurse was on duty all night. But her station was around a corner, out of sight of fourteen A.

He went to the door. Then where? There was an elevator several doors down; he took it. It opened on the ground floor near the emergency entrance. There was an admitting desk there; he spoke to the man behind it.

"Is this desk staffed all night?"

"When there's business." The attendant grinned. "When there isn't, the on-duty person naps in this room." He pointed to a door next to the counter. "There's a bell here on top of this desk. Usually we're called ahead if there's incoming, so we're up and waiting. If not, they bang the bell. That'll wake the dead. Makes a hell of a racket."

"How about outgoing?"

"If we're needed they tell us. This is a small, private hospital. We don't get much nighttime traffic either way."

"How about last night?"

The attendant looked at Hudson quizzically. "There some reason you're asking all these questions?"

"I'm a friend of the girl in fourteen A who's missing. I was out with the police all day looking for her."

"Sure. The Wheaton girl." How she would have hated her celebrity status. And the reason for it.

The attendant flipped open a large notebook; studied a page and swung it around for Hudson to see. "Nothing at all last night. Except her. After she came in that was it. Nothing in or out."

"Who would have been on duty? Not you."

"No. Roberto has the graveyard this month." He looked at the clock behind him. "He'll be by in an hour or so."

Hudson peered out the emergency doors. He'd heard vehicles — two? — during the night, coming into the clinic. He closed the doors and went looking for Dr. Wendt. The woman at the reception desk said the doctor was with a patient, but there was a call for him, a Mr. Krestinski. Said it was urgent. Hudson took the telephone number to his room and dialed.

"Are you at Wendt's?"

"Yes. Have you..."

"Stay there. I'm coming out." The connection was broken.

Krestinski was a well built, six foot redhead about Hudson's age. Right now he looked mean.

"Where can we talk?"

"My room? Or Wendt's office."

"It's you I want."

Krestinski took the chair in Two C, leaving the bed for Hudson. "Now give." His eyes were hard.

Hudson returned the look. "No, you. What made you change your mind and come running out here? You hear from the police?"

"Yeah. But not the way you think. Lander Margate. You mentioned him on the phone. How well do you know him?"

"He was my father-in-law's attorney. Now I guess he's mine."

"Guess again. His body was pulled out of Marblehead Harbor a few hours ago."

"Good Christ! You're sure? I was just with him yesterday!"

"When yesterday?"

"Late in the afternoon. Four maybe. How did it happen?"

"Drowned. Doctor says it was last night. End of the Eastern Yacht Club pier. He keeps a boat there."

"His office said he was getting it ready for winter." Hudson stopped. "You think there's a connection?"

"Do you?"

"There sure could be."

"You?"

"Me the connection? Hell, I don't know. I hope that's not the only reason one's dead and the other's missing."

"You said 'there could be' a connection as though you knew what it was."

"Yeah."

"You kill them?"

"Shit. Would I have called you if I had?"

"Maybe. People do funny things trying to be smart."

"Okay. There were four of us here working on what may have been a series of murders."

Krestinski raised an eyebrow.

"Sure. We were real smart. A bunch of amateurs investigating murder."

He looked at his hands. "Cilla and I came across some suspicious things connected with the deaths of her father and uncle and my father-in-law. We had no proof to go to the police. We would have been laughed out of the station. So we went it alone. Since then we've had proof enough for ourselves, but still no evidence. We've been gassed, shot at and had a house burned down around us. Margate was helping us. Now both he and Cilla are...not here." He paused. Then looked up. "There's a detective named Horace Plough who's been working on it. Here's his number. Call him and ask him about me. Then I'll tell you the story."

Krestinski studied Hudson. Then picked up the phone and dialed. The conversation was short. The agent hung up the phone and turned to Hudson.

"Mr. Plough states his client list is confidential. He further says, however, that he has no client named Rogers."

Hudson sank back on the bed.

Krestinski said softly, "And then there was one."

Chapter 20

IT WAS DARK. No, there was a faint glow someplace. Where. As though swimming up a long staircase, Tabi gradually came awake. Her body protested. More sleep. She started to drift off. Where? The question brought her back to the surface. Ashram? No, the bed was too soft, and too big. She stretched out a foot. Ouch. Something hurt. She reached a hand down and felt the bandage. Bandage? The arrow! Memory flooded in. Hudson. The tent. She'd been in a sleeping bag. And cold, until...he had warmed her. And then? Cars. Bumping and swaying, murmured conversations..." a great play". Why did she remember those words?

Was this a hospital? She listened; from outside the window there was the sound of automobiles. Many. City hospital? A door creaked open and a shaft of light crossed the foot of the bed. She closed her eyes against the brightness. Footsteps approached the bed. She slitted an eye; a large figure was standing next to her. She feigned sleep, without knowing exactly why. The person leaned over, and a strong odor penetrated her nostrils. Sicky sweet. She'd smelled it before, cheap perfume. A hand shook her shoulder, then withdrew, and the footsteps retreated. The door closed.

It was the door. Hospital doors either rumbled or were silent, they didn't creak. Not like this one had, sounding old and worn. She tried to raise herself and fell back on the pillow, her stomach turning over. So weak. From overhead came a thumping. Somewhere a woman screamed. What...? Her eyes closed and she slept.

There was someone in the room. She'd come awake in soft little cat's feet steps. Then suddenly there was a crash as though a chair had been tipped over, and a muffled muttering. She froze; her eyes wide open. The room was still dark and she could make out nothing. Then footsteps toward her. The woman again? Something bumped the bed.

"Move over, girly." A man!

She felt the covers being raised, and a body laid itself heavily on the bed next to her. She reached out a hand and felt a hairy bare chest. "What the hell...!" She gave it a push.

"Now Laury. Be good."

She scrambled out the other side of the bed and got her feet on the floor. An arm went around her waist and pulled her back. Raising up had drained the blood from her head; she nearly passed out again. Vaguely she was aware of a hand pulling up her nightdress, and a body pressing up against hers.

"C'm on, Laury." It was almost a whine. "It's been two weeks you been gone!"

Her head cleared a little. She turned her body so it faced him, reached down with both hands and squeezed as hard as she could.

"Ahhhhhh!" His body contracted in a spasm, his knee banging against her bandaged thigh then thrashing wildly in the bed, but she hung on, applying more pressure with a strength born of fury. The scream became higher and fainter, ending in a rattle, and the body collapsed.

She lay back, her breath coming in short gasps. After a minute she could feel energy beginning to flow. She swung her legs to the floor and stood up, cautiously. Her clothes. Where were they? She crossed the darkened room, tripping over an overturned chair. She felt a table and a lamp on it. She turned it on and looked around by its faint light. The man on the bed was snoring heavily, his hairy naked torso visible above the sheet. There was a smell of liquor in the room. What the hell had she gotten into! A dizzy feeling made her right the chair and sit in it, her head bent toward her legs. It wasn't a nightdress. It was one of those things one wears in a hospital. But this was no hospital! It was a dingy, seedy room with bare floor and old-fashioned furniture.

She remembered the thumping and woman screaming — not a real scream, a theatrical cry of someone pretending to scream. A whorehouse! She'd died and gone to hell, and this was her punishment! To spend eternity fending off the disgusting overtures of sotted males. Well she was going to get out of this one fast! But clothes. She couldn't go out on the street in this whatever-you-call-it. And there was nothing in the room she could wear. In desperation she considered the man's things piled on the floor. They were too big, fortunately. She could feel disgust rising in her throat at the thought. But what?

The door opened on a long, narrow, dimly lit hallway with thread-bare carpeting. All the doors off it were closed. On tiptoe she approached the first and put her ear to it. From inside she could hear a rustling; she moved on. The second was locked, but the third was quiet, and she eased open the door. No creak; also no people. She hurried inside and closed the door behind her, turning on a bare bulb ceiling light hanging at the end of a thin wire. She held her breath, thinking there might have been someone too quiet for her to hear. But no one.

The closet held a dress. She sighed with relief. A bureau drawer revealed lacy underwear. She shook her head. Not without washing them. She tried on the dress. It was a sheath with plunging neckline, spangly and black and at least one size too small. Short-skirted to begin with, it barely reached the top of her thighs, leaving the bandage exposed. Not the only thing exposed sitting down, she thought. But she still wasn't going to put on underwear that...There was a pair of black high-heeled shoes with open toes that she was able to squeeze her feet into; she grimaced as she stood up.

She looked at herself in an unframed full length mirror. Elvira, only witchier. Can't be helped. She turned off the light and closed the door behind her. There was no one in sight, nor did she come across anyone as she descended two flights of stairs. At the bottom was a small entryway, and as she peered around the corner, she could see a large woman sitting behind an old wood counter. Beyond was the front door. She paused as a wave of nausea swept over her, then looked again. The woman seemed immobile, as though a statue to scare away city crows. How get by her?

A couple came down the stairs behind her, the woman pulling the man by his sleeve. Tabi turned toward the wall as they passed; they stopped at the large woman.

"He wants to pay by credit card!"

"No."

"He says that's all he's got on him. I've already wasted twenty-five minutes on the slob. He hasn't even got the rent."

"What card?"

The man pulled out a wallet and spilled its contents on the counter. "Which do you want?"

The woman selected one and studied it. Then with some effort got up and opened the door to the room behind her. "Wait."

As she disappeared through the door, Tabi walked through the entryway and out on the street. It was a run-down neighborhood with the dark front stoops of houses and neon lit store windows intermingled. There were few people on the trash strewn sidewalk. To her left it was dark; to her right was a bar. Her high heels wobbled down to it. The tight skirt rose with each step of her long legs, making her feel she was walking naked. She stopped at the bar door and pulled the skirt down as far as she could. Then opened the door and entered with small almost mincing steps to keep it from riding up again.

Through a smokey haze she could make out a telephone on the wall between her and a long bar with silent, hunched over figures — pigs at a trough. The telephone must have been installed by Alex Bell himself and required a quarter. She went to the bar and waited until the bartender noticed her. He was tall and skinny with an apron that looked as though it had been last worn in a slaughterhouse.

"Help you?"

"Could I borrow a quarter for the telephone?"

The bartender showed disbelief.

"You can have it right back. I'll call collect."

"Ha. You bitches make twice what I do." He went back to the other end of the bar.

She went out. She needed distance between herself and the house where a man slept in the bed she'd vacated. She went two blocks down and three over, then two more down, as quickly as stumbling heels would take her. The neighborhood didn't change, nor did the garbage in the streets. Fortunately the temperature was mild, only becoming cold when a gust of wind wrapped itself around her bare legs. A hand grabbed her arm.

"How much, Baby?" A tubby little man with drooping mustache.

She looked at him coldly. "I need a quarter."

The man stepped back and looked at her. "Twenty-five bucks for a fox that looks like you? What's wrong with you?" He noticed the bandage. "Diseased." He scurried off.

"If you want to give it away try Roxbury." A fortyish woman with enormous breasts and an old fur piece was scowling at her. "This is a professional corner."

Tabi leaned against a lamp post and sighed. "What do you charge?"

"Fifty. Can't make ends with less."

"Fifty dollars."

"Yeah. The Standard," she pointed to a building across the street, "takes fifteen. Sometimes I ask a Benny. You know, the more you ask the more they think they're getting."

"A Benny."

"A Ben Franklin. A century." She looked more closely at her. "You green?"

"I'm...do you have a quarter? I've got to use a telephone."

"Honey, I just came on. Haven't a sou." Her eyes were appraising. "If you don't mind my saying, you got that dress too short. Keep the goods under cover till they buy."

"Thank you. I'll remember that."

"Looks of you, you don't need the streets." The woman eyed her envi-ously. "Used to look like that myself. Well, maybe not quite so good. You could model." A man walked up, patted the woman on the rear. "Bill! Thought you might be by." She drifted off with him.

Roxbury's part of Boston, she remembered. She took off a shoe and, holding onto a lamp post with one hand, rubbed her foot with the other. The shoe straps were digging into her and left a deep indentation on her foot. A convertible screeched to a stop in front of her. She froze. A man leaned across from the driver's side.

"Hey, Long Legs! Want some action?"

My God, she thought tiredly. He can probably see right up my dress, and I just don't give a damn.

"Always." She put her shoe back on.

"What's your best price."

"A couple Bennys." She leaned against the lamp post the way she'd seen old movies of Lauren Bacall.

"A couple...! You must put on quite a performance for that."

"An experience you'll never forget."

"Guaranteed?"

"Guaranteed. Or you only owe me a quarter."

"Deal. Hop in."

"No. Over there." She pointed to the Standard. "And you pay the room." He didn't like that as well. "Okay," he said reluctantly. "I'll park."

They crossed the street together, and Tabi looked in a lobby mirror as the man settled with an elderly clerk. The room was one flight up. As he closed the door, the man reached out to put his hands on her waist. The one I owe you, Hudson, she thought. With a thud the man hit the floor. He groaned once and was still. Tabi went through his pockets. Took a quarter and replaced the rest.

The clerk showed mild surprise as she came down the stairs. Another Bell Original took her coin. She dialed O and Kabir's number, told the operator it was a collect call and listened to it ring. And ring. After twenty she hung up, sat on the small lobby's sofa and put her head in her hands.

Chapter 21

KRESTINSKI HAD BEEN making telephone calls. He verified the accident that killed E. Wallace Carver and Sylvia Rogers. Hudson Rogers had suffered minor injuries and been released from the hospital less than a week after it occurred. Dr. Evans confirmed that the injury to Cilla Wheaton could have been made by an arrow. And the burning of the Carver house in Marblehead had been officially declared arson; any one with knowledge wanted for questioning.

"You're a wanted man."

"Me?"

"You, if they knew you'd been there."

Hudson had given the FBI man the complete story, skipping nothing. Interspersed with Krestinski's phone calls and questions it had taken well into the evening.

"I want you to come back to Boston with me."

"So you finally believe it's kidnapping."

"I want to keep an eye on you. The way people have been dying and disappearing, I'm not going lose *you*."

They had taken two cars. At Krestinski's office he'd thought of more questions so it wasn't until 3 AM that the FBI agent called it quits.

"I've booked a room for you at the Park Plaza."

"You're not going to clap me in a cell, material witness and all that?"

"That's what your room at the Park Plaza is. Just with carpeting."

Boston has a beauty at that hour of the morning that is spoiled by the addition of daytime people. Even missing some leaves, the Public Garden by streetlight looked inviting. Were there as many muggings as seemed constantly in the newspapers? Flashes from the front of city war zones. The hotel lobby was attractive, but even here in one of Boston's solid older hotels there was some sort of fracas taking place at one end. Had that sort of thing become a nightly occurrence? Hudson took a route to the elevators that avoided it. His room was on an upper floor. He climbed into bed wearily. Cilla. Just coming to Boston he'd felt he was somehow deserting her, leaving the last place she'd been. A cold numbness had invaded his body. Was she being held to silence him? Or had she already had her 'accident'? He had to hold on to the first.

Sleep came eventually.

Chapter 22

SHE RAISED HER head. The elderly clerk hurriedly looked away. Hudson, where are you? Did you just leave me here to...nonsense. He'd carried her — shouldered her dead weight — all the way up Nancy Pond Trail to their tent. And in the cold and the wet had sheltered her and made her warm...and then...? Automobiles, and ...a whorehouse?! She shook her head. The resulting nausea reaffirmed it; this was a nightmare, but no dream.

The front door was pulled open. Three unshaven youths about her age punctured the lobby with loud shouts and laughter. Tabi quickly got up and turned to pull down her skirt in the mirror. One of the three held the door open to shout at someone else outside. Tabi walked out it, and away. It was four blocks before she found another ancient phone. She tried the number for Wallace Carver's house in Bartlett. Where else could she find Hudson? No answer. Same with Kabir's. Then who? No point in trying Margate's office at this hour of the night. She asked for a home phone for him. Nothing. The detective, what was his name...Plough. Patten and Plough. She looked through the phone book. It was indeed a Boston directory. There! In the front of the book she discovered it was a local call. She dialed.

"You have reached the offices of Patten and Plough. At present we can not come to the telephone..." Her precious quarter in the machine to hear a recording. After the beep she said wearily, "Mr Plough, this is Cilla Wheaton. I'm somewhere in Boston and..."

"Hello? Hello? Miss Wheaton? Horace Plough here. Hello, are you there?"

"Oh, Mr. Plough!" A friendly voice! Her ordeal was over. "I'm somewhere in Boston. I don't know how I got here or where Hudson is. Can you come get me? I know it must be late, but..."

"Of course, of course. I hear a car. Are you outdoors? At a pay phone?"

"Yes, it's a slum, a Boston slum. And I don't know what I'm doing here."

"Can you see street signs?"

"Well...yes! Hold on a minute and I'll go up to the corner. You won't hang up, will you?"

"No, no. I'll be right here. Give me the telephone number in case we get disconnected for some reason."

She read off the number of the machine and ran to the corner. Outside of an occasional car there was no one on the streets.

"Barker and Moreno. Does that mean anything to you?"

"Hold on a minute. I have a map...yes, I see where you are...Okay. We don't want you hanging around that area. Here's what I want you to do. Go away from Barker on Moreno for one block and tell me what the name of the next street is. The next street that crosses Moreno. I'll stay right on the telephone."

"Mr. Plough, I just have the one quarter I put in to call you. It's going to run out."

"Then hang up and I'll call you back."

Feeling she was severing an umbilical cord, Tabi did as she was told and waited. As murderers must for a reprieve from execution. In less than a minute the ring came.

"Plough again. Now get me that street name."

She left the wobbly shoes by the phone, dangling at the end of its cord, and ran down the middle of the street, casting peeks over her shoulder at the booth. If someone else should come by and hang it up...The streetlight was out at the next corner so the name was hard to read. As she stood tiptoe on bare feet trying to make it out, an automobile slowed beside her. Oh God, not another one. Not now! She turned toward the car with a fierce scowl on her face. The driver accelerated and sped away. Burke. She ran back.

"Burke Street, Mr. Plough."

"Good. Go back in the direction of Burke on Moreno for...six blocks. To Sutton. Go one block to your right and there is a flower shop called The Flower Wheel on the corner of Sutton and Haverhill. Wait there. I'll be along in...fifteen minutes. I'm not far away. Can you remember that?"

"Of course...tell me the name of the shop once more."

"The Flower Wheel. I'll be driving a tan Chevrolet station wagon."

She hung up the phone slowly. Joe Namath. That was it. Sometimes she had watched televised football games. There was something that excited her about the tackling. Hitting a body hard — a man's body — and leaving it sprawled on the turf. Joe used to be an announcer who used to be a player and occasionally did commercials. Quarterback, she thought. They always talked a lot. Namath had a funny way of pronouncing the letter 'L'. As in 'a great play'. Only it came out 'plllaay'. Which is how the voice in the car that abducted her said it. And how Joe pronounced 'flower', as in 'The Flllaower Wheel'. Like Plough.

She put the tight shoes back on. There was sure to be broken glass somewhere on the way. For she had to go to the Flower Wheel. Enemy or not Plough was her only thread to what had gone before.

She encountered no one until she made the turn on Sutton. This was a little better neighborhood, which made her feel even more awkward in her skimpy dress. It was a small store, with lattice work on either side of the door. She studied it from across the street. The Flower Wheel squeezed itself between two triple-deckers. She crossed to the one on the right. From the railing on the first floor porch, she was able to grasp the floor of that above. She put her shoes behind a bush and climbed to the second floor. She sat on the porch and waited.

The station wagon came slowly down Sutton and eased to a stop in front of the store. Two men got out. Plough must be the shorter one with glasses, she thought. He was giving the instructions, motioning the other to the left while he went to the side of the shop right near her. She stretched out on the porch floor.

"Miss Wheaton?" A flashlight shone on the bush where she had deposited her shoes. "Miss Wheaton, it's Horace Plough." Though his voice was hushed in keeping with the hour, she could hear him clearly through the railing. Even 'Plough' had an elongated 'L'.

"Greg, come over here." He had picked up her shoes and held them out to the other. There was a flickering streetlight half a block down which gave a gaslight glow to the two men as they bent over their find.

"Cheap," said Greg.

"Hmm. Would she have shoes? Where would she get them?"

"At Frieda's? Looks like a pair one of her girls would wear."

"Why discard them? This is no place to go barefoot. No. These aren't hers." He replaced them under the bush. "But why isn't she here? My instructions?" He thought a minute. "I think they were simple."

"But is she?"

"Simple? I hardly think she would have attracted a man like Rogers if she were."

Tabi smiled to herself. She knew how she presented herself to the world of men. Everything she had done with Hudson had been to produce precisely the opposite effect of 'attracted'. Until...

"Still, she might have taken a wrong turn."

"There was *one* turn! Unless she miscounted the blocks. In her state that's certainly possible. Damn Frieda. This isn't like her, letting the girl get out." He reached a decision. "Let's cruise the side streets. Maybe we'll pick her up." He headed for the station wagon. "We'd better, or they'll bury me under an outhouse."

Tabi climbed down as they pulled away. Who is 'they'? Margate? She'd liked the lawyer; she shook her head. Then who? Who was Plough really working for? She peered down the street. There was a faint glow in the sky in the direction she'd been headed. That must be the city center. She put the shoes back on and started at a fast pace. Plough would keep coming back to see if he'd missed her.

Four blocks later she slowed. The city seemed as far away as ever. And she couldn't walk another step in those heels. Barefoot on streets that were apt to have broken glass was asking for trouble. A pickup truck stopped for a light. It was headed in her direction. The driver had long flowing hair. On impulse she climbed quietly over the tailgate and curled up behind some boxes.

The driver seemed unaware; the light changed and the truck took off. It was an older vehicle and it rattled and shook. After a long way the street lighting became brighter, they were coming to something. Tabi caught a glimpse of an expressway as they crossed over it. Then the driver turned off and stopped. She heard the truck door slam, counted twenty and hopped out. The first word she saw was 'Vermont'. It was on the side of a bus, and there were more behind it. Bus station. She pulled the skirt of her dress down as far as she could, opened the door and walked in. A cigar smoking clerk was the only person in sight.

"Do you have a bus that goes to New Hampshire?"

"Sure. Manchester. Portsmouth."

"Anyplace near Bartlett?"

"Nope. Concord Trailways does. Peter Pan terminal. Fifteen minute walk." He pulled a little map from under the counter and drew in the direction. "Here. They've got one to North Conway. It's already gone though."

"How about tomorrow? Or today I guess," as she noticed a wall clock which showed after three.

"Five forty-five this afternoon. Gets in to North Conway at nine o'clock."

There was a wall of telephones. As she went toward them, the mens room door opened and the pickup truck driver came out. He'd tied his long hair in a pony tail. His eyes flicked over Tabi. Then came back to her, and he ambled in her direction with the beginnings of a smile. She swerved from the phones and headed out the door she'd entered. When it closed behind her, she turned to her right and walked quickly toward a square with a large building that showed the only signs of life. The wind had increased, and she shivered. She needed a place until time for the bus. Fourteen hours. She had to get indoors. Her wound was beginning to throb and, now that she was in no immediate danger, an immense weariness was settling on her like an enveloping cloak.

She crossed a street to the large building, waited until there was no one in sight and went through the entrance. Around a corner to her left she found a bank of telephones that didn't require change. She dialed Kabir's number, holding her breath. Twenty rings and nothing. She came out of the booth and leaned against it. Her eyes closed. A hand took her arm. She came alert instantly. A man in uniform .

"There's no loitering here."

"I was making a telephone call."

"And now you've made it. Let's go." He started to pull her toward the door she'd entered.

"Let. Go. Of. My. Arm."

"Don't you give me any trouble. You floozies...hmmf!" His body went back, knocking over a long mahogany table with a crash. He shook himself and started to get up. "Why you..." The rest was forgotten as Tabi's foot connected with his chin. He sprawled over the table and was quiet. There had been plenty of noise, though. Tabi ran around a corner to an open area. There were stairs going up to her left, and beyond a door padded with dark red carpeting was just closing. She caught it before it shut and found herself in a brightly lighted corridor with bare floors. She followed it to the right, then took some stairs on her left going down. At the bottom she could go either direction, went right and right again into a large room. In a corner were large laundry baskets piled with soiled sheets and pillowcases. She selected the one furthest from the door and — too tired to care what sheets they were — crawled into it, pulling some over her so she was hidden. She curled up and put both her hands side-by-side over the bandage where the arrow had entered. And slept.

Voices. For a minute she couldn't make out where she was. Then it came clear. She cautiously pulled the sheets off her head, but kept lower than the rim of the basket. Two women in white dresses were twenty feet away.

"Housekeeping's short again. They want me to go. I say no way. I do laundry, I no make beds."

"Me neither. They know better than ask me."

They moved off, and Tabi climbed out. There was a room next to her with lockers. She went in. There was no one there. On a bench was a white dress like the others wore. She held it up to herself. It would do. She quickly changed into it, kicking the Elvira costume into a corner with a sigh of relief. It was a long dress; even in a size too small for her it came down well over the bandage and the knee as well. Am I ever going to wear underwear again, she thought. At least she didn't look like the streets. There were several bobby pins in a jar which she used to put her hair into a comforting bun. She searched the area but could find no shoes, so put on the high heels and walked through the large room into the corridor. Halfway down it was a service elevator. A young black woman in a grey uniform was striding from it toward Tabi.

"We got to get you right up to housekeeping. They're screaming. Where you been?" Without waiting for an answer, she took Tabi by the arm and walked her into an open elevator, pushing the button for four.

On the fourth floor she led Tabi to a desk and left her there. Tabi edged away as the large Puerto Rican woman behind the desk turned from a telephone and looked her over.

"You the girl from the laundry, honey?"

"Ah...yes."

"Done rooms before?"

Tabi nodded. Get to a phone. Any phone.

"Can't without a uniform. Muncie, get her something to wear and start her on Ruby's rooms."

Dressed now in grey, Tabi followed the elderly maid onto the elevator.

"You start with fourteen fifty-six and do the evens. I'll take the odds." The lift rose. "You can use this cart. I've got my own up there." She looked more closely. "What are you wearing those shoes for?"

"These are borrowed. Someone took mine."

"Ain't you got lockers in the laundry?" She shook her head in disgust. Looked again at the shoes. "You got big feet. Like Ruby. She keeps a pair in her closet. As her being out's why you're here I guess you can use them." The elevator stopped, its floor indicator pointing to fourteen. "Right around here." She led Tabi around a corner and opened a door revealing a linen closet. She handed a pair of sneakers, and pointed to a room. "What's your name, honey?"

"Tabi."

"Tabby? Sounds like a cat. Well, Tabby, there's fifty-six. Make it snappy, we're late enough as it is." She went off down the hall.

The sneakers also were tight, but so much more comfortable than the others that Tabi sighed with relief. Now a telephone. Kabir certainly should be home now. They must have phones in the rooms. Down the hall she could hear the other woman knocking on a door and saying, "Maid." She pushed the cart up to room fifty-six and knocked.

"Yes?"

"Maid."

"Okay. Come on." The voice was slurred. She visualized it spewing alcohol fumes.

Tabi looked around. What now. "Would you open it, Sir?"

"Minute." The doorknob turned, and the door was partially opened. "Come ahead. I'm in the bathroom."

Tabi caught sight of a back disappearing into the bathroom and heard the sounds of teeth being brushed. The bathroom door closed, and she scurried to the telephone. She quickly read the instructions and dialed Kabir. Busy! At least someone was there. She hung up. In a few seconds she tried again. Still busy. She looked at the bathroom door. How much time did she have? Nervously she started to make the bed, look as though she belonged. Then realized they'd make it up fresh. The hell with that. She sat on the bed and stared at the phone. Maybe if she concentrated on it they would get off the line and answer. She wrote the number on a piece of paper and focused on it, willing it to answer. On the third try it did.

"*Oui?*"

"*Kabir, il est là?*"

"*Non, je regrette.*" A child's voice.

"*Qui êtes vous?*'" Who are you?

"*Mike.*"

"*Mike, vous parlez anglais?*" Pray he speaks English.

"*Bien sûr.*"

"This is his cousin Muktabai Wheaton, Mike. Where is Kabir?" She could hear the electric razor from the bathroom.

"He's gone to New Hampshire."

"To Bartlett?"

"I think so. He call in the evening."

"He'll be telephoning you this evening?"

"Yes. At seventeen hundred hours."

"Mike, will you give him a message from me? Do you have something to write on?"

"Yes. I can take a message."

"Good. Tell him that I am in Boston but will be taking the bus to North Conway this evening. I don't know where it stops there. He can find out by calling Concord Trailways. It gets into North Conway at...twenty-one hundred hours. Would he please meet me. Got it?"

"I have it."

"Good boy. And Mike..."

"I'm here."

"If a man named Hudson Rogers calls, give him the same message. Otherwise tell absolutely no one. You haven't heard from me and have no idea where I am. Understand?"

"Kabir and Hudson Rogers and nobody."

"Right. Thanks, Mike." She hung up and stood thinking. Would Plough be watching that particular bus, knowing it's where she'd go? She scarcely thought about where the money for the ticket would come from. That was the least of her worries. Plough, though...

Where was Hudson? Had he himself been captured? Worse still, had an 'accident'? She lifted the phone again and dialed Margate's number. There was no answer. No answer? At a lawyer's office, on a...it had to still be a weekday. She couldn't have been out of it that long. What was happening? She sank on the unmade bed, suddenly feeling weak. Oh Hudson. What I wouldn't give to see your face and know you are all right.

The toilet flushed; she was off the bed in an instant and halfway out of the room as the bathroom door opened. She closed the room door behind her and walked down the corridor toward the service elevator.

Chapter 23

IT WAS LATE when Hudson woke, much later than he had intended. He scrambled out of bed. Why hadn't Krestinski called? He dialed the FBI number. The agent was on the telephone and would call him. He looked at his watch. 11:00. He quickly showered, leaving the bathroom door open in case the phone rang. But the only interruption was the maid whom he had to let in while he brushed his teeth. With her in the room he closed the bathroom door; she would let him know if the phone rang. When he came out after shaving, she scurried out the door. Probably nervous about him being in the room. Who could blame her in a city hotel nowadays.

The phone rang. Krestinski. "Come over." He hung up before Hudson could get in any questions.

At the front desk Hudson learned he was indeed a guest of the Federal Government. His only bill was for a phone call. He studied it. He'd made no long distance calls. He thought back. The maid? He'd heard talking while he was in the bathroom. And there was something else.

"Do your maids have keys to the rooms?" he asked the clerk.

"Naturally. How else would they clean?"

Leaving his bag sitting on the floor in front of the desk, he walked to the elevators. On the fourteenth floor a maid was pushing a cart down the corridor.

"Where's the maid for fourteen fifty-six?"

"That's what I'd like to know! There's her cart sitting right outside it. Honestly the help today! This your room?" She opened the door to an empty fourteen fifty-six.

"Yes. What's her name? The maid for this room?

"Ruby. She's the regular. Course today it's that new fluff. Her and her high heels."

Hudson went to the phone. Next to it was a piece of paper with a telephone number on it. A 514 exchange, Quebec. It looked familiar. Of course! It was Kabir's number! But how...? "The name of the maid today. Tell me."

She saw the look on Hudson's face. "Tabby, that's what she said. Just like a cat, I told her." She eyed the guest with the intense eyes. "If there's anything missing..."

Tabby? What the hell did that mean. But it had to be. "She was wearing high heel shoes?"

"Couldn't believe it myself. Let her borrow Ruby's. If she's run off with them Ruby will..."

"Where would she have gone? With her cart still here."

"Down for a sniff or a pop, you ask me."

"Down where?"

"The locker room. Or the laundry. Maybe I should call the house-keeper if..."

Hudson took a twenty dollar bill from his wallet. "Could you show me?"

"Guests aren't supposed to..." Hudson added another twenty. "But who's to know. Come on. The elevator's across the hall."

The service elevator with scraped metal door and heavily soiled metal walls eased its way down the building. Hudson could only come up with questions. Was he all wrong about the kidnapping? Had Cilla in fact wandered away by herself? Amnesia seemed the only answer. But even at that, last night she was an unconscious patient in a Salem hospital; today a maid in a Boston hotel. A maid named Tabby like a cat. How did she get here? How did she get this job overnight? And good God, why?

There was no one in the housekeeping locker room. It was a quiet time of day in the back of the house, and no one paid any attention to Hudson. Just another manager or inspector.

"You mentioned the laundry."

"It's in the basement."

"Let's look."

The laundry revealed no maid. There was something dark in a corner of its women's locker room. He picked it up. It was a shiny black dress. He was about to put it back when he noticed a small stain on the hem. He looked at it closely. He wasn't familiar with dried blood stains, but thought this might be one. He held the dress up to himself. The stain was above his right thigh. He put it aside and fished around in the corner. There was a bit of paper. A map. Outlined on it was a route from the Greyhound Bus Terminal to the South Station. He wrote the FBI number on a piece of paper which he gave the elderly maid.

"If she comes back leave a message for me at this number." Krestinski would just have to get used to being an answering service.

* * *

"Did you come by way of New Hampshire?"

"In a sense. I think Cilla was in my room this morning."

"And I was just beginning to put some credence in your fairy tale."

"So was I. Do you think I go around inventing fantastic stories to see how long it takes you to lose patience and lock me up?"

"Surprisingly, your background is devoid of such behavior. Tell me, Hudson. Did she appear as a hologram or in a flash of light?"

"As a hotel maid. Actually I think she wanted to use my telephone. I heard voices while I was shaving and thought she'd turned on the TV."

"And you didn't recognize this girl you spent six hours in the sack with?"

"I didn't see her, John. Not her face. She knocked on the door and asked me to let her in. What maid does that? They all have keys. I unlatched the door and went back to the bathroom. Do you look at maids? I mean could you describe the last maid — hell, any maid — that made up a hotel room for you? But for once I've got proof." He showed Krestinski the paper with the number. "This is Kabir's telephone number in Odanak. She must have....what a fool! Can I use your phone?"

Krestinski nodded. "If there's a charge, she must have reached the number."

Hudson dialed.

"Oui?"

"Kabir, s'il vous plaît."

"Il n'est pas ici." Kabir's not there. Who's this?

"Ou est'il? Ici Hudson Rogers."

"Oh Mr. Rogers, this is Mike. I am watching the house for him. I have a message for you. Muktabai Wheaton will arriving in North Conway at twenty-one hundred tonight."

"Mike, when did she call?"

"There is an hour."

"An hour ago?"

"Yes."

"How will she be going to North Conway?"

"She taking a bus."

"A bus from Boston?"

"She said Concord."

"A bus from Concord, Massachusetts?"

There was a moment of silence. "Concord, Trailways."

"Mike, did she say how she was?"

"She was in Boston."

"An hour ago, she was in Boston."

"Yes."

"Did she say anything else, Mike?"

"Not to tell anybody. You and Kabir and nobody."

"And did you tell Kabir?"

"No. He call last night before I know."

"Where is he?"

"New Hampshire."

"Do you have a telephone number where he can be reached?"

"No. He call again tonight."

"Thanks, Mike. If he does call again earlier, have him telephone me at this number." He gave the FBI agent's number and hung up.

"It might be easier if you had your own office here."

"Where's the Concord Trailways terminal?"

"Down by South Station. In the Peter Pan Terminal."

"John, that settles it." He showed him the map. "She's taking a bus from there to North Conway tonight. We've got to find her before that."

"Why? We can meet her there."

"So could someone else."

"Who else, one of what you call 'the enemy'?"

"She made a point of saying to Mike, the boy on the phone, not to tell anyone her plans."

"You would have said the same thing, considering."

"Think about it. If she left the clinic on her own no one knows where she is. Who would suspect she might be in Boston about to take a bus? But if she was kidnapped from Wendt's and somehow got away from them, she'd have every reason to keep them from knowing her plans."

"So we can still meet her at the bus, Hudson."

"If you're in Boston, without a car, how do you get to Bartlett? Sure you can rent a car. But she hasn't any money."

"The bus costs money."

"But not a lot. Maybe she'll highjack it. The point is if we can figure the bus, so can others."

"Okay. I can't spare anyone from here..."

"No need. I'll find her."

"You sound pretty sure of yourself. You know something I don't?"

"Her."

Hudson stood at the door of the Park Plaza and looked around. Traffic clogged the street in front of the hotel. The sidewalks were jammed with hurrying bodies. Most people probably feel the safest place to hide would be in a crowd. Not Cilla. Tabby? Where did that come from? He thought back. At the house on Bear Notch Road she said she had several first names. Cilla. Muktabai. What else. Cilla was a nickname for Priscilla. Muktabai, Muky? Tabai? Taby! The name she calls herself. He was a little deflated she hadn't shared it with him. But what *had* they shared intimately. A night of music, but no lyrics.

A woman with many parcels nearly knocked him over. Dangerous to stand still. Keep moving in self defense. He walked the mapped route to the Peter Pan terminal. Would she sit there five or six hours waiting for the North Conway bus? No way. Not with people after her who might figure her for the bus. Then where? He prowled the streets around the terminal. South Station? The smell was musty; he searched its waiting areas without much hope. Wood nymphs didn't inhabit man-made caverns. Or treeless streets he thought as he leaned against a traffic pole. He kicked a pebble down an asphalt gutter. His watch said three o'clock.

He widened his search circles around the terminal. Highway construction areas. Chinatown. At four he forced himself to stop and think. Maybe she planned on going to the terminal at the last minute. If so, she could be anywhere. No, not anywhere. He took out the little map. Greyhound Bus Terminal. He retraced his steps past the hotel to the other bus station. Street lights had come on. It was nearly dark.

"Is this one of your maps?" he asked the woman behind the desk.

She glanced at it. "Yes."

"Is there any way of telling when this was given out?"

She shrugged. "Could be anytime. We use them all day."

He walked back to the Park Plaza. Greyhound was the direction she'd come from. She wouldn't go that way again. If she didn't go to Peter Pan... He crossed the street and walked toward Boylston. At the corner where it met Arlington he paused, and a smile spread across his face. He knew where she was.

Ten minutes later he sat down quietly next to a discarded pile of clothes hidden under evergreen bushes and what a sign advertised was a Sargent Cherry tree.

"A good little hari krishna would be out working the street."

The pile gave a sudden lurch, and a dirty face peered out at him. "Hudson! My God! You're all right? How did you find me? Oh hell I don't care! You're here!" A passing elderly woman stopped to gaze at the sight of a well dressed man sprawled on the ground with his arms around a filthy bag lady. Probably has a wife at home, too, she humpfed. Hudson could

feel Cilla's tense body gradually relax underneath the soiled grey uniform.
There was nothing tentative about their kiss.

Krestinski never met the bag lady. A huge meal, new clothes and a bath
— and a fresh bandage on the wound — brought Cilla back to life. Hudson
had never seen anyone more beautiful and said so. Cilla responded with the
shy, half-smile he remembered from the tent and now recognized as acceptance.

Kabir had called and left the message he was back at Odanak. Cilla did
not go easy on him. "Where have you been? Do you know how many times
I tried to reach you last night?"

"Mr. Krestinski told me. Are you all right?"

"Yes, but you're not going to be. Why didn't you stay by the telephone
as Hudson asked?"

"Mike was supposed to. His mother got sick."

"Too much trouble for you?"

"Muktabai, I had a hot lead. Listen, I found some papers that supposedly were written before Rogers Raid and drove down to my father's house
to check them out. I was only gone a little over twelve hours."

"While I was being hunted by the people who murdered my father and
yours."

"I know, I know. It was stupid. Can you forgive me?"

"What was this great lead?"

"A letter written by a man named Pere Roubaud."

"A priest?"

"Yes. The priest at St Francis during the seventeen fifties."

"So?"

"You remember in the musée we've got a little statue? It's wood, I
think, painted a silver color. It's a duplicate of one that was lost."

"Of course. The Madonna."

"Made of solid silver, the original one was. Well Pere Roubaud wrote
that he was afraid something would happen to it and said...it was in French
of course...that he had taken steps to ensure the safety of the statue in those
troubled times. And despite what happened in the battles with the English,
the statue would remain on Abenaki soil. I did some reading on it. Do you
know how important that statue is to the Abenakis?"

"Tell me."

"Since it's been lost we've had centuries of bad luck. The elders feel it
will continue until the Madonna is back in Odanak."

"So you ran down to Bartlett to see if your father had been using it as a door stop."

"Aw, come on. I remembered my father showing me a picture of it and telling me it was not lost in Rogers Raid as everyone thought. I got excited and figured maybe father had more on it."

"And did he?"

"In a book — *Lost Virgin*, it's a novel — it says the statue was stolen by one of Rogers Rangers..."

"As it does in *Northwest Passage*. I'm glad you found some light reading."

"No! Listen! There were notes my father made. He felt what was stolen was a fake substituted by Roubaud, and the original is safe."

"So where is it?"

"Father felt it must be on the treaty land. And so do I! Just from the way Roubaud wrote about it, that it would 'remain on Abenaki soil.' Think about those words! He couldn't very well guarantee St. Francis would stay in Abenaki hands. That's what he feared, that it would fall to the English. So where else could it be hidden 'on Abenaki soil'?"

"Still, I..."

"Muktabai, listen. I know it sounds unthinking of me. But look at it from my point of view. My cousin who's more important to me than anyone has been kidnapped. Why? Because somebody wants the treaty. Here was the Madonna also missing and probably stashed on the treaty land. I find the statue, I find the land. And maybe the treaty that gets you back from the kidnappers."

There was more, but Kabir was one of those people it is impossible to stay angry with, and Cilla had come close to forgiving him by the time they hung up.

Krestinski had also been on the telephone. "I'll pick up Plough and, if Cilla can find it for us, this woman at the cathouse..."

"Whorehouse," Cilla broke in. "I like cats."

Hudson ran his hand through his hair. "This may sound crazy, but how about just keeping an eye on Plough. He must have a good reputation or Margate wouldn't have hired him. Right now it will be his word and the woman's against Cilla. And her story won't come off as the most believable ever."

Krestinski frowned.

"There are others mixed up in this, John. While these two are awaiting trial, Cilla will be in constant danger from them."

"She is anyway. You *both* have had attempts on your lives. That's not going to stop unless *we* stop *them*. Right?"

"Absolutely. And to do that we need evidence."

"And you have a plan to get it."

"I do. And it's got to be done fast. There's a time factor here. They're trying to prevent us from finding the old treaty before something happens. How do we know? They're becoming more desperate all the time. First it was just 'accidents'. Then it was poisoned arrows and now kidnapping. The next time we'll have proof."

"The next time you'll be dead. We may be able to get them for murder then. Good plan, Hudson."

"Exactly. You win out either way."

"What's the other way?"

"We find the treaty. Obviously whatever's in it will stop their plans or they wouldn't be working so hard to prevent it. In fact, it may itself furnish the proof we're looking for. Even if it doesn't, you know the players, Trimble and Plough. You have them watched and see what they do. If they make a mistake you'll have them and whoever's behind them."

"All you have to do is find the treaty."

"Right."

"Right?"

"John, I don't know where it is but I think I know how to go about finding it. As quick as Cilla is up to it..."

"Cilla is more than up to it," said the girl. "Now tell me what I've agreed to."

He did.

Chapter 24

THE WIND HIT them full force as they broke treeline. Warm in their long underwear, parkas and heavy sweaters, the cold blast was merely an inconvenience that made climbing a little slower. For the sky was clear, unlike the day before. Yesterday there had been a bright sun as they set off, but clouds moved in before they'd been on the trail an hour, making a change of plans advisable, and they'd stopped overnight at Mizpah Spring. They ran into no other hikers, as the AMC hut was closed for the season. Several times Hudson had noticed Cilla sitting with her hands over her wound as though in pain.

"It's not bothering me," she said in answer to his question. "I'm doing *Reiki*."

"What's that?"

"Healing."

"Laying on of hands? Like Christ did?"

"Like anybody can."

Sometimes he thought of the girl as native to an exotic planet where the effect of several whirling suns created strange and wondrous life forms with totally different conceptions of a quite different cosmos. Or maybe he was just an older generation...no, he liked the exotic planet better.

"It works?"

"Yes."

"By warming?"

"By energy."

"Hmmm."

"Do you believe in radiation?"

"Of course."

"It's a form of energy that can cure cancer. Why can't another form cure a wound?" She saw he was unconvinced. "Pragmatic Hudson. You'll just have to take my word it's working." She searched his eyes. "For now."

* * *

After leaving Krestinski two days before, Hudson had reclaimed his room at the Park Plaza and booked an adjoining one for Cilla. Plough's resources weren't unlimited, and it seemed safer than moving. The detective hadn't returned to his office. Nor had anyone else. Krestinski reported the door remained closed and locked, and only his machine answered the telephone. There was no one at Plough's house in Brighton. And no sign of Trimble.

Despite her protests that she was ready to go, Cilla slept eight hours, came alive for breakfast and slept another twelve. Hudson kept his impatience to himself. He needed her strong.

"How did you find me?" she asked when the room service waiter left.

"Mostly luck," he admitted. "Once I found myself looking at the Public Garden I was pretty sure you'd be there. You'd pick trees and bushes over people any time."

The next day they'd left for New Hampshire.

They sat on rocks at the summit. Cilla had kept a strong pace, resting only briefly at the Lakes of the Clouds before continuing on up the cone to the top. The wind was at their backs as they looked out over a hundred miles of jutting peaks.

"So this is Hidden Mountain?"

"*Kodaak Wajo.* Over the centuries the name got separated from the mountain it described. It was thought to be the home of the gods. That's what threw me off for a long time. No Indian dared mount it. But a white man was another story."

"Chief Gill?"

"Samuel Gill, his father. If it had been Chief Gill there would be no mystery today. *He* lived until the seventeen nineties. Samuel died while the Abenakis were focused on war with the white man. A home among the enemy would have had little appeal to the tribe. But our friend Samuel spent the first fourteen years of his life in New England. My guess is that it was still 'home' to him, though he became an Abenaki in every other way." Hudson shook his head. "I think he could see what was happening to his adopted people and made a deal with Benning Wentworth."

"But *he* couldn't arrange a treaty. He wasn't a Chief."

"I'm not sure there *was* a treaty. I think it may just have been a deed."

"Why would Governor Wentworth deed New Hampshire land to an Indian? Even an adopted one?"

"Think of what it must have been like living in New Hampshire in the mid seventeen hundreds. In constant danger from Indian raids. Maurault wrote that between seventeen fifty-four and fifty-nine there were almost continual expeditions by the Abenakis into New England. How many scalps did Robert Rogers find in Saint Francis? Six hundred?

"Benning Wentworth was a sly one. He deeded New Hampshire land right and left to his friends, and with each one he kept a chunk of a hundred acres or so for himself. But he soon discovered land has little value if it's worth your life to live on it. Along comes this white man, not an Indian, someone he can trust — as much as he trusted anybody — and offers to use his best efforts to calm down his warring brothers. Wouldn't it be worth a gamble to trade him for a godforsaken parcel of inaccessible and untillable mountain land? Don't forget there weren't many roads in this area then; most settled land was near navigable rivers like the Connecticut. Not in this area.

"The only ones who cared about the White Mountains were red...It seems strange to be able to see a hundred miles in all directions from a 'hidden' mountain."

"It *was* yesterday."

"That's right. Hidden by clouds."

"As it often is."

"What do they say about Mount Washington...the highest winds ever recorded on earth? Summer's not so bad, but in winter it becomes arctic."

"Emma Persons said it's known as the worst weather on earth. Uninhabitable. At least to the Indians."

"No wonder they thought it was a very special place."

"And why Gill picked it. It was the most special place in all the White Mountains. If the map were ever found, no white man would believe an Indian map would be drawn from this place."

"And now that we're here...?"

Hudson carefully pulled the paper from his pocket, sheltering it from the wind. "Now we look at the map. And hope it shows where the deed is."

"You figure the rumors about a hidden mountain and the promise of Indian land came from Samuel Gill?"

"Right. Here's what I think happened. He could see what was coming — the almost complete destruction of St. Francis and perhaps all other Abenaki lands. He couldn't get anyone to listen to him so he hid the deed in white man's territory — maybe on the deeded land itself — and sewed the location on the back of a holy cloth. Something with no material value to make it attractive to looters in a raid. In fact, because it was an icon, it was more likely to be spared."

"Why didn't Gill just come claim the land after peace was declared?"

"He died in seventeen fifty-eight, the year before Rogers Raid. And obviously before he told anyone where the map was."

"That doesn't make sense, not to tell his own son the location of something as important as that map."

"Probably a matter of timing. I suspect the younger Gill wouldn't have been too happy with his father's attempts to make peace had he known about them. He *was* an Abenaki even without a drop of Indian blood in his veins. And from what I've read, warlike. He'd sooner been drawn and quartered than bargain with the white man. I'd bet his father was keeping it to himself until whatever disaster he foresaw was over."

"And died before it came. Then how did the rumors start?"

"Who knows. Death-bed confession, Pere Roubaud. Maybe just a desire to let someone know everything would be all right in the end. That no matter what happened they had land they could live on."

"Sounds perfectly simple. That little piece of paper with lines on it is going to lead us to another piece of paper hidden two hundred years ago somewhere in a hundred miles of peaks and valleys. That no one else has found."

"You have a good grasp of the fundamentals." He held the paper up, comparing it with what he saw. "It should be Chocorua...and it is! Look! See that little blip in the line to the left? When we turn the paper sideways..."

"It becomes a mountain range!" Cilla took the paper from him and said excitedly, "Yes! There's Passaconaway...hey, this is really a drawing of the Sandwich Range!"

"Which I've seen so often recently that it looked familiar as soon as I saw it. That's why I felt we had something on the back of that altar cloth. If I hadn't spent the summer looking at it from so many different peaks..."

"But what about the rest? These peaks in front. And the eye."

They held the paper between them so each could study it. Hudson pointed to his right. "I think the squiggly line to the right is the Saco River. See how it winds just as the one on the paper?"

"That kind of frames in one end...then the other mountains should be...right there." She pointed to the distance. "What's that peak?"

"Hmm. I think it's Tremont."

"So the eye is right near Mount Tremont. Between it and the Sandwich Range."

"From its shape, it has to be a lake or pond..."

"Sawyer Pond!"

"Of course! The pupil is its little island! Good work!"

"Do you think it's there?"

"Why don't we find out."

For the middle of October in the White Mountains it was surprisingly warm. Carr sitting with his snow guns poised at Great Haystack couldn't have been very happy, thought Hudson. It had to be close to 32 degrees before they could operate, and colder for efficient snow making, Cilla pointed out. Hudson was comfortable in just chamois shirt and jeans as he poked a log on their fire. Sawyer Pond was fading into a muddy gray before them as the sun disappeared.

Hudson wondered if they weren't becoming too casual, making camp so close to a trail. With new equipment; the old was still at Nancy Pond. But it had been several days since they'd last seen members of the enemy, who now almost seemed to exist in another world. Plough was the darkened streets of Boston; Trimble someone running through lightless buildings soon to be burning. They were the nether world and had no place here in the beauty of the mountains.

He watched Cilla as she sponged off the plates from dinner. Had she grown more mature lately? Or was he just trying to justify his feelings for someone so much younger. Well, not that much younger. Fifteen years wasn't...or was it sixteen...?

She saw him looking at her and smiled her half smile he had come to treasure. He reached out a hand and took hers. They sat by the edge of the fire.

"I'm nervous," he grinned.

"Holding my hand?"

He nodded. "Just like a kid on a first date."

"I'm not a first date, Hudson."

He shook his head. "After what we've been through, I feel as though I've known you a long time." He looked into her eyes. "The question is, are you a date?"

"Do you want me to be?"

"Yes."

She nodded slowly. "And your...wife, Sylvia?"

"I still love her. She'll always be a part of me, with a room in my heart all to herself. Where I'll sometimes visit."

"You're a good man."

"Charlie Brown."

"Hudson Rogers."

He looked up at a sky that was suddenly night. "And now I've used the word, this will come easier." He turned to look into her grey eyes. "I've fallen in love with you, Cilla. I don't know how or why or what in hell brought it on, but..."

"Tabi." She pronounced the 'a' as in father.

"I...what?"

"If you're going to be in love with me, you've got to know the me underneath. Tabi not Cilla." She ran her fingers lightly over his hand. "She's a different woman, Hudson. You may not care for her."

"Tell me about Tabi."

"She lives in a cocoon, protected from the world — which she doesn't much care for. She's seen other women become butterflies, spread their wings and go flying off into the sunset. But she can't. Hasn't wanted to, because there's nothing out there but hurt."

"Still?"

She closed her eyes. "One day...she looked down at a man, lying naked and cold and shivering and helpless...a strong man...a man she had hurt, who hadn't hurt her, hadn't *wanted* to hurt her...She'd never taken her clothes off in front of a man..." She paused. "But this was something she *had* to do...and she did. Lying next to this man, feeling his...his body become excited, even though his mind was unconscious...Understand, sex was a word in her dictionary right next to disgust and fear. And yet here there was no threat. And to her surprise, no disgust."

She was quiet for so long, Hudson prompted, "What was there?"

"A desire to protect...No, a *need* to comfort. Maybe it's something all women have. A need to nurture."

"As a mother with her children?"

"Hudson, you don't need mothering. Not any more."

"I did in June."

She nodded. "In June you were a mess, physically and emotionally. This was different. A feeling I've never had before...And then when you carried me all the way up to Nancy Pond. And warmed me...Tell me again. What you feel for me."

"I love you...Tabi."

She looked at him closely in the flickering light of the fire. "What does that mean? To you? That you take me to bed and six months later we meet on the street as strangers?"

"I..."

"That's the behavior code, isn't it? It certainly is of my generation."

"And mine."

"Well, that's another thing with Tabi. She's old fashioned...To most of my friends being old fashioned means one man at a time. To me it means one man period."

"Tabi-Cilla, I want you to marry me."

She looked into his eyes for a long moment. The tenseness in her body gradually eased, and she sighed. "That's good. Because you're the one man."

And then there was no hesitation. They slid into each other's arms as if they had always done so. After a moment, her lips parted for the kiss as though it weren't the very first time they had ever so welcomed a man. Hudson held her slim body tightly, feeling butterfly wings beating beneath the shell. She shivered.

"Are you cold?"

"I think it's the excitement."

"Perhaps we'd better go in the tent anyway. The wind has come up."

"Hudson...?"

"Yes, dear?"

"I may disappoint you."

"Unlikely."

"I may disappoint myself...I'm not sure I can...do it."

"Then you won't. I'm happy with what we have."

"But I want to! I want to be able to...give myself to you. I don't want to be just a half woman for you. I want to give you pleasure; see your love at what I've given."

"I guess we've got to start right there. You don't give and I receive. We both give to each other. If sex is to be part of love — forget the times it isn't — both give and both receive. That means you've got to find as much pleasure as I, or nothing works."

"I don't know...my friends tell me they've...felt things. What did one call it? A bursting of ecstasy. All I feel is that's where I...go to the bathroom. That doesn't make me feel...sexy. But don't you see, it doesn't matter! As long as you..."

"That *is* old fashioned. Sometimes women used to go their whole lives without a climax — never knowing one was available. When only the man enjoyed sex."

"I don't care, Hudson."

"*I* do. I blew it with Sylvia for a bunch of years. I won't with you. So someday when..."

"No! You don't know what fears I'm battling to talk about this! Can you...help me to feel something?"

"Now?"

"Now. I may never get my nerve up again."

"Okay." He helped her up, and they went together into the tent.

"Hudson...?"

"I'm here."

"Tell me you love me again."

"I love you, love you, love you."

"That's right. Keep saying it."

Her new sleeping bag fit nicely with Hudson's. By the faint glow of the moonlight that crept through the tent flap they took off their clothes. It was chilly, and they wasted no time crawling into the combined bag. At first they just lay there. Then his arms went around her, as hers did him.

"Two weeks ago I would have broken the leg of anyone who suggested I might be lying naked with a naked man."

"And now you've done it three times."

"Now it feels you belong here."

He was very slow and gentle, kissing her face and neck, caressing her arms and shoulders, As his fingers crept toward her breasts he could feel her stiffen.

"I love you."

"I know. I'm trying." Gradually her tension eased. His fingers circled her breasts, and he felt the nipples harden. She started to tighten again, but, with an obvious effort forced her body to relax. She shivered as his tongue explored each nipple; it became a shudder as his hand moved down past her stomach.

"Listen to me, Tabi. I'm not going to come inside you tonight."

"You must!"

"And I will, but only when you're ready. You've got to learn to accept pleasure. Otherwise it becomes all one sided."

"But I want to please you..."

"You'll please me a hundred times more when I know you're feeling the same. Believe me when I say it. I do know."

"Where did you ever come from, Hudson."

He caressed each thigh, being careful of the now small bandage, and gradually her legs parted. She was very dry, and he moistened her with saliva. Then he tenderly explored her with his fingers. Finding what he wanted, the fingers of his left hand began a persistent massage. He kept his body close to her but not on top of her so she wouldn't feel smothered. His right hand kept contact with her breasts. In the dim light he looked down at her — her eyes held trust but not a small measure of fear.

"I love you, Tabi."

For a long time she just lay there, as though a body on an operating table. Probably the way she feels, thought Hudson. Her lips gradually became soft to his; the rest of her body unmoving. Then she gave a startled gasp and a sudden intake of breath. Her eyes opened wide and her legs twitched.

"Just relax and remember I love you."

For a long moment she froze, her knees together, her eyes searching Hudson's through a ten year shell. Then she gave a little cry as though of pain and opened her long legs. With eyes on his, she pulled Hudson's head down to hers and pushed her tongue between his lips. His left hand felt moistness. She leaned her head back, her breath beginning to come in small gasps. Between them she breathed, "Hudson, Hudson, Hudson." Her hips began to writhe. "Oh my God...!" Then nothing but guttural sounds until the dam broke.

The climax was long, and Hudson kept her in it until she could take it no longer. She lay back breathing deeply for a moment, then pulled him close to her, wrapping her arms around him, her head on his chest. "Idiot girl."

"What?"

"Maggie. A friend of mine at the ashram. She said women are ravished in pain, feeling nothing more than the eternal weariness of womankind. She talks like that."

"She wrong?"

"Dead wrong. She never been with Hudson." She raised herself on an elbow to look at him. "And she's never going to."

"Well...Can I consider that a formal acceptance of my earlier proposal?"

"Yes. And someday soon I'll notarize it."

They lay back in each others arms. From out on the water came a sound like the call of a loon. There were no loons on Sawyer Pond, Hudson was certain.

"What's our plan for tomorrow?" Where there had been a wall between himself and Cilla, Tabi seemed to enter his mind and read his thoughts.

"We put ourselves in the moccasins of Samuel Gill."

"Suppose the pond looked the same two hundred and thirty something years ago?"

"I'm pretty sure it did. At least the water level was about the same. The trees were much bigger."

"As big as the one pressing against me a while ago?"

"Not quite that size. But then they didn't have the enticement."

"I can't even visualize something as big as that inside me." She kissed his cheek. "But I want to. Soon." She paused. Then looked at him curiously. "Your finger never went inside. How did I..."

"Common misconception. Your sex gland is close to the surface."

She lay back. "I've so damned much to learn." Her hand stroked his chest. "Fortunately I've a good teacher."

"Ready for another lesson?"

Her half smile appeared, and she nodded.

Chapter 25

IT WAS THE hour just before dawn. Hudson sat on a rock at the shore gazing out at the pond. The wind was still, and a dense mist hung over the water. Behind the pond the ridge between Mount Tremont and Owls Cliff was faintly outlined by the lightening sky. I've got a precious deed; one that may mean salvation for my adopted people. Where do I hide it. It mustn't be found or destroyed by accident. So I don't put it in a tree that might be cut down. Presumably it's written on something perishable. So maybe I put it in a container. Do I sink the container in the pond? Too risky. Everything leaks sooner or later. Though I certainly don't plan on its survival for a couple hundred years.

Why Sawyer Pond? Why here instead of...It only made sense if this was part of the deeded land. Could the mountains here be Wabanaki Awiben? He studied their outline. Owls Cliff could be the head of someone lying on his back. But the col between it and Tremont made an ungainly neck, rising too abruptly to a puffed out chest. Sort of like the Cat in the Hat.

The mist had slowly evaporated, and the Pond was like a large mirror. As he looked, he could see Tremont and Owls Cliff reflected in it, and...He turned his head sideways. Yes! Owls Cliff added to its reflection became the head of some one lying facing him. With a feather protruding from the top! The double col then became a normal neck, and Mt. Tremont a pair of strong shoulders instead of the keg-like chest he'd seen before. Wabanaki Awiben. Indian seen when it is calm. With certainty he knew he was look-ing at what Samuel Gill must have gazed on so long ago.

Then where...Food. That must have been at the front of Gill's mind. The Indian could live most anywhere as long as there was food. His eyes followed the image down to where the stomach would be, and...Of course! There was the island! Deadhead! If you draw a circle and put a dot in it, where the hell else would the hidden object be!

Cilla was awake when he got back to the tent. "I'm supposed to be the early riser." She lay in the bag watching him as he sat to re-tie a boot.

"Come with me. I want to show you something." She wriggled out and stood, holding her clothes against her nakedness. He pulled her to him. "You're beautiful."

"You think so?" She shook her head. "That's a word I never connected with me."

"You wore that wonderful hair in an ugly bun and hid a perfect body under workman's clothes." He gently kissed her wounded thigh.

"Now I've been offered two hundred dollars for it."

"Not even an opening bid."

"And if your head moves one more inch you won't get me out to see whatever it is."

"I'll start a fire."

"Outside, not in here."

She was dressed by the time a few feeble flames licked at the twigs he used for kindling, and they went down to the pond. Hudson pointed out the image. Just then as they watched, a light breeze rose and the figure disappeared.

"And our Indian is hidden, like the mountain."

"So the deed is on the island?"

"I'll bet on it."

"How do we get to it? Swim?"

"Or wade. It's pretty close to the shore."

While Cilla cooked breakfast, Hudson followed a path that took him to the end of the pond opposite the island. From the shore the water looked no more than hip deep, though it was hard to tell whether or not it got deeper near the island.

They took little gear except Hudson's knife and the small folding shovel he wished were bigger. And a towel. It was chilly enough to make wandering around wet unappealing. Hudson took off his clothes and with Cilla on his shoulders holding them, started across toward the northeast corner of the island. Though the cold water nearly numbed his body, the footing was easy until they were about twenty feet from it.

"It drops off quite a bit," said Cilla.

"Keep your legs up. Let's not get the bandage wet." The frigid water came to his shoulders but no higher, and after a quick towel-off and with his clothes back on he felt warmer.

"Now where?" asked Cilla.

The island was a hill, a little more than an acre in size, populated mostly by softwood and shrubs. The side where they landed had a small flat area in the southeast corner. Other than that it rose on all sides to a point perhaps thirty feet above the level of the water.

"Look for a reference point. Some geologic feature that would be apt to survive for a number of years. A large rock if there is one."

There wasn't. They searched the entire island but could find nothing to guide a holder of the map.

"My guess is the flat area," said Cilla. "The clearing looks manmade, as though stumps and all were removed. Perhaps to plant something else." Hudson could come up with no better idea, so they dropped their gear and began to dig. The open area was only ten feet in diameter so they started in the middle and gradually widened the hole. The little shovel made progress slow, but by early afternoon they'd unearthed a few substantial rocks and nothing else.

They sat on the top of the island — the eye of the jellyfish map — with sandwiches for lunch, looking back down the grey-blue water of the little pond, crisply glistening in the late October sun, toward where their tent sat hidden behind trees. This area of the island was mostly open, with a scattering of winterberry bushes and small spruce trees. A tangle of underbrush nearly obscured the old stump of what had been a sizable tree.

"Do you suppose that was a tree when Gill was here?" There was no longer a suggestion of 'if' in Cilla's voice.

"Good thought. While a tree wouldn't have been chosen as the hiding place, the combination of tree and top of hill would have made good reference points. As a matter of fact, with nothing else available, the highest point on the island could be reference enough." He looked at her. "Shall we try a new dig?"

She nodded. "I think the first is a dry hole."

Hudson sized up the ground. "Assuming that tree was here, he'd have dug a few feet away to avoid roots."

"And on which side?"

"I'd guess facing Wabanaki Awiben, if we're locked into his thinking."

They took turns with the little shovel, and by late afternoon had a substantial hole dug.

Cilla leaned on an edge. "Shouldn't we have found it by now? Would he have gone deeper than this?"

"*He* mightn't. Layers of composting leaves, rotting trees and bushes may have built up. We've got an hour more daylight. Too late to start a third. Let's keep going."

There was momentary excitement several times when the shovel chinked against something hard, but each proved to be a rock. It was Cilla's turn in the now substantial pit.

"Hudson."

"Something?"

"Somebody's head."

"*What*?" He jumped down beside her.

"A little somebody. Made of something heavy. And I think I..."

Peeking through the dirt at the bottom was the head of a woman wearing a crown, on top of a veil that was pushed behind her shoulders. Further digging revealed she wore a robe which descended to her feet. She was seated in a massive chair and had a child on her knee. The whole statue was a little more than two feet high.

"The Madonna," announced Cilla. "The statue Kabir was after."

Hudson wiped away the dirt and scratched the surface with a fingernail. "Silver, all right."

Cilla's eyes were glowing. "A gift to the Abenakis from Chartres. Hundreds of years ago. When it left St. Francis our luck left along with it." She clapped her hands. "And now...!" A sudden doubt made her glance anxiously at Hudson. "I'm not wrong? It is the Madonna?"

He nodded. "It must be. This is what Pere Roubaud meant in the letter Kabir found. He kept the statue safe by arranging for Samuel Gill to hide it, probably putting a replica in its place as Becancour thought. Who would know there was a replacement? Holy objects aren't handled. Rogers Rangers stole a fake."

Reassured, Cilla joined in excitedly, "And Gill told Roubaud just enough about what he had done, so after Samuel died the rumors about Indian land and a hidden mountain started."

"Let's see what we've got."

It took a little doing. For its size, the statue was extremely heavy. Once uncovered, Cilla — with all her enthusiasm — could barely move it. Hudson lifted it clear of the pit and scrambled out after it. As he got to his feet there was the sound of an explosion from down the pond, and Hudson fell back on top of Cilla.

"Hudson! What happened?"

He was holding his left shoulder and grimacing with pain. "I think I've been shot."

"You're bleeding! Let me look at it!"

Blood was seeping through the fingers of his hand. "Not now. *Carefully* peek over the edge and tell me what you see. Christ, what am I saying. Stick the shovel up first and see if it draws fire."

She raised the tool. As it cleared the edge, a second bullet sent it flying. Cilla rubbed her hand and looked at Hudson. "Good shot. Would have air conditioned my head."

"From the sound, it's coming from down the shore near our tent. We *did* get careless. They must have found our tent off Nancy Pond Trail."

Cilla nodded. "And followed the trail."

"Yeah. To Carrigain. I'd forgotten the two connect. They'd come out on Sawyer River Road..." a spasm of pain crossed his face..." not far from our car."

"Let me look at you." Using his knife, she cut the shirt away from the wound, then tilted him forward. "There's an exit hole. Looks as though it went clean through." She eased him out of the rest of his shirt.

He flexed his arm. "Nothing's broken. I've got a handkerchief." He pulled it out of a pocket of his jeans. It was clean, and she placed it over the bleeding. Then cut strips from his shirt with the knife and wrapped them around his shoulder to hold the makeshift bandage in place.

Hudson had been thinking. "Wish I knew how many there are...Cilla, we've no weapons to compete with that rifle. We're going to have to give him a little overconfidence. Take off your shirt and stuff it with whatever you can find — the remnants of my shirt as a starter."

"And then?" She unbuttoned.

"We get you shot, too."

"So he thinks we're both down and climbs up to finish us off. At which point we break his neck."

"Something like that. The problem is they usually come in twos."

Cilla was stuffing the sleeves of her shirt with dirt. "Then we'd better have a plan for more than one...If they see two bodies, they won't be looking for anyone else."

"A dummy and me. Where will you be?"

"Wherever I can hide out there. It'll start to get dark soon."

"One reason they probably won't waste much time getting here."

"This shirt isn't going to fool anyone. It better have a bottom." Cilla took off her jeans and started filling the legs.

"You'll freeze."

She shook her head. "I'm too damn mad. Those bastards killed my father and have put us through hell. I can't wait to get my hands on them."

She used the knife to cut her belt in half and tie off each pant leg. The two then slid the dummy up the edge of the pit. The shot lifted the cloth of the shirt. Cilla screamed, and they let the 'body' drop to the ground just outside the hole.

"Think my sound effect was convincing?"

"Should think so. Scared the shit out of me."

Then all they could do was wait, hoping darkness arrived before the enemy. The temperature had dropped into the forties. Shirtless, Hudson was cold. But Cilla in just bra and panties seemed unaware. "How will they get to the island? The same way we did?"

"Probably...Listen!" The sound of a branch cracking came faintly. "They're moving along the shore. When they reach this end of the pond the island trees will hide us. You can slide out then."

Another ten minutes and they heard the sound of men's voices due east of them.

Hudson pulled Cilla down for a kiss. "Take the knife."

"What will you use? You're hurt."

"My right arm's okay. Get going."

She crawled out and down the westerly side of the little hill. Then circled back through the underbrush so she was behind bushes, only fifteen feet from the hole. Presently the voices came nearer. They were wading across to the northeast part of the island, the way they'd come. Suddenly there was splashing, followed by a string of curses.

"George? What happened?"

"*Merde!* It gets deep here. Keep your piece over your head."

Cilla froze. There was something in that voice. Something menacing...

"And shut up with the jabber."

More splashing. Then silence. Another five minutes and she heard them. She peered around the bush. In the gathering dusk she could make out two figures cautiously climbing the hill single file. She looked back at the hole. Hudson had kneaded the dummy into a fetus position and pushed it under bushes, so just where shirt and jeans met showed. They passed her only four feet away — two large men. The leader approached the pit where Hudson lay while the other circled to his right.

"Here's one!" said the latter in a loud whisper.

"And the other," said the leader. "Damn good shootin if I do say. And what in hell's this? A statue! Must be what we want. Meantime..." He raised his rifle and pointed it into the hole. "We'll just make...oop!" A hand reached out of the pit and grasped the rifle, pulling it and its owner in.

At the same time Cilla hit the other on the back of the neck as hard as she could with clasped hands. His heavy coat deadened the blow and he turned quickly, his rifle butt catching her on the side of her face. She collapsed in the bushes. Damn, she thought on the edge of consciousness. Should have used the knife.

"Fred! Over here!" The roar came from the hole. Fred scrambled over to it. Hudson had his right arm around the other's throat. Big as the man was, he was unable to break the hold and was gradually weakening. Cilla made it to her feet as Fred brought his rifle down on Hudson's head. He lifted it for another blow just as she shoved the knife into his back. He fell into the pit, taking the knife with him. The leader, released from Hudson's iron grip, clambered out coughing. He got to his feet, ham-size hands hanging like a gorilla. She kicked him hard in the crotch. He doubled up, and she kicked him harder in the jaw, sending him crashing to the ground. She jumped into the pit. Hudson was out cold. She shook him and got a groan.

"Hudson!"

She patted his face. His eyes blinked. "What...?"

A huge arm went around her shoulders and pulled her from the hole. "You bitch! I should have killed you before!" The big man threw her to the ground. As she scrambled to her feet, he put a hand on her throat and squeezed. With the other he ripped off her brassiere. "And now..." he grunted as she fought back. "Before I...Bitch!" Cilla kneed him but was unable to get enough force behind it. He squeezed harder. Cilla's senses were going. She felt herself thrown to the ground and the heavy body landing on top of her. A hand was pulling at her panties. Oh God, not again! she thought. Suddenly the pressure was gone. Through a haze she could see the giant form lifted clear of her body. Hudson!

Wounded shoulder and all he lifted the hulk as though it were a feather. A growl escaped his throat. With a savage movement he slammed the attacker to the ground. There was uncertainty in the man's eyes as he got to his feet. He turned to run. He'd gone fifteen feet when Hudson caught up with a hard blow to his kidney. The man fell again; got to his feet, was pounded with heavy blows to the body. Knocked down again by a vicious blow to his jaw. Tried to crawl. Hudson pulled him to his feet.

Cilla would never forget the picture silhouetted against the pond and the fading sunset. A half naked man standing with legs spread apart holding the huge body of her attacker over his head — a celebration of triumph at the finish of a jungle battle. The end was almost ceremonial; he went down on one knee and brought the hulk's back down hard on the other. There was a deadly snap. The body shuddered and lay still.

Cilla ran to him. He remained on one knee looking down at his victim. Then bent down and took the jacket and shirt off the crumpled figure as though they were the ears of a bull. Cilla helped him to his feet. Blood was oozing from his shoulder but not as badly as she had feared. He put the jacket around Cilla and shrugged into the shirt himself. With his right arm around her, and both of hers around him, they made their way back to the pit. The second man was gone. And so was the statue.

From down the hill they could hear splashing. It came from an area more to the south than the route the men had taken coming in. They followed the sounds. From the flat area on the shore they could see a figure struggling in water up to his waist. He was holding the heavy statue in both hands. No rifle was in evidence.

"I think he's stuck," said Cilla.

Hudson took off his boots. "It must be almost quicksand there. Maybe if I stay on the surface..." He launched himself into the water and in a few powerful strokes of his right arm pulled level. The man called Fred had made no progress. He couldn't seem to lift his feet, and the weight of the statue pressed him ever lower in the water. He saw Hudson coming, dropped the statue and thrashed frantically toward land. No matter how he struggled his feet were bound as if in cement. A blow from Hudson's fist ended his problem.

It was ten minutes work to free him from the muck. Another half hour's futile search found no trace of the statue. With Fred's wound bound and his arms tied to a tree, Hudson lay exhausted on the top of the island, his own wound tied tightly. He and Fred gave off an odd burned smell, apparently from the near quicksand.

"The man you...killed?" More execution, thought Cilla.

"Trimble."

"I knew him as Gagnon."

"You *know* him?"

She nodded slowly. "It's been coming clearer. Big. A lot of hair. It set off alarms in me. From ten years ago."

"He's the one who...?"

"Yes. I'd blocked it out. But I'm sure. I can see him bending over my mother..." She paused. "His name was Georges Gagnon. He lived right in the village."

"Bartlett?"

"Yes. He and his mother."

"But he's from Massachusetts."

"He wasn't then." She thought a moment. "They were only in town a year or so. Moved away shortly after... He fit in well with the local gang...They liked to make fun of my clothes."

"Your Indian clothes."

She nodded. "They were French-Canadian, the kids in the gang were. The only people lower on the social ladder were Indians."

"You and your mother."

"Yes."

"You think that's why?"

"I've always thought it was something like that." She exhaled. "If it hadn't been for my phony ethnic pride, it never would have happened."

"Hey. Ethnic pride is no reason for rape and murder."

"But don't you see, I flaunted my Indianness; became more Indian than a full blood." She turned her head away. "Mom would be alive today if..."

Hudson put his arm around her. "Maybe I did something like that too. The man who destroyed your family did the same to mine."

She turned quickly back. "Oh, Hudson. Here I am going on about things that happened long ago, and your wife...it's only been six months."

They were both quiet in their own thoughts for a while. Then Cilla said, "It's so frustrating to lose the statue. Just when we almost had the answer."

Hudson reached into the pit. "You mean this?" In his hand was a document.

There was just enough light for her to see the words, "By the authority vested in me by His Royal Majesty, George II..."

Chapter 26

"MY GOD! WHAT did you do to this guy?" John Krestinski was looking at the battered, twisted body of George Trimble stretched out on a table at North Conway's Furber and White Funeral Home.

"He made the mistake of attacking me," said Cilla coldly.

"*You* did this?"

She slowly shook her head. "Just the bruise under his jaw." She smiled faintly. "I think it was a wild animal did the rest."

"The wild animal that's getting his shoulder repaired at the hospital?"

She looked at Krestinski. "Hudson is the gentlest man I know."

"But...?"

"Are you married, Mr. Krestinski?"

"Yes."

"Do you love your wife?"

"Very much. But this...! It looks like he got in a cage between mating gorillas!"

She nodded. He stared at her a moment. Then called over one of the agents that had lugged the body out from Sawyer Pond. "What's the official cause of death?"

"Broken back. Internal organs are a mess. I guess they had a choice."

Krestinski folded his arms across his chest; tilted his head sideways and studied Cilla. "You *could* say it's our fault. We let Trimble slip." Apparently reaching a decision, he took her by the arm. "Let's go see King Kong."

Memorial Hospital was only a quarter of a mile away. Hudson was making his position clear to Doctor Evans.

"No way. Nothing good happens to people in hospitals."

"You've lost a lot of blood, young man."

"I've lost a lot of people in hospitals. And a hundred years ago in hospitals they considered the letting of blood a treatment." Hudson continued to dress.

"Not for a patient who'd just been shot." He spied Cilla and the FBI agent approaching. "A bullet and an arrow. Hadn't you two better stay out of the woods for a while?" They had seen no reason to disabuse Evans of a conclusion — however tenuously held — that Hudson's injury had been sustained while hunting. He peered at Cilla. "You didn't have that bruise on your face when I saw you. Is there a war going on out there?"

"Just carelessness." And stupidity, thought Cilla. But learning. The knife is mightier than the rabbit punch.

"Don't think I've seen anyone more 'careless' than our friend Fred in the next room. Must have fallen over backwards on his knife, wouldn't you say?" The doctor's tone was heavy with irony.

"I know it's confusing, Doctor," Krestinski took control of the conversation. "But you've done your duty and reported the accidents to the police. Let's leave it at that."

The older man shrugged and turned to Cilla. "No after effects from the poison?"

"None."

He nodded. He looked at Krestinski. "I assume you want to see your other 'hunting accident' now?"

"Yes. Are you finished with him?"

"He's all yours," Doctor Evans was giving ground none too cheerfully.

The agent on guard outside Fred's room opened the door for the three. Fred was lying in his side facing them. His eyes were closed. It had been a difficult trek getting Fred out to the car by flashlight. With the need to fight passed, and blood oozing from his own wound, Hudson had left their new tent where it was, along with most of their equipment. He gave Cilla the rope tied to Fred's bound wrists and devoted his remaining energy to hauling his own body down the trail by the flashlight's fading glow. They'd reached Krestinski by phone still in his office, and the agent had a crew into Sawyer Pond by daybreak.

Cilla made Hudson sit in the only chair the room offered. Krestinski didn't waste words. "Fred, you're in enough trouble to put you in prison for life. The only way you have a chance of seeing daylight again is to answer my questions."

Fred, whose last name was Dubois, opened pale blue eyes that looked as though they'd been washed with the colors instead of the whites. Though his driver's license put him still in his twenties, his face was grey and sagging. "I'm hurt. What do you want?"

"You're charged with attempted murder, assault with a deadly weapon and attempted kidnapping. How did you get into this mess? You work at Great Haystack, don't you?"

"When they's work, which they ain't much of lately. Been there twelve years. Cilla knows me." His Swamp Yankee whine ran the gamut of the tone scale.

"I recognize you now. You were on the ski patrol when I worked there," she looked at him with distaste. "You were a good skier. What happened?"

"They cut back on patrol. Economize they said. Dangerous I say. People gettin hurt..."

"How did you get involved with Trimble?" Krestinski broke in.

"George? Known him since school. He was Gagnon then. Till he moved down country. Is he dead?"

"Yes. Did he hire you for this?"

"He said he was after something, and others were after it too. Gave me some money to come along. He didn't say nothin about shootin."

"Then why did you bring a rifle?"

"I always got a piece; carry it in my pickup. Didn't use it though, you can check for yourself. Haven't fired it this week. It was George shot them two."

"And Floyd Carr?"

"What about him?"

"Were you working for him, too?"

"Sure. At the mountain when they's work."

"Did he know what you were doing with Trimble?"

"Naw. All he knows is business."

"How about Larry Cook."

Krestinski glanced at Hudson curiously.

"You goin to make trouble so I don't have a job?"

"Did he know Trimble?"

"I guess he knowed George, but he didn't know nothin about Sawyer Pond."

"And Bear Notch Road, where you committed an assault at the Wheaton house?"

"We was just goin to rough 'em up. Kinda a warning George said."

"Rough them up with chloroform?"

The head dropped back on the pillow. "Maybe I better get me a lawyer. I talk too much."

And with that he closed up. More questions were greeted with silence. In the hospital cafeteria Hudson handed the FBI man the paper he'd found and an explanation. "I drew the description of the deeded land on a map. Wabanaki Awiben is Owls Cliff and Mt. Tremont."

"Which we'll have to prove."

"There must be other references in historical documents. The peak behind it is Great Haystack, and Bartlett Lumber is right next door. According to the Hart's Location town clerk they're the only large properties involved. A couple of houses, but all the rest is National Forest. Carr has one of the big tracts and Larry Cook owns the other. When that deed is recorded whoever it is is blocked."

Krestinski read it over. "Well, it's a deed to Samuel Gill from Benning Wentworth, representing the English Crown, seventeen fifty-seven...'the lands deeded to said Samuel Gill and the Abenaki nation'...Gill to use his best efforts to bring peace...Signed, witnessed...All the elements of a legal deed. I'm not up on colonial documents, but this will certainly stir up the pot. What's your county seat, Ossipee? I'll get it down there this afternoon." He put it in his pocket and turned to Hudson. "Now tell me. Where did you find it?"

"While Cilla was getting in position for our visitors I examined the statue. The deed had been sealed in the bottom with wax."

"Trimble seems to have done all the dirty work," mused Krestinski. "Maybe we can get the one behind him for conspiracy."

Hudson shook his head. "Murder."

"Whose?"

"Chief Becancour."

"Trimble could have done that too. The night before he killed Mr. Wheaton and your father-in-law he could have been in Sorel eating with the Chief."

"Not Trimble. I think the Sorel trip was a last try that wouldn't have been entrusted to a numbhead like him. The murders show we're dealing with desperation. On the facts we have, it could be either Cook or Carr. The collapse of the housing market in the early nineties put most lumber companies in trouble — particularly the small ones like Bartlett Lumber. Some never recovered. Bartlett Lumber's only asset now would appear to be its land. It's got a lot of it, but it's been well logged and buyers for it were scarce. If they did find one it could be their last chance to bail out."

He turned to Cilla. "Would you say the same thing's true with Great Haystack? Fred is down to part time work with them. Sounds as though they may be suffering."

"Size again. Over the past ten years most smaller ski areas have gone out of business. They can't afford the investment in snowmaking, detachable quad lifts and stuff like that, that skiers are demanding."

"Then why would anyone want to buy Great Haystack? It's not exactly a small area, but it's no Vail with whole town attached."

"Potential. It could be a big area. It's actually built on Little Haystack mountain. Carr owns about two thousand acres right next door on Big Haystack."

"Why hasn't it been developed?"

"Money. The last few years haven't been good to him weatherwise. One was a disaster, it rained all Christmas week. And the Forest Service. Carr's land is mostly on the flat, it only runs halfway up the mountain. The top is all National Forest. They've practically frozen expansions in the White Mountains; it can be done, but it takes time and money — which Carr hasn't got."

"But the flat land could be a whole new resort village. Interesting enough to attract an international buyer?"

"I've walked it. It's great land."

"So Cook or Carr goes to Sorel. If Becancour couldn't be bought off, then the three would die the next day. They had to kill them all at once; one survivor would have been as dangerous to their plans as would three. They could see what had happened with the Mashpees and Passamaquoddies. As soon as word got out there was an Indian claim all land transfers would have been frozen until there was a settlement. That could take years."

"Trimble could have made that try."

"No, this was financial stuff, over Trimble's head. Remember the Chief's last words?" Hudson asked Cilla.

"'No better stock than Abenaki.'"

"Becancour spent a lot of time in the States. His English was good enough for him to make a play on words. He'd been offered *capital* stock in a corporation — maybe Great Haystack or Bartlett Lumber — if he would give up his potential claim. He was saying to Azo that Abenaki stock was better than that of a corporation — one Uncle Joe might have thought was financially shaky."

"That hypothesis's a bit shaky too."

"What other interpretation makes sense?"

"I'd hate to be the one selling it to a judge."

"You don't have to. It only convinces me there's someone behind Trimble who knows he's now vulnerable."

Krestinski pulled an ear lobe. "We're out of my jurisdiction up there. I suppose we could get some of our Canadian friends to trundle photos around Sorel restaurants. But six months is a long time. Most people can't remember a face from last week."

"So we make him come to us." Cilla said quietly.

"Exactly," said Hudson.

"Hold it." Krestinski leaned forward.

"We get word to Carr and Cook that we've got the deed," Hudson continued. "Today's Friday. The Registry will be closed over the weekend. On Monday we're going to record it. That will flush the guilty one, and the FBI nets him when he comes after us. What's wrong with that?"

"Two things come immediately to mind. There are probably a dozen more." Krestinski was having difficulty restraining his exasperation. "I think you both have a death wish. No, that's not point one. That's an observation. Here's one: what makes you think your behind-the-scenes man would risk showing himself? He's always worked through others before."

"Our boy can't afford the risk of others in on his plan. I don't know how much Fred and his other thugs know about what's going on. I'll bet nothing. Now he's lost Trimble, the one person who did know and who could be counted on for the dirty work." He looked at the agent.

"So you're saying with Trimble gone he has to come after you himself."

"Right."

"Why does he have to kill you?"

"Hopefully he doesn't. That's where you come in."

"No. That's point two. I can't protect you."

"Illegal, immoral or don't want to?"

"Can't. We're right in the middle of a major case in Massachusetts. The only reason I was allowed to run up here with a team was the connection with Cilla's kidnapping. The murders are a local affair. In any case we've got to be back in Boston tonight."

"And we've got to go for it anyway. Recording the deed may stop a sale, but this may be our last chance to get a murderer."

Krestinski sighed. "I suppose I can't stop all fools who want to put their heads in nooses. There are too many of them nowadays. I'll ask the local police."

"Not necessary..."

"Necessary. Or I take the deed and record it."

Hudson looked at Cilla and shrugged. "Can you get us a bug?"

"A what?"

"A listening device. Don't tell me all the detective stories I read this summer have it wrong. Something we can put in Fred's room to see if our plan is working."

"I think you read too many of them. You're going to have Fred overhear us saying you have the deed, and have him tell Carr."

"Or someone else on his crew."

"And Cook?"

"Fred works for him, too."

"Why not just put it on the radio? Or shout it from the street corners? Not convoluted enough for you? Spare me from chess players."

"It's got to be done quietly, John. Don't forget a rumor of a claim could do as much damage as the actual filing. And once he sees he's lost he might skip."

"So he comes slinking through the night to what? The Carver house?"

"It's where Fred will say the deed is."

"Then let the local police handle it. There's no need for you to be there."

"And if *he* has a bug in *that* house? Hey, I know it's unlikely. Maybe even ridiculous, but someone seems to have known a lot about our plans, and I sure don't want to lose the one chance we have of trapping him."

Krestinski rubbed his forehead. "So how do you get word to send someone to see Fred? Call and invite them?"

Hudson grinned. "Jungle telegraph."

It was a few minutes before five o'clock as Hudson swung open the door to the Bartlett Post Office.

"Well!" Emma Persons had key in hand. "What on earth have you been up to? Fall off a cliff?"

"A bad accident in the woods. George Trimble was killed. You know him?"

"Better than I'd want, not to speak ill of the dead. Used to be Georges Gagnon. A mean one he is, or was. You look as you should be in bed. What happened?"

"There was a misunderstanding. Fred Dubois was also hurt."

"Bad?"

"He's in Memorial Hospital."

"Poor Freddie. Never been the same since the fire at Spot."

"What?"

"Spot. Table Mountain you probably call it. You're going to have to learn the language if you're going to live around here." She eyed him. "Or *are* you planning to stay here? You've been away a spell."

"I'm back. At Wally Carver's place. I've a deed that needs to be recorded first thing Monday, but other than that I'm going to take it easy for a while there."

Emma studied him shrewdly. "With Cilla Wheaton I'll bet."

"Think she's too young for an old gaffer like me?"

"Not Cilla. In some ways she's older than you. Kid's had a tough life, as I guess you know by now."

"I do. I'm going to marry her, Emma."

"Well, hoo-ray! I've been hoping things would turn up for her. You must be quite a man to tame her."

"I hope she never is tamed."

"And so do I. That girl has what it takes. I want an invitation to the wedding. I've known her longer than most anyone."

"You've got it." Hudson hoped she'd gotten all the rest.

Chapter 27

CILLA PULLED UP the collar of her turtleneck. She could hear the wind tugging at the corners of the house like ocean waves lashing the shore. It was a cold wind, sweeping from Mt. Washington, and gusts pushed their way down the chimney making flames dance in the fireplace. The fire was atmosphere, eventually sucking more heat from the house than it produced. There was no need to shiver in this house. The heating system was good, and there was more than enough oil. Wally's 2,000 gallon tank had been filled the week before — with the little amount of winter usage Wally had given the house it was just the fifth such order since the property was built. Hudson had, in fact, had to show the driver the woods road on the south end of the property that served as access to the over-sized tank.

Cilla's shiver wasn't from the cold. Saturday had passed uneventfully as had the daylight hours of Sunday. Would he come? Someone had gotten the message all right. The 'conversation' arranged for Fred to overhear had been successful. He'd repeated word for word the story about the deed and its location to a 'visitor', who turned out to be the other man Hudson had seen at Great Haystack on his blueberry visit.

She was seldom impatient and never fearful. For herself. She now had someone else. She smiled at her thoughts, that she should be worrying about a man like Hudson — strong as an ox — who had proven he was more than capable of taking care of himself, and any others who happened to be around. But his shoulder had stiffened up, and his anger hadn't cooled. Cilla, for the first time in as long as she could remember, was at peace with herself. As was Tabi underneath. Most unexpectedly, she'd found a man — no, *the* man, for she couldn't picture another — who restoreth her soul. She paused at the thought. She had always been able to walk through the valley in the shadows and fear no evil. Was she now able to put trust in other men? She shook her head. No way. That would come much later, if at all.

She analyzed it. What was she fearful of. Two men from the Bartlett Police Department were hidden someplace outside. The Chief had supervised their posting. Granted they were 'specials', extras put on for part time work. But they were expecting only one intruder. There was general agreement that the one behind the scenes wouldn't want anyone else in on this errand. And the four of them were surely a match for one.

Yes, it was Hudson. She'd broken her protective shell and embraced another. Even the tiny chance that harm should befall him brought out strong protective instincts. She guessed some of it was selfish, like what others felt about the acquisition of material things. When they got them, they spent the rest of their lives worrying about losing them...There was truth to the Swami's philosophy that the only truly happy person is one who has nothing. Attachment to the things of this world causes worry. But with Hudson it was something else...something much more...

At eleven they banked the fire and mounted the stairs to what had been Wally's bedroom. Cilla still felt strange crawling into bed with a man, as she had the two previous nights, though they'd promptly crawled out to the darkened downstairs and sleeping bags — Cilla on the main floor, Hudson in the finished basement — leaving the bedroom lights on a timer to go off at midnight. Her spot was behind the couch in the big living room, from where she could see the french doors leading to the main deck, as well as the kitchen. The wind rubbed a tree against the building, and a dead branch skittered across the roof. They'd alternated naps during the day to stay alert during the hours most likely for a prowler. A sudden gust rattled the french doors. She didn't envy the men outside, though they were dressed for the weather.

Would it all be for naught? Maybe that was even for the best. Now that she had Hudson, did anything else really matter? She stretched out on her back. She could feel his hands on her, his fingers exploring her, and her becoming moist. Good God! She was Pavlov's dog responding to an imagined mental stimulus. Embarrassed, she curled up on her side and thought about the ashram. Warm feelings, but also a strangeness. It was no longer home. Home was here. She thought back to the first time she'd been here and the discovery of the X on the map where her father had died. Hudson had acted such a wimp — flabby body and humble spirit. How could this personality have cloaked the man she loved. But then she also knew the cold, witchy face she'd shown the world. And Hudson had just lost his wife whom he loved and on whom he'd come to depend. Did he love her, Cilla, as much? Was she just a rebound to him? She knew the answer before she'd finished the question. They had been bonded in battle, by a fire so intense it left no seam between them.

When had it started? For her it had come on the banks of the St. Francis

River with wind like a knife slicing its way down from the Arctic. It was not a wimp she saw, though he was lying nearly naked and helpless outside that gas-filled cabin. Perhaps the scene did tug at some motherly strings she hadn't known about. But the feel of his body against her own had nothing to do with motherhood. The flab was gone, and hard muscles rippled beneath the surface of surprisingly un-hairy skin — which for the first time made her embarrassed by the hair she'd allowed to grow on her legs. Though still unconscious, his arms had gone around her and pressed her to him. The feeling of protection they gave was exciting, even realizing it was meant for another.

And him. When had the spark of love been kindled in him? It was hard to say; he was by nature a person who protects, and that can obscure what else lies beneath. She thought that first kiss, in the sleeping bag at Nancy Pond before he was fully awake, had come as a surprise to him. It wasn't to her. She had been studying his face for an hour before his eyes opened. Would she have initiated it if he hadn't? No. She was quite sure of that.

A tenacious acorn, hanging on long after its relatives had fallen, lost its struggle with the wind and fell to the roof, rolling down and off the edge. She could hear the furnace come on. And the smell of oil. No. It wasn't oil. Gasoline. Gasoline? She quietly opened the door from the living room to the bottom floor. The smell was stronger. "Hudson?" she whispered. She heard a rustling but no response. The carpeted stairs gave up no sound as she descended. "Hudson, where are you?" As she reached the bottom of the stairs there was a crash and a thrashing around as though she'd come upon an alligator pen. Then the sound of a solidly connected blow. And Hudson's voice.

"There's a light switch next to you, Cilla. Let's see what we've got."

Light revealed Hudson standing in the middle of the room, blood seeping from his forehead — a chair overturned, a video camera and tripod on its side — but by the collar he held the slumped body of a stocky, red faced man dressed in dark clothes. It was Floyd Carr.

"You're hurt," she exclaimed.

"Forehead cut. Lot of blood; little damage."

"Is he dead?"

"Not yet. I want a few answers first. Get some water."

Cilla filled a plastic wastebasket in the downstairs bathroom and brought a hand towel to Hudson, who let the body drop to the floor and pressed the cloth to his wound.

"What happened? How did you get hurt?"

"He must have a key. There wasn't any noise." She looked at him skeptically. "And I might have closed my eyes for a minute," he admitted sheepishly.

She nodded. "You forgot you were shot only a few days ago." She noticed a large red can on the floor behind Carr. "Gasoline?"

"Don't strike a match. He's soaked the whole downstairs. I caught him coming out of the furnace room."

"Should I get the police?"

He shook his head and threw the contents of the wastebasket in the unconscious man's face. There were spluttering sounds.

"W...What?"

"Why, Carr?"

"What?...Where...?"

"You know where you are. I asked you a question."

Carr struggled to a sitting position. "What question? I don't have to talk to you. I..."

Hudson reached down with his good right arm and pulled Carr to his feet by his collar, then steadied him with his left hand. "Why. Did. You. Kill. My. Wife." Each word was accompanied by the slap of his open right hand across the man's face — right to left then left to right — and each harder than the one before.

Carr tried futilely to fend him off. "Stop! Stop! I didn't kill her!"

"You were there."

"I wasn't! I..."

Another slap. "You had to be. You followed us home and alerted Trimble by car phone when we approached the street he was waiting on."

"I didn't. I don't know..."

Slap. "You do and you did."

"Stop!" There was fear in his eyes, but bluster still on his tongue. "You have no right..."

Slap. "And you had no right to kill my wife. Or her father." He nodded toward Cilla.

"Trimble! It was Trimble! For God's sake! *I* couldn't have climbed Owls Cliff!" He stopped suddenly.

"Go on." Cilla's voice was cold and hard. "What about Owls Cliff?"

"I've said all I'm going to." Hudson raised his hand. "Go ahead, beat me up! I'm through talking."

"In that case." Hudson swung him around and encircled Carr's throat with his right arm. He applied pressure. There were sounds of choking; the body started to thrash frantically.

"Hudson..." It was almost a question from Cilla.

Rasping sounds from Carr.

"What's that?" Hudson asked interestedly. "Speak up." He eased the pressure.

"All right! All right!" He gulped air. "They gave me no choice. I *pleaded* with them. The Indians don't need my land. They're all up in Canada." The words were gushing now. "What did they want with a bankrupt ski area."

"Bankrupt?"

"We would have been. The washout..., the bank was on me..."

"You could have sold it," Cilla broke in. "With all the land on Big Haystack..."

"I *have* it sold! A Japanese group. They're going to sign a purchase and sale next week!" He looked frantically from one to the other. To Hudson, "They got interested last March. I was surprised myself, I didn't think they were still buying here. But they are, at least these people!" To Cilla, "Then I found your...father on my land with his damned instrument. Said it might not be my property after all. Crap! I spent fifteen years building it. He laughed at me! Can you believe that? He laughed. Said the mountain was going to be an Indian encampment. What could I do?" He turned to Hudson, his voice pleading. "Everything I own is in that ski area."

"You could have discussed it rationally, instead of..."

"I tried! I went down to see your father-in-law in Marblehead. I *begged* him just to give me *time!* Let the Japanese buy it. Then he could do as he liked."

"And he told you to take a hike."

"Stubborn old farts. All of them. I offered Chief Becancour a share of the business. Stock in Great Haystack! Would have been worth real money when the Japanese buy. Did it on my own! What did they have, a worthless piece of paper. A draft for Christ's sake of a deed! And no guarantee there *was* a deed. And I offered him a share of my business that I'd worked years..."

"And he turned it down, so you poisoned him."

"You can't prove that. You can't prove I did anything."

"Let me tell you what I *can* do. There are two policemen outside. For starters I can have you held on a charge of attempted murder; the gasoline can and your presence here will keep you safe and sound while we arrange to have Chief Becancour's body exhumed for traces of poison. That's one murder you committed all by yourself, and there'll be people in Sorel who will have seen you together the evening of April thirtieth." Carr's eyes flickered, and Hudson could see him searching for holes he could crawl through. "However. I don't have much faith in our present court system. You might find a way to con a jury. So I'd much rather you just confessed, while we make a videotape that it's of your own good, repentant nature and free will."

"Hah. Call your officers. I'll talk through my lawyer."

"I think you misunderstand the situation. You are not in control of it. There is a way I can guarantee punishment for what you've done to my family and Cilla's."

"What do you mea...n...?"

"You've undoubtedly seen movies or on TV how simple it seems to be to break a neck with a sharp twist of a head." Hudson's tone was conversational.

"What...?"

"I've always been curious if it is really that easy, but opportunities to practice that sort of thing are rare, and one hasn't presented itself to me. Until now."

"You...can't seriously..." Carr backed away.

"I've never been more serious."

"But that would be *murder!*" A horrified gasp.

"Oh I don't think people would see it that way. An intruder in my house. Spreading gasoline. We fought, I have no weapon." He moved closer. "I think..." Carr opened his mouth to yell. Hudson jammed the end of the towel in it and pushed him into a chair. He stepped behind it and put Carr's head in a lock. "Let's see now...a quick snap and..."

Frantically Carr pulled the towel from his mouth. "No, no, no! Don't! I'll tell you everything! *Please!* I promise!"

"Control yourself, Floyd. You're wetting my chair. Would you like to speak to us?"

"Yes! Yes! Please let go of my head."

"Cilla, put that camera on him. It's all set to go." She righted it and adjusted the tripod. "Now, Floyd, I'm going to take my hands away and step out of the picture. You just tell us what you've done in your own words. If you falter, it will be my turn to practice. Ready Cilla? Camera. Action!"

"I...Where should I start?"

"Why don't you give us your name."

"Floyd Carr."

"Now tell us what you've done."

"Ah...Trimble..."

"No. Not Trimble. What *you've* done. Start with your visit to Chief Becancour on April thirtieth."

"We had dinner. I pointed out to him that he might never find the *real* deed, but his searching could be fatal to *my* plans."

"Why is that?"

"Business deals are delicate. In areas where Indian claims have been made all transfers of property have completely stopped. For years! Whether the Indians won or not! Even a *rumored* claim would scare off my buyers. Who would buy with the possibility of losing it after putting in money?"

"But you got another 'no'. Not much of a salesman were you?"

"Damned old fool. I offered him something *real*. Not an Indian fable."

"So you poisoned him."

"I...I was angry. I gave him something to make him feel sick. So he'd understand how *I* felt."

"So sick he died. Is that how bad *you* felt?"

"That was an accident! He must have had a weak heart. I never meant to hurt him. I *liked* him!"

"Cilla, this makes me feel all warm inside. Let's take a break...sorry, Floyd." The smile didn't rise above his lips. "I just want to give you a big hug."

"All right! All right!... It was him or me. I *had* to stop him or I was *ruined*! You can see that."

"So you killed him. Then what did you do?"

"I called Trimble, told him...the Chief had suffered a heart attack." He looked at Cilla. "He couldn't wait to...take care of your father. I don't know what he had against him."

"That he was my father." Carr stared at her uncomprehendingly. "Tell me exactly what happened."

"You sure you want...?"

"Yes."

"Well...Trimble called him that night and told him we were ready to make a deal, and that I asked him — Trimble — to go look at the line described in the deed. The next morning Wheaton took him up Owls Cliff. Said he and the Chief had figured out that the line runs through there and Mt. Tremont before cutting over to my place." He stopped.

"And then he killed him."

"He bungled it. It was supposed to look like an accident. They *all* were. He said there was a fringe of saplings there so he couldn't just push him off. He had to *throw* him. Stupid clod. That's a sheer cliff! He could have found another place on it without trees."

"And the stake."

"Yes! He was so eager to murder your father he didn't wait for his explanation! He never knew about the stake. I had to send him back for it."

"After you found we'd seen it."

"Yes."

"Then you drove to Massachusetts."

"We had to rent a bigger car. Trimble only had a little Honda. We followed you to the restaurant. On the way found the perfect spot for Trimble to wait on your drive home."

"Which we never reached," said Hudson softly. "Then you sent Fred and the others to kill us."

"No! Those were Trimble's friends! They did what *he* told them to. Sure, some of them worked for me. But I didn't send them after you. They didn't know I even knew Trimble...May I use the bathroom?"

"I suppose it's that or replace the chair. Go ahead. You can't get out the window."

Carr went into the downstairs bathroom and closed the door. Cilla shut off the camera. "Suppose he'll do something to himself?"

"Do you care?"

She shook her head wearily. "I just want it over."

The toilet flushed, and the door opened. Carr came out with a cigarette in his hand.

"Hold it...!" Hudson was a second too late. Carr dropped it on the floor. There was an explosion of flame which quickly leaped across the large open area. Within seconds the room was a sheet of fire. Carr made for the back door, pulled it open and went through on the run. Hudson's first thought was Cilla — the flames had leapt up around her. She darted away from them. Hudson picked up the towel and smothered some that were licking at her jeans. "Get to the phone. Nine, one, one. There's an extension in that room. Carr won't get far."

He took the wastebasket and filled it from the bathroom tub. Leaving the water running, he emptied it on the flames and went back for a second as a louder explosion came from the furnace room.

There were sounds of yelling outside, then shots. Cilla finished her call and took the wastebasket from the spare bedroom.

A policeman poked his head in the door. "We...shee-it!" He dashed out again.

Hudson and Cilla alternated filling at the tub. The cop returned with a garden hose he'd attached to an outside spigot. Between the three of them they got the fire under control before the fire department arrived. As they peered at each other in the smokey room, the second policeman staggered in looking dazed, and they sent him out to the road to tell the fire trucks many thanks but they wouldn't be needed. The fire had been its fiercest in the furnace room, nearly consuming a timer that had apparently been attached to a small explosive device. This was the conclusion of the fire chief, who said he had to make an inspection whether the fire was out or not. The younger policeman had received a blow on the head much like Hudson, though not as bloody.

There was a body outside. It was Floyd Carr. And he was definitely dead.

Chapter 28

"WELL TELL US how you two got together?" Lois Gately's slow drawl carried above the murmured conversations of the group that gathered at the Carver house for the coming out of Cilla Wheaton, the coming alive again of Hudson Rogers and the announcement of the engagement of the two. "Looks like the young lady beat you up." Don Gately's wife had a dry, amused voice that started on high C and eased its way down to F.

"They let her out without her collar," Tanya Shaw — Cilla's dearest friend from the ashram — murmured in a low voice. The surface Lois was much as Cilla would have pictured Sylvia, attractive, at ease in social situations, but she was sure the similarity ended there. Hudson could never be married to someone with the sharp tongue of his former partner's wife.

"She fought me off for a while, the mountains gave me staying power. When are you going to get out hiking, Don?" Hudson turned the conversation.

"He doesn't have an inheritance from a wealthy father-in-law to let him wander the woods in a pair of shorts. Isn't that right, Donald?"

"We could get out more, dear. Maybe Hudson will invite us up skiing."

He'd be more apt to invite John Krestinski, thought Cilla, studying Gately's graying hair and face and tentative body movements — a little like Hudson in June. The FBI man, in conversation across the room with his wife and the Larry Cooks, had become a friend, one who fit more with the new Hudson — who despite wounds and bandages gave the feel of an athlete-in-prime — than did the Gatelys.

"And freeze our little buns off? Are you two really going to hide away in this godforsaken wilderness?"

Hudson exchanged grins with Kabir, who was pouring cider for John Fanstock and his wife.

"This is home to most of these people, honeybunch," quickly put in Don Gately. "I'm sure they don't share your thoughts about it."

Emma Persons, in a group with Augustus Mooney and Bartlett Police

Chief Carl Solomon, whose men had brought in Carr's body, winked at Hudson. "The way we look at it, God forsook the flatlanders. Wilderness is how we like it."

There was a knock at the door, and Doctor Evans came in. "Sorry to be late." He shrugged out of his coat. "Looks like day out there with all those lights." Two dozen floodlights illuminated the Carver house and grounds. Wally had loved the woods, wanting to be able to see them night or day. From Swallow Hill Road it could have been an alien spaceship about to blast off.

As if his arrival was a signal, Cilla went round the large living room offering fresh glasses of cider or wine. Lois Gately carried a vodka martini. Tanya Shaw carried a purring Juniper.

"Are we going to get a peek at that draft?" Larry Cook asked Hudson. Not many of the details had become public, but Larry's bank as holder of the Great Haystack mortgage had held worried conferences after the Abenaki deed was recorded.

Hudson opened a desk drawer and handed the paper to the banker. "It's not much like the executed deed, all scratched out and written over, but it's what got Wally started. We just followed after."

"How did Wally get it?" asked Augustus Mooney.

"Don't know. Tracing the genealogy of a Wentworth family descendent, I'd bet."

"What's Wabanaki Awiben?" asked Emma Persons, reading over Larry's shoulder.

"An old name used to describe Mount Tremont and Owls Cliff," said Hudson. "Wally'd never heard it either, so he asked Cilla's father. Between him and Kabir's father they figured it out."

"May I see," asked John Fanstock. He held it almost gingerly. "So this is what Carr was after."

"That was just a clue pointing in a dangerous direction for him. It was the deed itself he needed to destroy."

"Because it included Great Haystack."

"Right. Just when he'd found a way out of the ski area's problems."

"After the rainout a while back," said Emma. "We all wondered if he could survive that."

"Luck was on his side, for a while. He needed someone to bail him out, and at the end of the winter he came across a buyer — a Japanese firm interested enough to start negotiations."

"Damn," said Fanstock. "Japanese, huh. I didn't know they were back buying here. With all the problems they've got..."

Hudson gave a half smile. "Carr was probably rubbing his hands with anticipation on the very day last April he found Ben Wheaton surveying a line east of the ski area. Ben's problem was he was too up front with people. He also didn't like Carr. I think he took some pleasure hinting that Great Haystack might be Indian land. It was a mistake. That would result in five murders."

The room was suddenly quiet.

"Five murders?" Don Gately was stunned.

"Carr poisoned Chief Becancour in Canada and had Trimble kill Ben Wheaton and drive a car into the one Wally, Sylvia and I were in. All supposed accidents."

"What went wrong?"

"Unfortunately for him, Trimble wasn't the most gifted of God's creatures in the thinking department. He made a mistake that made Cilla suspicious. He had Wheaton accidently fall off a cliff where he couldn't have fallen off by accident.

"And I had come across a map at Wally's the three had apparently used. After Wally, Ben and the Chief determined that Mt. Tremont and Owls Cliff formed Wabanaki Awiben, Chief Becancour identified it with an 'X' on the map I found and labeled it with an Abenaki word — sort of planting his totem." Hudson fell silent. Cilla slipped over to him and took his hand in hers.

"You said *five* murders." Dr. Evans had been listening intently.

"Cilla and I and her cousin Kabir thrashed around trying to piece together what had happened to their fathers and my father-in-law. Along the way we enlisted the help of Wally's attorney, Lander Margate. I asked too many questions and was lucky to escape an attempt on my life in Canada...Trimble had a French-Canadian heritage and had no difficulty melting in with the people there while following me. Margate wasn't so fortunate. Trimble got to him in Marblehead and drowned him."

Doris Cook shivered. "What a dreadful man, Trimble. How did you catch him?"

"He caught us. With the help of a two hundred and thirty something year old map we found the deed. Trimble had been following and tried to take it from us. We had a disagreement. He lost."

"A disagreement," said Don Gately looking at Hudson's bandaged shoulder.

"And Carr?" Dr. Evans would make a good stage prompter.

"He'd passed from desperate to frantic. The thugs he'd used were all friends of Trimble's, part of the gang he'd run in at school. None of them knew Carr was involved. To keep it that way he had to go it alone. He tried to get rid of both of us and the deed at once. He caught me dozing and sprayed the downstairs with gasoline, timed to go off after he'd gotten well away from the house. He was shot making his escape."

There was a burst of conversation. Most had pulled up chairs to listen to Hudson, and now chattered excitedly with their neighbors.

"What happens to the ski area now," asked Don Gately.

"Larry?"

"We've put someone in to run it this winter. The next move is up to the courts. The Abenaki deed is apparently genuine."

"So Carr was the leader; the one who planned it all," said Don.

"No."

"Trimble was a numbhead! You said so!"

"There was always something else. Rounded corners where there should have been sharp edges. The whole thing showed an inordinate fear of Indian claims. Almost as if someone had been burned before by them." He looked around the group. Someone changed position. "John Krestinski did some checking, and low and behold there *was* someone. Larry, you came here from Maine, right?"

"Yes, I was with a bank there."

"A bank that got caught in the Passamaquoddy suit."

"Sure. We were tied up for years."

"A bank you owned stock in."

"I had some, but..."

"Just as you do in Bartlett Lumber Company. How much do you stand to lose this time?"

"A lot. But I won't. We have a purchase and sale agreement, thank God. The Nature Conservancy's buying all our land."

"You knew Carr also had a buyer?"

"Yes, but I didn't know anything about the Indian claim."

"Can you say the same, John?" This to the real estate agent.

"I knew you were going to get to me! No, I didn't know a damn thing about Indians. You're just ticked at me for the things I said about your...the Wheaton girl here. Well maybe I was a bit out of line. People change. She was pretty kooky when she was young. No offense, Ma'am."

"None taken." Cilla smiled. "Kooky's okay."

"You *did* know something about what was going on. I got a copy of the deed of the Great Haystack land to Carr. You're on it as witness."

"Sure, I sold it to him. No crime in that."

"You were spooked when I mentioned Wheaton's stake on Owls Cliff.

So you told Carr about it."

Fanstock rubbed his nose. "Carr had the wind up. I didn't know what about. Came to me practically wringing his hands. He said Wheaton had found a problem in the title, not only to the land I sold him but the land all around the ski area, and he was going to hold me liable for the part he bought through me if it proved true. Owls Cliff is in the next range to Great Haystack. What was I to think? Sure I was nervous about Wheaton and told Carr what you'd found. Wouldn't you have?"

"Maybe that was one reason you came down hard on Cilla?"

"If I never heard the name Wheaton again..."

"But the one who knew the Wheatons best was their next door neighbor." Hudson turned to the postmaster.

"Since before Cilla was a wink in her daddy's eye," said Emma Persons.

"I think you know a lot more about a lot of things than you let on. Gossip runs quickly through a small town like Bartlett. But I had to be *sure* word would get to Carr and one other person that Cilla and I and the deed were here over that weekend. It was our last chance to catch him. Did you call them directly?"

Emma folded her arms on her chest. "I'm not saying I did. But what of it? It's what you wanted, isn't it?"

"You called me, Emma," said Larry Cook. "Was I the other suspect, Hudson?"

"A lot of things pointed to you, Larry. And yes it did work, Emma. Carr came. But the manner of his coming made no sense. The question was not only *how* did he have a key to the back door but *why*? Had he known days or weeks ahead that he might need it and snuck in here while I was away to have one made?"

"Maybe planning ahead," offered Dr. Evans. "In case you *did* find the deed."

"And what did he do when he came? He set a silly little fire that three of us put out in ten minutes. Would any sane man think he was going to destroy us and the deed with that? Would he leave something that important to chance?"

"Sounds more like Trimble than Carr," said John Fanstock.

"Trimble," Hudson shook his head. "For a long time I couldn't understand why *he* was involved. He was from Massachusetts and seemed to have no connection to Mount Washington Valley. I found out why last week." He glanced at Cilla.

"Murder," said Cilla quietly. "Ten years ago he murdered my mother."

"George Trimble? He did it?" Emma Persons' eyes narrowed in thought. "He wasn't Georges Gagnon then, was he?" Cilla nodded. Emma threw back her head. "Oh my! I should have guessed it." She brought her head forward with a snap. "Then he also..."

"He probably hadn't intended it to go that far," said Hudson looking straight in Emma's eyes. "He was a big kid who wanted to bully the only people in town he considered on a lower level than himself."

"Some big kid!" said Don. "Who liked to go around murdering people."

"He may have enjoyed it, but that's not why he continued murdering. He was being blackmailed."

"By Carr."

"Carr didn't know about Cilla's mother."

"How do you know?" asked Don.

"He told me. In his confession just before he bolted."

"Can you trust that?"

"Sure. He was *looking* for reasons to blame Trimble."

"Georges was a loser all the way," said Emma Persons. "He *did* leave town soon after the murder. I never connected it."

"Had to leave, and..." He shook his head. " Strange the way the human mind sometimes works. He blamed Cilla for it. So much so that he shot her with a poisoned arrow. Give the Indian a touch of her own medicine. All other deaths had been carefully arranged to look like accidents. There was no way a death from an arrow in a leg or an arm wouldn't be highly suspicious."

"Things are making a little more sense now," murmured Dr. Evans.

"So you're saying somebody brighter was involved," said Don. "Somebody not Carr, who was blackmailing Trimble."

"What convinced me was Lander Margate's death. How would Carr have known he was even involved? Margate never came to New Hampshire — didn't even know what Wally was working on."

"You going to tell us who did?" asked Fanstock. "Or don't you know?"

"I know. I'm almost sorry I do."

Don Gately leapt to his feet. "Jesus Christ! It's someone here!" He looked wide-eyed from face to face, as if expecting the word 'guilty' to be emblazoned on the forehead of one of them.

Heavy velvet curtains might just have been drawn across the room. The group sat still as statues, all staring at Don, who sank back in his chair, no one willing to look at a neighbor. Lois Gately pressed her hands tightly together. Outside an oak creaked in the November night wind.

Hudson nodded at the sound. "It all came down to a tree. Wally planned his house to fit in with its surroundings, not usurp them. He also changed some of his plans as he went along. Originally he was going to install a gas furnace, but along the way changed his mind and switched to oil. That was Carr's downfall. His foolish fire should have been deadly — open gas line, fumes filling the house before the timer went off. And it again might have been considered an accident. What a shock it must have been to him to discover an oil furnace. Why did he think it was gas? Someone got a look at Wally's early plans. Coming from the city where gas arrives in a line, I never knew what a country gas truck looked like until I saw one. As I'm sure most of you know, they're big, like oil trucks. There's a beech tree next to the front driveway with a limb that extends across it. Wally would never cut it, even though cars can barely scrape under. A gas truck couldn't have. Yet Mr. Mooney told me he'd seen one right out front of the house, a physical impossibility."

"I could have been wrong. It might have been the telephone company." Mooney sat stolidly in his chair.

"That's what you should have said. You weren't feeling the need to think it through just having met me. And why fib at all? I think it shook you to find someone at the house who knew Wally well enough to notice the house had been searched. There wasn't much out of place, but it was more than Wally would have permitted.

"Which took me to the next step, keys. It would have made sense for Wally to have left a set with the next door neighbor. As a matter of fact, I can't picture him *not* taking that simple precaution. In case of a problem at the house they'd be right there. Available for searching the place. And loaning to Floyd Carr."

"This is nonsense, you know." The old man was upright. "What reason would I have to hurt Wallace, or any of the others?"

"Money. Same as Carr. I think we'll find *you're* the real owner of Great Haystack. Carr didn't have a dime when he arrived here. He was from Greenwich, Connecticut so everyone thought he did. But my friend John Krestinski found he was divorced just before he left and provided a financial statement for the court there showing a net worth of less than twenty thousand dollars. The money for Great Haystack came from you. Money you were ready to murder for."

"Bullshit!" Mooney exploded. "I've had enough of this. You haven't got one damn thing to back up what you're saying. I'm leaving."

Krestinski sauntered over in front of the door. "If he doesn't, he's building you some strong grounds for a suit. And I'll testify for you. So why don't we let him dig his grave."

Mooney glared at the Bartlett Police Chief who looked away. He sat down. "I want you people to mark what's said here. You'll all be subpoenaed."

"I didn't want to believe it was you, Augustus. I'd actually begun to feel quite neighborly. You're right, proof has been hard to come by. You've covered your tracks well. But there are indications. The instructions to kill Margate must have come from you. You either overheard my telephone conversation or called the operator after I'd gone, to ask for the charges, and the number.

"Complete and utter speculation. Even if I were involved, why on earth would I want to do away with this Margate person?"

"I hate to think it, but it was a foolish little comment I made about being ordered to bring Cilla to Massachusetts — said only to spare Dr. Evans' feelings — that convinced you Margate was the motivating force behind me. You'd undoubtedly heard his name from Wally. You saw me as a pussycat. And you were right. My world had fallen apart, and I hadn't the stomach for putting it together. But you were wrong on Margate. He was an administrator, but not a leader in this."

Mooney twisted his head. "Carl, have I got to sit and listen to this?"

The Police Chief puffed out his cheeks. "I'm taking notes, Augustus."

"There were other things. I showed you the map with Owls Cliff identified. Carr followed me to Lost Pond to make sure I was away from the house while you nipped in and took it. He was no hiker. He damn near had a heart attack from that little walk.

"Then an English couple stopped by the house to ask for directions. Why did they come all the way down here to the end of the road when you were in your front yard raking leaves? Answer: because even though a wind had come up that threatened to scatter the leaves, you'd gone inside to telephone Trimble and set his thugs in wait for us at Cilla's house. It took me a while to understand why they were at Cilla's instead of here. But she'd *told* you we'd be going there to pick up her clothes. Perfect. You didn't want any violence right next door to you.

"You lived on the Cape, Augustus. What does the name Mashpee mean to you? Plenty I'd bet. John Krestinski found you were a big loser when the Indians there laid claim to land you tried to sell."

The older man stared straight ahead as though nothing of interest was being said. "It's true. I lost a little money there, but that's life. I laughed it off."

"Marie Delacroix. Did you laugh her off too?" Cilla broke in, her eyes pinning Mooney in his chair. "That cute French-Canadian visiting on the Cape who refused to have an abortion." Mooney closed his eyes. "No matter how much you offered her she was going to have your child. This was a real problem." Her voice was cold and sarcastic. "Illegitimacy carried a bit more of a stigma then, and Marie wanted a husband not money. But there was already a Mrs. Mooney, wasn't there? So this wasn't an option for you even if you'd been willing to marry her, which I doubt."

Mooney drew back in his chair, as Hudson took over, calmly but with steel in his voice, "So you found a husband for her who was more than willing to take money to marry a good looking girl. His name was Rene Gagnon. He came from Lynn, and the child was named Georges. Fifteen years later, after Rene died, Marie and he moved to Bartlett to bleed you for more money. Was some of his rage against you? Rage that built up to an atrocity against Cilla's family?

"Did he come to you with what he had done, or did you suspect from the fury built up in him? An unstable kid with a grudge. In any case you shipped the two of them back to Lynn and found Marie another husband. But young George Trimble — murderer — was now yours to command, and ten years later you did."

There was complete silence, as the group waited for Mooney's reaction. It wasn't long coming. He opened his eyes and looked over at the Police Chief. "All right. I covered up for George back then. And I suppose that's a crime, even if it is your own flesh and blood involved. He was wild. I couldn't control him then, and it's absurd to think I could now. What he did he did himself and with Carr. Yes, I have stock in the ski area. A lot of it. But there is absolutely nothing to connect me with any of the horror the two of them created. They committed the five murders. You, yourself said that."

"Not exactly." A man entered the room and spoke quietly in Krestinski's ear. The FBI man looked at Hudson and nodded. "I imagine about now Chief Solomon is beginning to have second thoughts about his old friend. He told you about the trap being set here for Carr, didn't he?" The policeman rested his forehead in his hand. "Even where his special officers would be stationed. Carr had lost his head. Panic had left him useless to your plans and a danger to you personally. You made sure he could never implicate you. It wasn't Carr who knocked out one of the cops, it was you. You took the unconscious man's pistol and when Carr ran out the back door and the other fired at him, you used the weapon to make sure he was dead.

"You left the pistol there, thinking the policeman wouldn't know exactly what had happened when he recovered consciousness. He was new to the force — his first encounter with a real live criminal. He'd be embarrassed he'd been ambushed and, since Carr had been stopped, there was no reason to say anything about it."

Chief Solomon stared at Hudson. "Kevin said nothing about finding his pistol fired."

"For the very good reason that he didn't find his pistol. He never thought of it when he staggered into the house or when he went out to Swallow Hill Road to meet the firemen. It was only later he found his weapon was gone, but by then he couldn't find the place he'd been stationed."

"So he left without his pistol and didn't tell anyone?" Solomon was incredulous.

"I found it the next morning lying in plain sight. I apologize for not getting right on the phone to you about it. Frankly I thought you might be involved with Mooney."

"I might as well have been," muttered the policeman.

"How were you to know. Mooney fooled everyone. What I did do was give it to John Krestinski. He checked it for fingerprints."

"No one nowadays would leave fingerprints on a gun," exclaimed Lois Gately. "Not if they've ever read a detective story."

"And Mr. Mooney is anything but foolish. But he wasn't used to murdering people himself. Have you ever tried to shoot a pistol with gloves on? Unless they're the surgical kind, it's difficult to get them through the trigger guard. He may even have tried. But when you do force your finger in, the glove reduces accuracy, and that's one thing he couldn't sacrifice."

Krestinski said, "There was evidence the pistol had been wiped off. But it was a sloppy job as though done in the dark, and one print remained — perhaps ignored from fear of an accidental firing. When Cilla brought you another glass of cider, Mooney, we lifted the prints off your old one. Can you think of any reason your print would be on the trigger of special policeman Kevin Abbott's pistol?"

With a bull-like roar, Mooney launched himself at Hudson, his hands reaching for his tormenter's throat. Cilla kicked him in the knee and chopped hard on his neck with the side of her hand. He crashed to the floor, and before he could rise, Krestinski and Solomon each had him by an arm.

The Police Chief could be heard telling Mooney his rights as the old man was led stumbling from the house.

"So the villain is unmasked, and they lived happily ever after," said Don Gately.

"Hold on." Dr Evans was still in his chair thinking. "If Carr and Margate were murdered, that makes six. You said five murders."

"My compliments, Doctor. You're right on the ball. That was the part that had me scratching my head. Mooney is no dummy, but he didn't seem to learn from his mistakes. He put warning notes on the door for Wally, who ignored them. Once I became a person instead of a widowed wreck, the note put on the door for me just got me angry. Mooney could see that, that I was going to come after him even harder. Then why kidnap Cilla? I had just about decided to give it up. The finding of the deed and the solution to a series of murders became unimportant compared to losing her. How many poisoned arrows or automobile accidents would she find happening to her if I continued to push. I told Margate that. Told him I was going to quit. That night she was kidnapped. Why?

"The only answer to that was, someone wanted me to continue, not stop. So I came to Margate. Plough was his agent — wouldn't even acknowledge me, I wasn't the client. The owner of the clinic she was taken from was his man; only he could have arranged *that* smoothly. It was a desperate move, and it worked. It made me realize I couldn't just walk away from it all. Cilla and I would never be safe unless we got to the killers. All along I was being motivated, directed on a course someone wanted me to follow. Margate?"

Hudson looked out the french doors. "Living here has been a strange experience. Things kept disappearing or being moved. I've heard thumps inside, seen trees outside wave without wind. At times it almost seemed as if I wasn't alone in the house. As a matter of fact, right now I can look out and see by the trees that there are lights on downstairs, and I didn't turn them on."

"Sure, they go on by sound," Don Gately was grinning.

"No, these were turned on by human hand. Shall we just take a look?" He walked to the door to the lower floor and opened it. "Will you come join us?"

The group looked blank. Don and Lois gasped, as up the stairs came an elderly man with greying hair but a firm, precise step. He stopped at the top and put out his hand.

"You burned hell out of my old office, Hudson."

"Good to see you too, Wally."

Chapter 29

"THE HEADLIGHTS GAVE it away." Wallace Carver was in his favorite chair, the bemused group around him. "I saw the other car flick them on just before he hit us. I shouted at you, Hudson, almost as we crashed." He stopped, and his eyes looked beyond the horizon. When he continued his audience had to lean closer to hear him. "How many times over the past months have I wished I had been in the passenger seat instead of Sylvia." Then he seemed to gather himself. "But I was sitting in the rear behind you and never even lost consciousness. Sylvia took the full force. She died instantly." He put a hand on Hudson's arm, though whether seeking or giving support was not clear. "You weren't hurt too bad; I'm not a doctor, but I can feel a pulse. From the headlights it was obvious to me the collision was intentional, and after the notes I'd received, I could guess its reason. But who was behind it, and what could I do about it? What I *did* was a plan born in desperation."

He took a breath. "Men think of themselves as immortal until they reach sixty. At seventy-five you know you're never going to run a marathon. Or hunt down a murderer. Joe and Ben and I had hit a nerve. The trouble was I didn't know whose. We had just figured from the way the line ran that Great Haystack was involved. But so was Bartlett Lumber, and there were probably others. Somebody was so panicked by our research they'd tried to kill me. And instead had..." His voice drifted off. Then stronger again...

"As long as I was alive I would be a target — yet I had nothing but suspicions to go to the police with. Sitting in that wrecked car, I decided to be dead." He looked into Hudson's eyes. "My only chance — *the* only chance to avenge Sylvia's death and catch a murderer — was you, and let me tell you that was one hell of a long shot. You were soft; the comforts of married life had put a pot on your stomach and dulled your reactions. Why I'd even taken a few games of chess off you. I'm pretty good, but I was never in your league in that foolish game. Yet it was that chess mind I needed. The mind that created the puzzles that made your business with Don a success would have to work out the puzzle of who had 'killed' me. Would you crawl into a shell with the loss of Sylvia, or would you take control of your life? From that day on, all I could do was push with a long pole from offstage. The rest was up to you."

Hudson grinned. "Or Cilla as it turned out. I'd still be a vegetable if it hadn't been for her."

Cilla smiled and gave an almost imperceptible shake of her head. Carver continued.

"The car phone still worked. I called Margate." Carver paused. "Probably signed his death warrant at the same time."

"That was me, Wally. Mooney got to him when I used the telephone in his house."

"Lander was a good friend. When we were lugged into the hospital he and ..." He looked around at the group listening..."a doctor friend of his were there to spirit me away. They told the hospital the doctor had been treating me for a problem that required special care and got me to his clinic. If it hadn't been the middle of the night and a relatively new crew on duty it never would have worked. The doctor and Margate were the only ones to know I was alive. I gathered the doctor wasn't all that comfortable carrying the secret."

"So whom did they bury?"

"An unidentified corpse. That was also the medical department. It made him nervous. At one time I thought he might give us away."

"And I never thought to inquire *where* you had 'died'."

"Why should you? You had enough on your plate, a new widower — injured at that." He looked at Hudson with an appraising eye and a little smile on his lips. "I knew you'd had guts when I first met you. Thank God they hadn't been buried too far under twelve years of soft living."

"You're a cold blooded bastard, you know that? Letting me think you'd died, and then jabbing me with warning notes to get me moving."

"You knew that was me? Good work." Carver's face lit up with approval. "Just a little motivation. And only when Margate felt you were packing it in." The old man fixed Hudson with a curious stare. "When did you figure out I was still alive? Or was it just a lucky guess a while ago?"

"No. I knew."

"What gave me away?"

"The books, Wally. They were what got me started. When we came back from Odanak looking for your safe, the house was 'just as you kept it' as the cleaning woman, Mary Walton, put it. The books were all lined up right at the edge of the shelves. I don't have your obsession; books go on shelves any old way. Mary had only dusted and vacuumed. If she hadn't straightened them, who had. For sure not me. And by then Mooney had other things on his mind than books. It had to be you. The only person who couldn't stand seeing them just sitting there casually, as they would in anyone else's bookcase."

Carver nodded. "A failing. I won't apologize for it. Anything else?"

"Little things. You were in Room Two C at the clinic."

"How...?"

"The doctor felt there was a rightness to my using it. Said it was 'fitting'. Odd choice of word. Just because I was one of Margate's clients? No. A *particular* client. Who 'fit' with another.

"And then there was the phone bill. There was one too many calls to Margate on it. At the time I let the telephone company convince me it was my error. My mental fuzziness. But there were other signs...The house burning in Marblehead. It was like the house fire here. Inefficient. When Trimble tried to gas me in Odanak, he gave me a knock on the head to be sure I wouldn't wake up. He was no brain, but he wouldn't have attempted to kill us by setting fire to that house unless we were immobilized. Only someone who didn't want us to die and made sure we didn't."

Carver interlocked his hands on his stomach. "You sleep a little sounder than I'd thought. I practically had to shout to wake you in time."

"But why burn down the house?"

"I had to keep the heat on you, if you'll pardon the expression." He leaned forward in his chair. "Damn it, I'd been twiddling my thumbs for months waiting for you to get off your duff and start doing something about my problem. I wasn't going to let you follow your muse again, or whatever the hell it was you were doing all summer. I'd have blown up *this* house if I'd felt it'd do any good." He sat back with a little smile on his face. "Besides, I didn't want you to find I'd removed all my genealogical files."

Hudson considered several strong comments, decided to be charitable. "Why? I mean why take your files and nothing else?"

"What would you expect me to do, sitting around waiting for you to come up with answers? I worked on them."

"But your house!" exclaimed Cilla. "It was such a beautiful place!"

"Nonsense. Pretty location, but the house itself was going to pot. Evelyn enjoyed it, so I kept it up while she was alive. The Neck isn't what it used to be."

Hudson looked at Cilla. "That word again. Motivation. This man stops at nothing for it. It was on his instructions Margate arranged to have you kidnapped."

"What?" Cilla turned a fiery eye on Carver.

"Damn it Hudson!" Carver put up his hands and started damage repair. "My dear. It sounds horrifying put like that. But consider it from my point of view. Let's first acknowledge that I am as Hudson says a cold blooded bastard. But we weren't playing parlor games. This was all out war. For keeps. And when you were shot Hudson wanted to walk away from it! So you wouldn't be in more danger." Wally's tone was scornful.

"And what's the matter with that?" Cilla burned brighter. "He'd just lost one person he loved — due to your *own* detective playing, do I need to remind you? He didn't want to lose another just a few months later. Too human a reaction for you?"

"Too ridiculous. He couldn't keep you from danger! You and Hudson were in it. You'd never have been allowed to survive. You knew too much, and they'd committed too many murders for two more to make a difference. Help me on this, Hudson!"

Hudson shook his head. "Time you took your own medicine."

Carver turned back to Cilla with exasperation. "He was letting his feelings for you cloud his judgement. I couldn't permit that, for any of our sakes. I had to make him see he couldn't just walk away from it, or take you away and hide someplace. And you weren't kidnapped. I merely asked Lander to have his man Plough hide you someplace where you'd be safe."

"A whorehouse!"

"I know, I know. A bad mistake. I'd no idea of Frieda's...sideline. Or that she was simple enough to assume she could control you as she did her girls."

"But Cilla had been poisoned!" said Hudson. "She was taken right from a hospital. You took a big chance with her life, Wally."

"Doctor...the doctor said she was out of the woods. And weird as she is, Frieda Patten is Plough's partner and a registered nurse. She just makes more money in another service field." He took Cilla's hand in both of his; it lay there, unresponsive. "I'm as fond of this man as if he were my own son. I was delighted with his marriage to my daughter Sylvia. They were good together. But I know a little about you from Ben and I've kept track of you these past long months. You and Hudson have something special, something maybe even more...Look at it this way, maybe the two of you wouldn't have realized how much you mean to each other if..."

"That's enough," said Cilla. "You'll just keep talking until you convince me. I'm not sure I want to be convinced just yet."

"What I don't understand, Wally, is why you didn't leave me some clue about the wall safe," said Hudson. "It would have shortened my work a lot."

"Would it? I doubt it. And I couldn't chance it. In the beginning you were mashed potatoes, all the drive of a baby carriage. You might even have thrown that first draft away. When you finally got moving you moved too fast for me. If you hadn't found it I would have arranged it."

"*How* did you keep track of us since the crash?" asked Cilla. "Where were you?"

"Across the river from here. There's an abandoned shack in the woods. I'm damn glad you solved this before the snows, Hudson. There's no heat, light or cooking facilities."

"Then how did you eat? Or contact Margate?"

"I think he's used this house more than we have," grinned Hudson.

Carver nodded. "There's a little pine-paneled room downstairs with a telephone. I used it as an office when Evelyn was alive. Come the fall, I spent more than a few damn cold hours in the woods outside waiting for you to leave, so I could get into that nice warm room and talk to Margate. He called me there after the funeral. From then on you were using the house so I had to call him," he grimaced. "Except once, always collect." He peered up at Hudson. "You nearly caught me one time when I tipped over the telephone table. I made it to the hemlocks, and you rushed by only two feet from me." He chuckled as he stood and put a hand on Hudson's shoulder. "I didn't decide wrong, boy. You saved both our tails. I bet you even know how I got food without showing myself in town."

Hudson glanced at the postmistress. "It had to be Emma. She was too quick knowing who I was, even for a small town."

Emma Persons glared from her chair. "You knew all along I'd pass the gossip on. You were playing with me."

"As you were with me, Emma."

"You're smart all right. I hope not too smart. That doesn't go over too good in Bartlett." She got up. "Well, Wally, it's over. Thank God. I for one am tired. Where's my coat?"

That was a signal for the rest to start moving to the door. Those not local had been put up at a nearby inn. Wally insisted Hudson and Cilla keep the master bedroom. He took an upstairs guestroom which he said would be like a palace compared to the shack where he'd been living.

When they were alone, Cilla looked thoughtfully at Hudson. "You're lucky."

He took her hands in his. "In so many ways."

"I mean with Mooney. He's a shrewd man. We never would have caught him if it hadn't been for that fingerprint."

"What fingerprint?"

"The...you're not going to tell me there were no fingerprints on his glass."

"Loaded with them."

"Then...the gun?"

"It's not a field I'm into, but I doubt if you can get a usable fingerprint off a trigger. Krestinski couldn't."

She looked at him a long time. "I hope you never have reason to come after me."

"I have, and always will."

They mounted the stairs.

"That limb on the beech tree out front. That really was the beginning of it for you?"

"Yep. Wally's tree. Why?"

"'Fitting', Doctor Wendt might say. That Wally's problem be solved by one of his trees."

"How so?"

"I read an inscription on one of his books from someone who said he's like one."

"Wally like a tree?"

Cilla nodded. "'Tough on the outside and just as tough in'. It said his life is really in his roots."

"They've got a point there. Genealogical roots. What a nut. Can you imagine him sitting in that little shack for months with nothing but papers on family trees?"

"Umm hmm."

"Yeah, he...Why do I get the impression you don't think that's a little weird?"

She peeked up at him shyly, "Me too."

"You too what?"

"Want a family tree. Ours."

END

Epilogue

IN DECEMBER A festival was held at Odanak, celebrating the three hundredth anniversary of the receiving of the statue of the Madonna from Chartres. Only the new Chief knew that the replacement displayed in the musée had itself been replaced by the original, dredged from the muck of Sawyer Pond and hidden beneath a painted plastic wood surface. The young leader of the Abenaki felt it was the only way to ensure the permanent safety of the solid silver relic, which he believed had already changed the tribe's fortunes. And his cousin and her friend with the hateful name agreed. The new Chief began a movement to encourage his tribe to relearn their ancient language and customs, pointing out what might have been lost by neglecting their heritage.

The Abenakis decided to accept free and clear title to Great Haystack Ski Area as settlement of the deed negotiated by Samuel Gill, provided only that the United States government keep the remainder of the land, not privately owned, in National Forest. In turn, said United States government found it to be in its own interest — i.e. the preservation of many thousands of White Mountain acres — to pay off the Great Haystack mortgages. With its heavy debt removed, the ski area could become a money maker for the Abenakis, and the cousin of the Chief was put in to run it for the tribe.

When Mooney's house came on the market to raise money for attorney's fees, Hudson bought it and deeded Wally's house back to him. But the older man would accept none of the funds Hudson had inherited, saying he had plenty more that Margate had not reported in the estate.

In February, regular skiers at Great Haystack Ski Area noticed a lithe man with a wrestler's build had become a new addition to the Ski Patrol. Any that wandered into the woods on the westerly side of the mountain might have seen him ribboning trees for a new, unusually twisting and curving trail from the summit, to be cleared come spring. The man seemed a little old for ski patrol work, but the General Manager said he'd had lifesaving experience, and she had every confidence he could handle any problems that came his way.

* * *

If you enjoyed this book ...

its sequel

THE SNOWS OF MT. WASHINGTON

is scheduled for publication in 1999.

We'll be pleased to put you on our mailing list
for when it's available.

Name _____

Address _____

Any comments you'd like to convey on *THE HIDDEN MOUNTAIN*:

_____

_____

_____

Return to MFDC Press, P.O. Box 543, North Conway, NH 03860